MULBERRY PARK

**Center Point
Large Print**

**This Large Print Book carries the
Seal of Approval of N.A.V.H.**

MULBERRY PARK

JUDY DUARTE

CENTER POINT PUBLISHING
THORNDIKE, MAINE

This Center Point Large Print edition
is published in the year 2008 by arrangement with
Kensington Publishing Corp.

Copyright © 2008 by Judy Duarte.

The text of this Large Print edition is unabridged. In other
aspects, this book may vary from the original edition.
Printed in the United States of America.
Set in 16-point Times New Roman type.

ISBN: 978-1-60285-178-8

Library of Congress Cataloging-in-Publication Data

Duarte, Judy.
    Mulberry Park / Judy Duarte.--Center Point large print ed.
        p. cm.
    ISBN 978-1-60285-178-8 (lib. bdg. : alk. paper)
    1. Large type books. I. Title.

PS3604.U24M86 2008
813'.6--dc22

2008005696

"To my Heavenly Father, who didn't respond in writing to the letter I left for Him when I was a child, but who answers each of my prayers with wisdom, power, and love."

Jeremiah 29: 11–13

Chapter 1

Analisa Dawson stood in the center of Mulberry Park and stared at the biggest tree in the whole world, with branches that reached all the way to Heaven.

She fingered the gnarly trunk, then looked way up to the top, where the dancing leaves poked through the cotton clouds and waved to the sun and beyond.

It was perfect. If she put her letter high enough in the branches, God could reach it. But there was one little problem. She was going to need some help.

She glanced across the lawn where Mrs. Richards was sitting on a green park bench under the shade of another tree—one a whole lot smaller. The nanny's eyes were closed, her head was drooped, and her hands rested in her lap.

Sometimes, when Mrs. Richards brought Analisa to the park and she didn't have another lady to visit with, she dozed off while Analisa played, which is what she was doing now. But even if Analisa wanted to wake her up—and she didn't—poor Mrs. Richards couldn't walk very good because she had arthritis in her knees. So no way could she climb up a tree, especially that one, which meant Analisa would have to find someone else to help.

As she searched the park, she spotted the man who always sat at the same picnic table by the winding walkway that led to the restrooms. Today he was wearing a yellow baseball cap and a green shirt with brown suspenders, and as usual, he was playing a game all by himself.

Mrs. Richards called it *chest*. It didn't seem like a fun game, though, because the man hardly ever smiled.

He did smile and say hello once, but when she started toward him, Mrs. Richards pulled her aside and said, "Analisa, we don't talk to strangers."

So she wouldn't ask him for help.

Trevor was here again today, sitting by the monkey bars and digging a hole in the sand. He didn't usually talk to her. At first Analisa thought that was because she was a girl, but then she realized he didn't play with boys very often, either.

Mrs. Rodriguez would help, if she was here. But she only brought her children to the park in the afternoons or on Sunday mornings, after they went to Mass, which was the same as church but with a lot more candles.

Analisa missed going to church, like she used to when she lived in Rio del Oro with her mother and father. At least people talked about God there and could answer her questions.

It was different in California. So far, she hadn't been able to find anyone who knew anything about Heaven. So she'd written a letter to God, which was why she had to find someone to put it in the tree.

And the only someone she could see was Trevor.

He wasn't a whole lot bigger than her, but he was

older and might be a good tree-climber. Besides, asking him to do a favor wasn't the same as playing, so she walked back to the playground toward the boy.

He wore a red shirt and jeans, and when the summer breeze blew a piece of his hair away from his forehead, she spotted a scar over his eye. She wondered what had happened to him, but knew better than to ask. Mommy had taught her not to stare at people who had something wrong with them.

As her shadow covered him and his hole, he looked up but didn't talk or smile.

Analisa nibbled at her bottom lip, kicked at the sand, then cleared her throat. "Excuse me, but when you get done with your hole, can you help me do something?"

He shrugged. "Depends. What kind of help do you want?"

She turned and pointed toward the branches that reached clear to Heaven. "I need someone to climb that tree."

His gaze followed the direction of her finger, then he scrunched his face. "How come?"

She reached under her shirt and pulled out the envelope she'd tucked into the waistband of her shorts. "I need to put this way up high."

Trevor glanced at the bright pink letter she'd worked hard on last night, then looked back at her. "How come you want to put it in a tree?"

"Because I wrote it to God. And this morning at breakfast I asked Mrs. Richards if the mailman took letters to Heaven, and she said no."

Trevor rubbed the knuckle of his pointer finger under his nose, leaving a dirty smudge on his upper lip. She opened her mouth to tell him, so he could wipe it with his shirt, but decided not to.

"You know," Trevor said, "you're wasting your time. God isn't going to answer you."

"Yes, He will. If I get it high enough." Analisa crossed her arms and shifted her weight to one foot.

That tree was going to take her letter all the way to Heaven.

As the sun cast a fading glow over the San Diego suburb of Fairbrook, Claire Harper ran as if the devil were closing in on her, and sometimes she swore he was.

Her feet pounded a lonely cadence on the path along First Street, as her breath came out in sharp huffs and her heart pulsated in time.

Left, right. Left, right. In and out. In and out.

Supposedly endorphins gave a runner a natural high, but Claire ran only in an effort to relieve stress—and Lord knew she had plenty of it.

Grief, too.

So each day after work, she drove to Mulberry Park, where she slipped out of her power suit and into a pair of shorts and an old T-shirt that had once been Ron's, kicked off her sensible heels and put on a pair of sneakers. Then after a bit of stretching, she took off down the jogging path, hoping to escape the depression that had dogged her for the past three years, the broken heart that kept her from getting a full night's sleep.

She had medication to help with that, pills prescribed by the shrink Ron had insisted she see, but she quit taking them because the side effects made it difficult for her to function at work, especially in the mornings.

Claire turned down the path that lined Applewood Drive and headed back to the park.

There was a light wind today, a heavenly breeze her grandmother used to call it. The kind that carried God's whispers to those who took time to sit and listen.

As a child, on days like this, Claire would close her eyes and try to hear the voice Nana had talked about. But that was eons ago, back in a time when she'd actually believed dreams could come true.

People told her time would heal, but it hadn't. Grim memories still followed her, haunting her.

The lifeless body of her son. The stuffed bunny held in cold hands. The shovelful of dirt landing upon the small white casket that had been lowered into the ground.

"Focus on the sweeter images," the shrink had said. And she'd tried.

Erik's first smile. His first tooth. His first step.

It felt like a lifetime ago that she'd ruffled his hair, brushed a kiss across his brow. And no matter how far she ran, how hard, she couldn't escape the fact that he was gone.

Yet each day after work, she continued to follow the same path, sticking to the same routine and returning home with the same results—a body that was toned, a soul that was battered, a heart that wouldn't mend.

As Mulberry Park came back into view, she slowed to a stop, exhausted. Trying to catch her breath and cool down, she trudged toward the massive mulberry that grew in the middle of the lush green lawn.

Near the tree a concrete bench had been erected, a memorial to Carl Witherspoon, dear departed husband, father, and friend. Claire had never heard of the man, but each day, at dusk, she claimed the quiet spot as her own.

Leaves littered the concrete slab, and she brushed them away before sitting on the cold stone seat.

The heavenly breeze continued to blow, to rustle through the branches.

"Close your eyes," Nana used to say. "Listen to the wind and you can hear God's voice."

A couple of times, Claire could have sworn she'd heard it, too. But she no longer spoke to God, no longer listened for His voice. No longer expected anything from Him.

And why should she? He'd quit listening to her three years ago.

From the corner of her eye she spotted a flicker of pink overhead. She glanced up to see an envelope flutter down, just missing her lap as it landed on the ground. It was the color of a flamingo, with glitter stuck to uneven globs of glue, and a child's handwriting on the front.

Unable to quell her curiosity, she bent and reached for what looked like a greeting card.

To God From Analisa was etched on the front.

As Claire lifted the envelope from the ground, a sprinkle of shiny gold and silver rained onto the grass. Then she glanced up at the mulberry, at the expanse of branches and leaves.

Odd.

She perused the envelope, then turned it over, where the flap had been licked to the point it was barely secure. Inside, she felt a small tube-sized lump.

The strangest compulsion to open it settled over her. The urge to see the little girl's picture, to read the painstaking scrawl of her words.

It had been three years since Claire had seen anything this precious.

Erik's efforts to draw and write never failed to touch her, which is why she wouldn't remove his last pieces of art from the refrigerator.

Ron used to complain about that.

"For cripe's sake, Claire. I loved him, too, but he's gone. Dwelling in the past is making me crazy, not to mention what it's doing to you. Can't you take those drawings down? Put them in storage someplace?"

That had been the beginning of the end of their marriage.

Well . . . No, that wasn't exactly true. But it had been

the beginning of the realization that without Erik to bind them together she and Ron no longer had anything worth holding onto.

"It isn't healthy," Ron used to tell her. "Sitting in Erik's room for hours on end."

Maybe it hadn't been.

But for some reason, Ron had been able to forget their bright-eyed son and she hadn't.

"You need to move on, Claire."

Like he had?

Ron's half of the wrongful death settlement had already been spent or invested.

But Claire hadn't touched hers.

How could she, when she considered it blood money?

She fingered the pink paper and the flap on the back began to lift. To open.

It wasn't a conscious decision. Not really. But she found herself reaching into the envelope, pulling out the folded letter and a blue marker. Reading the words.

Dear God.
Tell Mommy and Daddy I am being good. And that I love them. And you. Will you rite back and tell me what Mommy and Daddy are doing in hevin? I asked Unkel Sam and he doznt no. I will put a marker in the invalop for you in case they dont have pens in hevin.
Love Analisa

Tears blurred Claire's eyes, and a knot tightened in her chest. Her heart, which she thought had become permanently numb and lifeless, quivered.

She scanned the park, her gaze settling on the swing set in the playground, where a dark-haired boy sat alone, his hands on the chains, his toes dragging in the sand. If there'd been a little girl in the area, Claire might have reached out, might have considered embracing her. Might have succumbed to the compulsion to offer sympathy.

But Analisa, whoever she was, had left her letter and gone.

Claire tried to imagine what it would have been like for Erik had Claire been the one to die in the accident, leaving her son to grieve for her.

She would have hoped that someone would have reached out to him, told him that she hadn't wanted to die, hadn't wanted to leave him. Insisted that she would love him forever and do her best to look out for him always, to be his guardian angel—if there were such things.

Her own faith had been shattered by his death and her unanswered prayers, so she'd never been able to envision a smiling Erik with wings and a halo. Yet for some reason she wanted little Analisa to have some peace, to embrace her hopes and dreams—at least until adulthood brought along an inevitable wallop of faith-busting reality.

It's what Claire would have wanted for Erik, even if she couldn't have it for herself. So she uncapped the blue marker as if someone else had stepped in to guide her hand and respond to a child's plea for answers when there weren't any to be had.

Someone else who, for the next couple of minutes, scratched out a note on the back of the child's letter and pretended to be God.

The next day, Claire sat at her desk at Fairbrook Savings and Loan, wishing the clock would kick it up a notch.

She hated her job, hated getting up each day and going to work.

But she hated weekends, too. Days when she didn't have to punch a time clock.

Her stomach growled, reminding her that she should have had more than coffee for breakfast.

She glanced at the clock on the wall. It was nearly noon and she was ready to head to the café down the street and pick up a salad, but there was still a call she needed to make and one more customer to see. So she closed the file she'd been working on, put it in the wire basket that held the other loan applications she'd been processing, and picked up the phone. She dialed her supervisor's extension.

He picked up on the first ring. "Joe Montgomery."

"It's Claire. Have you got a minute?"

"Sure." His voice softened immediately, although she wished it hadn't. He'd always been a bit more sympathetic than she was comfortable with. "What's up?"

"I'd like to take an early lunch on Thursday. I need

to see an attorney, and eleven-thirty is his only time slot available."

"Is everything okay?" he asked.

"Yes and no. I received a letter from the parole board, and Russell Meredith's hearing is on July twenty-fourth."

"Do you have any say about him being released early or not?"

"According to the notice, I do. And I want him to stay behind bars as long as possible."

"I can understand that."

Could he? Claire wasn't sure anyone who hadn't lost a child could.

Russell Meredith had been responsible for Erik's death. He'd run him down on the side of the street, then kept driving, callously leaving the scene.

A jury had convicted him of vehicular manslaughter, which, as far as Claire was concerned, was just another word for murder.

"Who are you going to see?" Joe asked.

"Samuel Dawson. He represented Ron and me in the civil suit against Meredith."

At first Claire had felt funny going to the attorney who'd worked more closely with her ex-husband than he had with her, but Sam was already familiar with the case.

"Do you need to take a longer lunch?" Joe asked.

"No. His office is in that new six-story brick building next to Mulberry Park, so it's nearby. I shouldn't be long."

"Take all the time you need."

"Thanks."

After hanging up the receiver and disconnecting the line, she glanced at her appointment list, rolled back her chair, then stood and walked to the waiting area, where a petite Latina woman with a toddler on her lap sat next to a small, school-age boy.

"Maria Rodriguez?" Claire asked.

"Yes, that's me." The woman stood and shifted the little girl in her arms, revealing a distended womb.

"This way." Claire escorted her back to the office, but couldn't help glancing over her shoulder.

Maria, her big brown eyes luminous, carried her paperwork in one arm and the toddler in the other, while the boy—about seven or eight—followed along. "I'm sorry, but I had to bring the children with me. There wasn't anyone who could watch them for me this morning."

"That's all right." Claire pointed to the chairs that sat before her desk, watching as Maria told her son to take one and chose the other for herself. "What can I help you with?"

"I recently inherited a house on Sugar Plum Lane," Maria said. "It belonged to my *tía*—my aunt—but several months before she passed away, she quitclaimed it to me. It's an old home, but very clean and comfortable."

Claire nodded, assuming the woman meant to use the house as collateral. It was a simple enough procedure, especially if there wasn't a huge mortgage or if there weren't any liens against it.

This appointment was just the first in a prescreening process the bank had recently instituted, and if the initial paperwork was in order, Ms. Rodriguez would be given a full application packet.

"Did you fill out the form you were given at the front desk?" Claire asked.

"Yes." Maria handed over the paperwork.

Claire looked at the neat, legible writing; it appeared to be complete. "Where do you work, Ms. Rodriguez?"

"I've been cleaning houses, but after my aunt passed away, I no longer had a sitter." She caressed her stomach, then cleared her throat. "I'm a hard worker and plan to get a job as a waitress. Once that happens, I'll make double payments and get it paid off in no time at all."

"How much money are we talking about?"

"I need fifty thousand dollars to see me through the next two years."

"You don't intend to work for two years?" Claire asked, realizing she might have to give the woman bad news before they went any further in the process.

"With the cost of daycare, especially for infants, I'm afraid it wouldn't do me any good. But as soon as Sara enters kindergarten, the expense should be easier to handle."

When Erik had been a baby, Claire had wanted to stay home with him, but Ron had gotten caught in the credit card trap, and she'd been forced to return to work immediately after her maternity leave. It had torn her apart to leave her infant son in the care of others when he'd been so tiny. But at the time, even though she'd worked at an entry-level job and the cost of his sitter had taken nearly half her paycheck, there had been no options.

Claire looked at the Rodriguez children, a blue-eyed boy with a head of thick dark hair and a squirmy toddler. Her gaze naturally drifted to the woman's belly. In a couple of months, maybe less, Maria would have another little one.

"What does your husband do?" Claire asked. Maybe there was a big enough income and it wouldn't matter that she'd be out of work.

"He's . . . we're . . ." She cleared her throat. "Separated. Legally."

"My daddy went to prison," the boy added. "And for a very long time, but he can send me letters."

The man was a convicted criminal?

Every day Claire met people wanting loans, couples hoping to refinance the house—to send a child to college, to remodel, or to pay off credit card bills. It was her job to calculate the risks of loaning them money, whether she sympathized with the applicant or not.

And in this particular case, Claire *did* sympathize. The poor woman had a rough row to hoe—and apparently no one to help. But the newly instituted loan regulations were sure to bind Claire's hands.

She scanned the application again, looking for something on which to base a decision to preapprove the loan.

Education? Just high school.

Work experience? None to speak of.

A savings account? Just a couple of thousand dollars.

"Actually," Maria explained, "I'm very frugal. So I've considered my living expenses plus the monthly payment in the loan amount I'm requesting. But maybe I can get by with less."

"I believe you," Claire said, "but I'm not able to approve your loan."

"Why?"

"Because you have no income and no significant savings."

"But I have a house. It's worth a whole lot more than what I'm asking for. If I didn't make the payments on time, you could take it from me."

As tears clouded the woman's eyes, an awkward sense of guilt settled over Claire. This wasn't personal. She was only making a decision based upon the bank's best interests. Didn't Ms. Rodriguez understand that Claire wasn't sitting in judgment here, granting loans on a whim? Playing God?

What about yesterday? a small voice quizzed. *Isn't that what you did at the park?*

Again, she cleared her throat, hoping to shed the guilt that had settled over her as well as the sense of impotence. "I'm truly sorry, Ms. Rodriguez. We're in the banking business, but we can't loan money when the risk to do so is too high."

"But I'm a hard worker. And honest. You can talk

to the priest at my parish, he'll tell you . . ."

Again Claire felt the uneasiness, the discomfort. The guilt. "Have you considered selling the house outright and living off the proceeds until after the baby comes and you can go back to work?"

"I don't want to sell the house," Maria said. "It's all I have."

It wasn't all she had. She had her children.

Claire would have traded places with her in a snap, if it would have brought Erik back.

Maria slumped back in her chair. "So there's nothing you can do?"

"I'm afraid not. Fairbrook Savings and Loan has a reputation for being conservative, so you may have better luck at another financial institution in town." Claire stood, signaling the discussion was over, the judgment made. "Unfortunately, my hands are tied."

The woman nodded, then touched the boy lightly on the shoulder. "Come along, *mijo*."

"Are we done?" the boy asked.

"Yes."

As Maria guided her children out of Claire's office, her shoulders hunched, yet she held her head high and led her little family to the door.

The boy slipped his hand in his mother's. "Can we go to the playground now? Please?"

"Yes, *mijo*. For a little while."

Claire would have given anything to turn back the clock, to have her son at her side again, asking to go to the park.

Yet that fact didn't make her feel the least bit better about dashing another woman's dreams.

Chapter 2

Walter Klinefelter parked his red Ford Ranger at Mulberry Park, then withdrew the worn leather game case and locked the door.

Two spaces down, the old woman and the blond-haired little girl climbed from their white Honda Prelude. They weren't what he'd call regulars, since they'd just been coming to the park the past couple of weeks, but they showed up about midday. Like he did.

He'd approached them once, trying to make small talk, but the woman snubbed him like he was a dirty old man or something.

Heck, he was harmless. But he supposed they didn't know that.

"Oh, yay," the blond pixie said. "He's here again today."

"Who, dear?" the granny asked.

"Trevor." The girl moved the tan-skinned dolly she carried from one arm to the other, then pointed to the child who'd been hanging out at the park a lot this summer, the kid who appeared as though he didn't have a friend in the world.

In that sense, the boy and Walter had a lot in common.

"I told you before," Granny said. "That boy is too old to be your friend."

"He's not exactly my friend," the little blonde said. "He just helped me do something yesterday, and I might need him to do it again."

"He'd better not be helping you climb on those monkey bars. If you fall, you'll get hurt."

"I'll be careful, Mrs. Richards," Blondie said, as she dashed off. Yet she didn't run toward the older boy who sat in the shadow of the slide, drawing with a stick in the sand. Instead she skipped toward the center of the park, near the mulberry tree.

Walter probably ought to mind his own business, which he seemed to do a heck of a lot of these days, but sometimes he got sick and tired of hearing himself think.

"I don't suppose you play chess," he said to the old woman.

She turned, and the sun glistened off the silver strands of her hair. He suspected she'd been pretty when she'd been younger, but now she wore a pucker on her face that suggested she'd weathered her own share of disappointment over the years.

"No," she said, "I'm afraid I don't play."

"Too bad."

They fell into step together, walking slowly.

"You're here all the time," she said. "And you've always got that game with you."

"My last chess buddy passed on a couple of months back, and I'm hoping to find a new opponent." There hadn't been many takers, though. Either they were too young or couldn't be bothered with an old man. That was to be expected, he supposed. There came a time when folks just outlived their usefulness.

The woman glanced at the midday sun, then reached a hand to her head and patted the springy gray curls as though feeling for something and finding it missing.

He did that sometimes, too. Got absentminded and forgetful.

"Oh, dear." She clucked her tongue. "Wouldn't you know it? I left my hat in the car."

Walter watched as she headed back to the white Prelude. The girl had called her Mrs. Richards, so the two weren't related. He supposed that made her a babysitter then. But what the heck. None of his business.

He made his way toward his favorite table, the one that sat along the path to the restrooms. He figured that particular spot saw more traffic than the others and would present more opportunities for him to find an opponent. It happened once in a while. Often enough for him to keep hanging out at the park, rather than whiling away the hours at home, which was merely a short walk from Paddy's Pub. Too short of a walk, actually.

Walter had no more than set up the game board and playing pieces, when Mrs. Richards approached. "I don't suppose you know how to get into a locked car?"

So maybe he hadn't quite outlived his usefulness after all.

"As a matter of fact, breaking-and-entering vehicles

is one of several handy tips I picked up while in the pen."

Obviously not one to appreciate his sense of humor, she placed a hand on her chest and sobered.

"Not to worry," he said, getting to his feet. "That was just a joke. I've never been in prison."

He had, of course, spent quite a bit of time in the local jail when you added it all up. The last arrest occurred after he'd gotten drunk while the city had held their annual Founders' Day parade, but he supposed Mrs. Richards, who appeared too prissy to get a chuckle out of it, wouldn't appreciate hearing the details.

His old buddies at the pub had thought it was a real hoot. They probably still did. But three years ago, Walter had experienced a sobering epiphany when Russell Meredith hit that kid on the bicycle. Russell swore he hadn't had a drop to drink that day, but had been so distracted that he hadn't even known that the bump he'd felt had been a child.

At first, before Russell had come forward and turned himself in, most people assumed the driver had been drinking. Why else would the guilty person have left the scene?

Naturally, since the accident had taken place just a couple of blocks from Paddy's, the cops had questioned everyone who patronized the pub.

For a while, all the regulars had eyed each other a bit suspiciously, wondering whether the guilty driver had been one of them. In fact, Walter suspected they'd all cast surreptitious glances at the vehicles in the parking lot, looking for new dents or streaks of paint—whatever.

Even Walter, who'd driven home completely bombed plenty of times, had been relieved to see that his truck hadn't suffered any damage.

He blew out a weary sigh, hoping to shake the memory that had caused him to admit what no one else had ever been able to. That he ought to quit drinking for a while.

One day led to a second, then a third.

And, thanks to Carl Witherspoon, a do-gooder who'd come to Paddy's passing out AA fliers after Meredith's arrest, Walter had kicked it.

So far.

Still, a good laugh and someone to share it with was what he missed the most. More than the booze.

Walter cleared his throat as he shuffled toward the woman's car. "As luck would have it, I have a coat hanger in my truck. Let's see if I've still got the touch."

"I appreciate your help," she said as they reached the parking lot. "It seems as if I'd forget my head these days if it wasn't connected to my neck."

"No problem." Walter went to the toolbox in the back of his pickup, then dug around until he found the bent wire hanger he kept on hand. Every once in a while one of the patrons at the pub had gotten locked out of a vehicle—maybe a good thing, he now realized. So years ago he'd tucked a coat hanger into the toolbox in the back of his truck. It had come in handy a time or two, which seemed to be all he was good for these days.

Hard to imagine that was his sole purpose for being on earth.

Walter Klinefelter, Parking Lot Superhero, who helped people out of a jam, then watched as they sped away in a cloud of dust, leaving him standing by his lonesome.

As he strode toward the Prelude, he wasn't so sure he could help. These newfangled models had antitheft systems that made it tough to get in. They might have to call the Automobile Club, if she had their service. Or a locksmith, if she didn't.

"By the way," he said, reaching out to the seventy-something woman. "My name is Walter Klinefelter."

"Hilda Richards," she said, taking his hand in hers.

Human contact was a funny thing. Just an occasional touch could make a man feel alive again.

He nodded toward the blond pixie and asked, "You babysitting?"

"I'm a nanny," she said, as if there was a big difference.

As she leaned against the side of the car, she winced, and he looked up from his work.

"My arthritis is acting up like old fury today. I hadn't wanted to come to the park, but Analisa was insistent, and I hate to tell the sweet little thing no. She's been through enough already."

He glanced over his shoulder at the child who was

now standing near Carl's memorial bench that rested at the base of the mulberry tree. "Are you new in town? I've been coming to the park for a long time and have just recently noticed you."

"No, I've been living here for years. And so has my employer. His brother and sister-in-law died about six weeks ago, and he's now the guardian of his niece. He's a busy man, an attorney with a big law firm." She pointed to the red-brick professional building that sat adjacent to the park. "That's his office there. On the sixth floor, with a view of the city. Anyway, he needed someone to watch over the girl, and I came out of retirement to do so."

Walter glanced again at the orphaned child, poor little thing. He didn't normally dig for information, but death seemed to be an ever-present reality these days, and he couldn't help his curiosity. "What happened to her parents?"

"They were missionaries in a remote village in Guatemala, where the nearest medical clinic was far away and sorely lacking. Her mother died of blood poisoning, something that could have been easily treated in the States."

"And her father?" he asked.

"He was going to bring little Analisa back to California, but while giving a tour of the neighboring villages to his replacement, he and the other man made a wrong turn on a narrow mountain road, and the Jeep rolled down a ravine. Her father was killed."

Walter shook his head. "That's terrible. Poor little tyke."

"She's pretty strong," Hilda said. "As far as kids go."

Walter returned to his work, wiggling the hanger between the window and the door.

"Oh, for goodness' sake," Hilda said. "Would you look at this? I had the keys in my pocket all along."

Walter carefully pulled the hanger free, then looked at the key chain that dangled from her hand.

"I'm so sorry for troubling you," she said.

"No problem." Heck, he didn't have anything better to do. If he did, he'd be doing it.

As he left Hilda to open the car and retrieve her hat, he headed back to his table, back to his game.

But not before scanning the park for the orphaned child—poor kid—and spotting her looking up at the mulberry, her mouth open wide.

Analisa couldn't believe what she saw. Her bright pink envelope now rested on the lowest branch, one that reached down to earth.

Had God read her letter? Had He answered?

Her heart skipped a beat, and she placed her dolly on the bench. Then she dashed off to the playground to get Trevor's help. Even though the envelope wasn't nearly as high as they'd put it, she still couldn't reach it all by herself.

As she drew to a stop near the slide, where Trevor sat in its shadow, he looked up. He didn't smile or speak, but he didn't seem to be annoyed, either.

"I need you to climb the tree again."

"You writing another letter to God?" he asked.

"No. Not until I get His answer."

"That's dumb. You're going to be waiting forever."

She kicked her shoe at a gum wrapper in the sand, then glanced at Trevor. "Don't you believe God talks to people?"

"Why should I? He doesn't talk to me."

Still, the boy stood and brushed the sand from his pants. Then, with Analisa happily tagging along, he walked toward the tree.

"See?" She pointed. "It's much lower now because God wrote me back and put it where I could reach better."

Trevor climbed on the bench, then stuck the scuffed toe of his sneaker into a little hole in the trunk. He reached for a branch, pulled himself up, and plucked the envelope from the spot where it rested.

The flap was open, like it had been read.

Trevor dropped it to her, but she missed, and it landed on the lawn. So she picked it up and pulled out the folded pink paper.

She gasped when she saw the writing below her own. God *had* answered. But there was a big problem.

Trevor jumped to the ground. "What's the matter?"

"God wrote in cursive, so I can't read it."

The boy took the letter from her hand and looked at the handwriting on the bottom of the page and also on the back.

"What did he say?" Analisa hopped and clapped her hands. "Tell me."

Trevor scratched at his head, then read God's words to her.

Dear Analisa,

I'm sorry that your mother and father couldn't stay long enough on earth to see you grow up, but I needed their help in Heaven. They miss you very much and send their love. We all hope that your uncle is giving you lots of hugs and finding time to take you to the park.

Your mom and dad have met an angel here. His name is Erik, and he looks a lot like you. They told him how they miss you and want to know that you are happy and safe.

Erik asked if he could be your guardian angel, and I have granted him permission to watch out for you. But please be careful when you're climbing trees or crossing streets. Erik is still learning how to use his wings.

Your mom and dad send their love. And so does Erik.

Love,
God

Analisa quickly scanned the treetop in search of her angel, but all she saw was an empty bird's nest and a broken kite. Then she searched all around her.

"What are you looking for?" Trevor asked.

"Erik."

"Aw, come on." Trevor scrunched his face and shook his head. "You don't really think God answered that letter, do you?"

Analisa scrunched her face right back at him. "Yes, I do. Who else would know the name of my very own guardian angel?"

Trevor opened his mouth to say something, then clamped his lips shut.

Maybe he realized he was wrong.

She looked from one side of the tree to the other, checking all the branches and hoping to spot a flutter of white wings or the sparkle of a gold halo.

"You're not going to see anything," Trevor said.

Analisa crossed her arms and frowned. She opened her mouth to stick out her tongue, but decided not to.

Once, when she and her friend Soledad were arguing about who got to keep the pretty blue marble and who got to keep the plain brown one, Analisa had gotten mad and stuck out her tongue. But Mommy had scolded her, saying it wasn't very nice.

"Even if there *is* such a thing as angels," Trevor said, "I don't think you can see them unless they want you to."

Trevor might be right about that. She wondered if Erik would ever decide to show himself to her. She hoped so.

As Trevor stooped to tie his shoe, she picked up Lucita from the bench.

"Do you believe me now?" she asked.

He shrugged, then got to his feet. "It's going to take more than one little letter for me to believe God can do things like that."

Analisa laughed. "Then I'll meet you back here tomorrow and the day after that."

"Why?"

"I'm going to write another letter to God tonight."

"How come?"

"To thank Him." She hugged the letter and Lucita close to her heart. Then she looked at Trevor. "Want me to find out if you have a guardian angel?"

"Nah. Don't bother. There isn't anyone looking out for me."

After her usual five-mile run, Claire made her way across the lawn at Mulberry Park, her body cooling down from another heart-pounding workout.

Yesterday, while catching her breath and resting, she'd sat beneath the mulberry, looked up and scanned the foliage for the neon pink envelope. But she'd seen only leaves fluttering in the afternoon sun and a torn, wind-battered kite dangling by its tail.

She had no way of knowing what had happened to the letter she'd left for Analisa. The little girl could have taken it, of course. Or it could have blown onto the ground, where a park maintenance worker might have found it and tossed it into the trash.

There were a hundred different scenarios, and she

decided it was ridiculous to give the unconventional correspondence more than a passing thought.

Still, as she neared the stone bench that rested in the shade of the tree, she couldn't help but search the vast array of leaves and branches again. This time something small and blue caught her eye.

Another letter?

Whatever it was rested too high to reach unless she climbed the tree, which Claire wasn't about to do. Talk about unconventional. Climbing a tree to retrieve a letter to God bordered on crazy.

Yet she continued to study the blue scrap of paper overhead, the message to her.

Well, not exactly to *her*, but since she'd answered Analisa's last letter, this was a response to what she'd written.

Claire scanned the park and found herself alone. A vacant red pickup sat in the parking lot, but there was no sign of the driver. It looked as though everyone who'd visited the park today had already gone home.

But Claire had no one to rush home to, no one to smile at her from across the table.

For reasons she didn't want to contemplate, that scrap of blue paper continued to call to her, and a strange compulsion settled over her, a growing urge to do something she wouldn't normally do.

Without any further consideration, she stepped onto the bench and reached for the lowest branch, then she placed a sneaker on the concrete backrest and pulled herself into the tree.

The bark scraped against her knee, and she grumbled under her breath. Still, she pressed on.

Claire hadn't done anything remotely unladylike in ages, not since she'd been a kid. This was *so* not like her.

What would her coworkers at the savings and loan think if they could see her now?

She braced her feet on the sturdy bough and rested her fanny against a slanting branch. Then, even though she felt like a nosy neighbor opening someone else's mail, she reached for the card-shaped envelope, withdrew the letter, and read the child's words.

Dear God.
Thank you for Erik. I tried to see him but he hides good. Is Erik sopose to be a seekret? I dint tell any one abowt it. But Trever nos cuz I cant read cursev. Trever is nice, but Mrs. Richerdz doznt want me to play with him cuz he is old. Can you give him a angel to? No one looks out for him.
Love Analisa

Claire studied the rudimentary handwriting of a stranger, a little girl seeking God and finding Claire instead.

The first letter had gripped her heart, had made her want to protect the child from grief, but now she feared for Analisa's safety.

Who was *Trever?* A dirty old man who'd set his sights on an orphaned child?

Claire shuddered at the thought. Good Lord. Little Analisa was worried about Mr. Trever, but who was looking after the trusting child?

Before she could ponder her growing concern, a graveled voice sounded from below. "Lose something?"

Claire's heart thumped, and she jerked back, nearly losing her balance. She grabbed a branch to steady herself, inadvertently crushing the letter in her hand.

On the ground, an elderly man stood, one hand on his hip, the other holding the leather handle of a worn brown satchel. His hair was white and thick, and he needed a shave.

Her embarrassment ran amok.

"Crazy fool woman. What are you doing up there?" A sparkle in his eyes suggested he was teasing, although she couldn't be sure.

"I'm . . ." She glanced at the blue letter and envelope she'd crumpled in her hand. "Just reading."

He humphed, then shook his woolly head. "There's probably a law against climbing trees in the park. And if there isn't, there ought to be. You could fall and break your neck."

The man looked as old as creation, and an aura of bright light lit his head like a halo or some kind of heavenly crown. She could almost imagine that God had taken human form and come down to earth to

37

punish her for reading His mail, for pretending to be Him.

When the man shifted his weight to one hip, eliminating the reflected glare from the sun and revealing a pair of wire-rim glasses perched on his head, the pseudo-divine aura completely disappeared.

"I don't suppose you have a ladder?" she quipped.

"Not *with* me."

She watched him for a while, expecting him to move on and go about his way, but he continued to study her. "You're watching me as if you haven't been entertained in years. Don't you have a television at home?"

"Nope. Got tired of all the dang reruns." A teasing glimmer lit his eyes, and humor tugged at his lips. He nodded toward the case he carried. "I don't suppose you play chess."

"Afraid not. I never could figure out how to balance the game board in a tree."

"Too bad." His grin broadened to an outright smile. "If you ever get it figured out, just give me a holler. My name's Walter."

"Mine's Claire. And I'll do that."

He nodded, then turned toward the parking lot, heading for the red pickup with the American flag decal displayed on the rear window. She'd seen it here before. It had a bumper sticker that claimed he was one of The Chosin Few.

A Korean War veteran, she suspected. A man who'd proudly fought at the Chosin Reservoir.

She tried to smooth the letter, then carefully tucked it into the waistband of her shorts.

As the pickup roared to life, she lowered herself to the ground. Her legs were still a bit rubbery from her run, and her foot slipped, causing her ankle to twist slightly and her knee to scrape against the bark.

"Ouch." She regained her footing, but grumbled again at the stupidity that had put her in this position.

The old man had called her crazy, and she had to agree. All she needed was a broken neck. Or to get laid up and be unable to work. Or worse. God forbid she'd be unable to run anymore. The rigorous daily jog was what kept her sane and her life on track.

Once safely out of the tree and seated on the bench, she pulled out the letter, reread it, and considered her response. Then she took the marker Analisa had again provided, printing this time so the girl could read the words all by herself—without *Trever's* help. When she finished, she dropped the marker back into the envelope, folded the wrinkled paper, tucked it inside, and placed it on the lowest branch.

As Claire drove toward the small condominium complex just off Chinaberry Lane and the three-bedroom place she called home, she again recalled the old man's words: *Crazy fool woman.*

For a moment, she'd wondered if maybe he'd been right. After all, how many grown women climbed into trees and responded to letters addressed to God?

There was a time when Claire might have called Vickie, the woman who'd once been her best friend.

"Hey, Vick," she would have said. "You'll never guess what I found today. And what I did."

But Claire had lost her connection to Vickie when Erik had died. Not that Vickie had been the one to pull away; she hadn't. It's just that one of the many things they'd had in common had been children the same age, and Claire hadn't been able to face the constant reminder of what Vickie still had.

And what Claire had lost.

Chapter 3

Walter turned down First Street and headed for the house he'd lived in for the past twenty years. He didn't often chat with people he'd met in the park. Why should he? Folks just seemed to think he was either feebleminded or a dirty old man, so he pretty much kept to himself.

But that shapely brunette jogger reminded him a lot of Margie when she'd been a sweet young thing and full of spunk.

He'd never said a word to the jogger before today, though. Women like her didn't want to be bothered by a worn-out old man like him. But when he'd walked out of the restroom and spotted her climbing a tree, he hadn't been able to resist.

It had been ages since he'd kidded a pretty little gal who knew how to tease back.

Margie, with her quick wit and playful side, had been like that. She'd had a way of making him smile and laugh at the simplest things. And when she'd died in the prime of life, Walter had been devastated.

He'd tried to shake the grief that had dang near killed him by drowning himself in the bottle, but it had been only a temporary fix.

How long had it been? How long had he been without the woman who'd shared his life and loved him in spite of his flaws and the demons that plagued him in the middle of the night?

Nearly twenty years, but it seemed like forever.

He supposed a man got used to fixing his own dinner, mending his own shirts. But living alone—or rather, sleeping alone—was tough.

And he wasn't talking about sex. It was more than that. It was the intimacy they shared, the conversations they had while lying close, holding each other.

They said time healed grief, but he wasn't so sure about that. After seeing the attractive young woman perched up in a tree, having a chance to talk and hear her voice, to catch a glimpse of her smile . . .

For a moment, he'd let the years roll back and had pretended she was his sweet wife.

And where had that gotten him?

Now he had an overwhelming urge to toast Margie's memory, to tell her again how sorry he was for the times he'd fallen off the wagon and let her down.

Maybe he ought to talk to someone. But who? Blake or Tyler? The kids who hadn't spoken to him in over ten years and had told him to lose their phone numbers? Or Carl Witherspoon, his best friend and mentor who'd died six months ago?

Walter looked up in the dusk-tinged sky and shook his head. "You left me in one heck of a fix."

He wasn't exactly sure who he was talking to, but as usual, there was no response.

It seemed that even the Ol' Boy Upstairs had forgotten him. Maybe He'd deemed a reformed hellion unworthy of entering the Pearly Gates. Not that Walter was looking forward to death. He suspected that all those years he'd been stubborn and had refused to accompany Margie and her sons to church had finally caught up with him. And that when he finally passed on, his tombstone would read: All Dressed Up And No Place To Go.

But heck, here he was on the right side of the cemetery lawn, and he still had no place to go, nothing to do.

Up ahead, flanked by an empty, weed-infested lot and a vacant building that had once housed a feed store, Paddy's Pub waited to pour a flood of scotch on a man willing to drown.

Happy Hour would be in full swing, which was tempting, but three years ago, Walter had made a promise to take one day at a time. A promise he hoped to keep.

Carl had more or less become Walter's AA sponsor, although Walter had refused to attend any meetings. "You'll have to get me rip-roaring drunk first, Carl. Crowds make me skittish when I'm sober."

The two men had become friends anyway and met almost every afternoon at Mulberry Park to play chess. Now, even though Carl was gone, Walter still showed up and set up the board on a picnic table.

Hanging out at the park alone was a stupid thing to do, he supposed, but it was a heck of a lot better than reverting back to the old ways, going back to the time when the pub had been his home away from home.

When he felt weak, he willed himself to think again of the tragedy that had struck about three years ago and had been so instrumental in causing him to take that first step into sobriety when nothing else had.

There but by the grace of God go I, the old saying went. And it was true.

It could have just as easily been Walter behind the wheel that afternoon, his reactions dulled by Jack Daniels. Walter who'd hit that little boy riding his bicycle along the street. Walter who'd have to live out the rest of his days behind bars.

At least he'd been spared that.

Still, there was enough other remorse to wallow in, other guilt to trudge through.

He kept the steering wheel straight, his eyes on the road ahead, but the urge to stop at Paddy's was growing stronger. He could make a turn down Main and change his route, but each day on his trek to and from the park, he chose to drive by the pub, forcing himself to face temptation and pass it by.

Today he was driving slower than usual, though. He

glanced at the speedometer. Yep. Well under the twenty-five-miles-per-hour limit.

He was practically at a standstill when he came to the pub, where a yellow neon OPEN sign flickered like a porch light, welcoming a tired old soul home, offering rest to weary bones, a place to unload a few burdens for a time, to share a few laughs.

Yet in spite of the overwhelming impulse to stop, Walter pressed down on the gas pedal, increasing his speed. He'd beaten it again today, but he feared there might come a time when he'd give in, when he'd take the easy way out.

As he passed the bar, he spotted a young boy walking along the sidewalk, kicking at a rock along the way. It was that kid from the park, the one who didn't appear to have anywhere else to go, anything better to do.

Again Walter suspected he and the boy had a lot in common, that they were both miserable and alone.

He had half a notion to befriend the kid the next time he ran into him, but Walter didn't have anything to offer anyone.

And he was a fool to think he might.

At quarter to ten, Sam Dawson grew tired of watching television and decided to read for a while. He clicked off the power on the remote, then headed to the room that had been his den before his niece moved in.

She'd gone to bed hours ago, but checking on her before he turned in had become a nightly ritual. He wasn't sure why, though. Maybe because he used to sneak off at night when he was a kid—not that anyone knew or cared when he did.

Sam supposed that might not become a problem with his niece, but peeking in on her still seemed like the kind of thing a responsible guardian should do.

From the doorway, he studied Analisa's sleeping form, watched her chest rise and fall in peaceful slumber. She'd tucked a worn-out doll under one arm and a brand-new teddy bear under the other.

His niece was a real cutie, and he was going to have his hands full when she grew up. But he was up to the task, even if that meant going head-to-head with any of the teenage boys who followed her home.

Sam raked a hand through his hair, then glanced at the little table and chair set that Hilda, the nanny he'd recently hired, had suggested he purchase.

Analisa sat there for hours, pretending to host a tea party for the queen or imagining a classroom for a couple of dolls and a few stuffed animals.

Tonight scissors, paper, markers, glitter, and glue littered the white wooden tabletop.

Analisa was usually pretty good about picking up after herself.

He'd have a talk with her about it tomorrow, which was a much better solution than his old man would have come up with. Sam would have been jerked out of bed, asleep or not, and slammed against the wall for making a mess.

In a strange twist, his own father had become the

antithesis of a role model when it came to parenting.

As Sam turned away, allowing the light from the hall to add more illumination to the child's room, the bold writing on a light green envelope on the little table caught his eye, drawing him back.

To God, it said.

She was writing another one? Wasn't the last one bright pink?

A subtle wisp of concern blew over him, and he wasn't sure what—if anything—he should do with it.

A couple of days ago, she'd come up to him and asked, "What's it like in Heaven?"

Her question had thrown him off balance, and he hadn't been sure if he should have given her a Santa Claus explanation or his own cold, hard spin on the afterlife.

"I don't know" was the only response his conscience had allowed.

She'd looked at him as if he'd kicked a puppy, and he'd felt as if he had, too. Maybe he should have made up something, mentioned the Pearly Gates, streets of gold, and a mansion in the clouds.

Her blue eyes had glistened to the point he feared she might start crying, then she'd crossed her little arms and shifted her weight to one foot. "Well, if *you* don't know, and since Mrs. Richards doesn't, either, we need to ask someone else."

No, they couldn't ask anyone else. First of all, Sam no longer knew anyone even remotely religious. And secondly, he wasn't about to flip through the yellow pages, call some minister out of the blue and ask a question like that.

Instead Sam had reached for one of Analisa's long, blond curls and gave it a gentle tug. "I probably should have asked your dad. I'll bet he knew all about it."

She'd nodded. "My daddy knew *everything*."

At times Greg Dawson had come across as a know-it-all, which had led to a second falling out between the two brothers nearly six years ago. Just one more rift they'd failed to mend.

But Analisa didn't need to know anything about that.

Sam leaned against the doorjamb of her bedroom and raked a hand through his hair. At times he wished he'd been on better terms with his brother, but it was too late now. Fate—or Whoever—had dealt them a fatal blow.

But hey. He'd get through it. He always did. And even though he couldn't make amends with his brother, he would do everything he could for his niece.

All right, so he didn't feel especially competent about being a parent, but money solved a slew of problems, and he had plenty of that. So the first thing he'd done was hire a nanny to take care of all the things a mother would do.

Jake Goldstein, a friend who'd attended law school with Sam, had recommended Hilda Richards, so that had solved the first dilemma.

Sam already lived in a nice house in one of the best

neighborhoods in Fairbrook, so he'd hired a professional designer to create a pink and frilly bedroom that was every little girl's dream. Then he'd provided his niece with all the dolls and toys she would ever want, all the things she would ever need.

It was a galaxy far, far away from the rundown neighborhood in which Sam and Greg had grown up. A fairy-tale world away from the childhood he and her father had experienced, a life Sam had done his best to escape.

Greg had escaped, too, but he'd chosen a religious path.

"You ought to come to church with me," Greg had told him more than once.

"Forget it." Sam hadn't needed the religious crutch. Instead, he'd pulled himself up by the proverbial boot-straps, excelled in college, utilized student loans, and went on to law school.

Rather than admire Sam's achievements and acknowledge that he'd kept his party-animal nose to the grindstone until he'd become an attorney, Greg had downplayed it all.

At the time, Sam had chalked it up to jealousy, but Greg had never seemed the least bit interested in money or success.

Six years ago, Greg had started in on Sam again. He'd told him that he still had an eat-drink-and-be-merry attitude and that his parties had merely gotten classier, the drinks more expensive.

Greg, who'd always found fault with Sam's self-reliance and drive, had criticized him to no end, preaching about the importance of placing one's trust in God.

A lot of good that had done Greg. With all his lofty ideas about the hereafter, he'd neglected to consider the present by drawing up a will or naming a guardian for his child.

Trusting God to the very end, Sam supposed. But who was looking out for Greg's daughter now?

Sam was.

Greg would be rolling over in the casket Sam had purchased for him if he had any clue that his hell-bent, self-centered brother was the one answering Analisa's questions about Heaven. Answers Sam didn't have and couldn't quite bring himself to fabricate.

"Welllll," his precocious niece had told him that day, "then I'll just have to ask *God."*

Sam had been happy to pass the buck to whoever would take it, but he hadn't meant to send her on some quixotic quest nor expected her to strike up a one-sided correspondence.

Or to offer God pictures she'd colored.

This evening she'd sketched an angel who looked a lot like the drawings she made of herself. The blue-eyed cherub—a boy—had glittery wings and wore a gold halo perched on blond, spiky hair. She'd even named him Erik.

Again, concern niggled at him. For a man who'd prided himself on his ability to solve any problem, he wasn't used to feelings of inadequacy, even when he was clearly out of his league with this sort of thing.

The angel was just artwork, he told himself. An innocent childish creation. That's all. But he would talk to Hilda about it in the morning.

That's why he'd hired the woman, although he had to admit being a bit apprehensive about her age. She had to be nearly as old as God himself, and, quite frankly, a good sitter ought to be able to keep up with the kid she was watching.

Jake had sworn up and down that Hilda was the best nanny in California. Not that she wasn't, but Sam hadn't seen anything to impress him to the point of singing her praises yet. Still he knew he ought to be thankful she'd come out of retirement and taken the job. His law practice was busier than ever, and even if it hadn't been, Sam didn't know squat about parenting, about what was normal for kids to do and what wasn't.

Struggling with the urge to shake it all off and retire for the night, the compulsion to step inside Analisa's room and study the artwork on the table won out.

He peered again at drawing of the angel, then turned the picture over. On the back side she'd written God a note:

Thank you for Erik. Can you give unkel Sam a angel to? He needs one to help him get his work all done so he can be home more.

A knot the size of a fist formed in Sam's chest, but before he could ponder what was going on in the little girl's mind or whether he ought to find a child psychologist for her, the telephone rang.

Who could be calling him at this time of night?

In an effort not to let the noise wake Analisa, he hurried into the hall and quickly answered.

It was Jake Goldstein.

"Hey," Sam said. "What a coincidence. I was just thinking about you a couple of minutes ago."

"Oh, yeah? I hope you were also thinking about golf. I called to ask you to play in the member-guest tournament we're having at Costa Serena."

Sam hadn't played golf in months, and Jake belonged to a prestigious club that boasted a challenging course that overlooked the ocean. There wouldn't be much arm-twisting going on. "I'd love to."

"Great."

That knot in his chest throbbed.

No, Sam realized, it *wasn't* great. He had a niece who was writing notes to God and asking for more of Sam's time and attention.

What kind of guardian would ignore that?

Only one who had a big LOSER sign pasted on his forehead.

Sam cleared his throat. "Wait a second, Jake. When is the tournament?"

"Next weekend. I would have called sooner, but I've been busy working on an appeal for a new client of mine, Russell Meredith."

"I'm aware of the case," Sam said.

A couple of years ago, the software exec's vehicle had struck a child on a bicycle. For more than twenty-four hours, while little Erik Harper had been on life support, the police had scoured the community looking for the driver who'd left the scene of the accident. Finally, Meredith had turned himself in, saying he hadn't realized his car had even hit the kid.

"Oh, that's right," Jake said. "You handled the civil suit the boy's parents filed."

Sam had managed to get the Harpers nearly five million dollars, which he'd hoped had helped them get on with their lives.

"The jury must have been putty in your hands," Jake said. "It's hard not to sympathize when the victim is a kid and the parents are grieving."

"The Harpers lost their only child. Plus they were at the scene and watched the accident happen. The jury would have needed cast-iron hearts not to be moved by that."

"Yeah, I know. And I'm afraid the parole board is going to see it the same way. But it was a tragic accident that could have happened to anyone."

"*Accidents* happen all the time. But *this* was a case of hit-and-run."

"There were mitigating circumstances."

"Meredith might have been intoxicated," Sam countered. "Drunk drivers are prone to flee the scene of accidents. And by the time he turned himself in, it was too late to prove one way or the other. Besides, he had a prior DUI causing bodily injury."

"That prior had been on his twenty-first birthday, and the injury was minor. He hasn't been in any trouble since, and I have witnesses who say Meredith was as sober as a nun and as law-abiding as an Eagle Scout."

"You probably should have defended him in the criminal trial."

"I wish I had."

A wry grin pulled at the corner of Sam's mouth. He and Jake were both practicing attorneys who could take either side in a case and present strong opposing arguments. In fact, they often did, even cases they discussed between shots on the golf course. "So what are Meredith's chances for parole?"

"It's hard to say. He's been a model prisoner, and I've never seen anyone more remorseful."

"Well, he *ought* to be sorry," Sam said. Meredith had slammed into Erik, knocking him and his bicycle into the shrubbery that grew along the road, then continued on his way.

The line grew silent.

Normally Sam made a point of distancing himself from his cases, yet this one had been particularly tragic and unsettling for everyone involved.

"Anyway," Jake said, "About the tournament—"

Sam cleared his throat. "You know, as much as I'd love to play, I can't take the time off right now."

"Work keeping you too busy, huh?"

"I'm afraid so." Sam glanced over his shoulder at the open door to Analisa's room. He also had an unexpected problem on the home front. "But I'll make time soon. Maybe next month."

After they ended the call, Sam started down the hall toward his own room, but paused momentarily by Analisa's open doorway. He took one last look at the picture she'd drawn, the angel named Erik. For a moment, a goose-bumpy shiver ran up and down his arms.

How weird was that?

He shook his head, quickly disregarding the coincidence. Even if he were foolish enough to believe in fairy tales or some spiritual *Twilight Zone*, Erik Harper had curly dark hair, not spiky blond.

And a bright-eyed smile that Sam suspected would haunt the boy's grieving parents forever.

Claire took the elevator upstairs to the sixth floor, strode to the solid double doors of Vandyke, Delacourt, West, and now Dawson, then entered a spacious lobby that boasted black marble, polished wood panels, and leather furniture—a validation of the firm's success and prestige.

She took a seat that allowed her to peer out one of several floor-to-ceiling windows that offered a view of Mulberry Park and the city beyond. The office didn't seem too familiar, but she'd only been here once to sign papers. It had been Ron who'd usually met with Mr. Dawson.

Of course, back then, Claire had been a zombie, barely able to put one foot in front of the other.

After checking in with the receptionist, she took a seat on a black leather sofa in the waiting room, crossed her legs, and reached for a *Psychology Today*. She thumbed through the pages, but couldn't find a single article to pique her interest, so she returned the magazine to the table where she'd found it.

An appointment with Samuel Dawson had been a good choice, she decided. Now there was no need to rehash the painful details with a new attorney who would have to be brought up to speed on the case.

She glanced at her wristwatch: 11:28. Surely someone would call her soon. She was anxious to get some solid legal advice, yet for some reason, she felt a bit uneasy and self-conscious.

Maybe it was just her reason for being here that made her hands clammy, her nerves taut and on edge.

She brushed her damp palms across the top of her lap, then opened her purse and withdrew the letter from the parole board.

Before she could read it again, a baritone voice called her name. "Mrs. Harper?"

"Yes." She glanced up to see Sam Dawson, a handsome man in his thirties, wearing a black suit. Expensive, she suspected.

He was tall, well over six feet, with broad shoulders and a square chin. His light-brown hair appeared to be sun-streaked, as though he spent more time outdoors than in the office, yet she doubted that was the case. Attorneys who'd just made partner probably didn't have much free time on their hands.

She stood, and he clasped her hand in greeting, a grip that warmed the chill from her fingers.

His confident touch was a balm to her frayed nerves. "It's good to see you again, Claire."

"Thank you."

"Let's go to my office."

She followed him down the hall until they came to an open door, where he paused and stepped aside, allowing her to enter first. As she passed by, she caught a whiff of his cologne, something ocean-fresh and musky.

It had been ages since she'd noticed scents. Not just a man's; a lot of things no longer smelled the same. The morning coffee for one. And even the rosebushes that lined Mrs. Wilcox's picket fence on Applewood Drive.

"Please have a seat," Sam said.

She chose one of the black, tufted-leather chairs that sat before his mahogany desk.

Had this been his office before?

She couldn't recall.

"What can I do for you?" His gaze locked on hers for the briefest of moments, and the intensity in his eyes—a vivid green in color—made it difficult to speak.

She handed him the notification she still clutched, holding onto the envelope. "Russell Meredith is up for parole on the twenty-fourth of July."

"Actually, I'd heard that." He took the letter and read the contents.

"And I want to make sure he serves every day of his sentence," she added, thinking it only fair. After all, Meredith had gotten off easy. It was Claire who had received the harshest punishment, one that would last a lifetime.

Sam lifted his eyes to hers and nodded. "I can understand why."

She might be wrong, but he seemed to recognize her pain. She'd felt it in his handshake, seen it in his eyes, heard it in his voice.

"The letter says I don't need an attorney, but I think that's the best way for me to go. Don't you?"

"Yes, of course. I can either represent you or advise you so that you can go before the board on your own. Either way, I'll do whatever I can for you and your husband."

Her chest tightened and her stomach clenched, reminding her that there was still some rehashing that needed to take place, still a few things Sam didn't know.

She cleared her throat, buying a moment for her emotions to rally. "If Ron wants to object to the parole, he'll have to get his own counsel. He and I were divorced about a year ago."

"I'm sorry to hear that."

She shrugged. "It was all pretty simple. We divided things as fairly as possible and had a single attorney draw up the papers. He . . . we . . . just wanted it to be over."

A little surprised at herself for sharing the details,

she didn't elaborate any further and was glad he hadn't pushed for more.

They discussed his retainer and fees, and she signed the standard paperwork. When he'd finished explaining what she could expect at the hearing and had answered her questions, she felt much better. Having someone in her corner, especially one so knowledgeable, was reassuring.

She stood, indicating that their meeting was over. "Thank you, Sam. I appreciate you helping me with this."

"You're welcome. In the meantime, I'll do a little research in case there's something we're missing. More details on that prior DUI might be helpful. I'll give you a call later in the week and let you know what I found."

"All right."

As Sam stood to escort her out, she faced him. "What do you think? *The truth.* What are our chances of swaying the parole board?"

"Actually, it's hard to say. But we'll give it our best shot."

She nodded as though he'd offered her what she needed to hear.

He hadn't though. Not really. There was a gaping hole in her life and her heart.

A hole nothing could fill.

Chapter 4

Claire might end her run each evening at Mulberry Park, but she made it a point to arrive after most people had taken their children and gone home for dinner.

So what was she doing here on a Saturday at noon, her car idling in one of only a few empty stalls?

She glanced across the console to the passenger seat, where a crayon-sketched angel named Erik rested. His gold halo was askew on a Bart-Simpson-style head of yellow hair, while big blue eyes with spiky black lashes looked up at her, and a crooked red grin tweaked her heart.

Yesterday, while peering up into the mulberry, Claire had spotted the picture on the lowest branch. Analisa's depiction of Erik-the-Angel didn't even remotely resemble her sweet, rough-and-tumble son, a boy with dark curly hair and golden-brown eyes.

In fact, Claire had reason to believe Analisa had drawn a male version of herself.

Erik looks a lot like you, she'd written in her response to the first letter. She hadn't meant that literally, but had been suggesting a commonality, since both of them were innocent children who'd been unfairly separated from their parents by death.

She blew out a ragged sigh. If Ron were still a part of her life, he'd tell her she was crazy, that she'd been foolish to quit seeing the shrink. And she'd be hard-pressed to argue with him.

Again she had the urge to leave, but scanned the park instead. The only person she recognized was Walter, the white-haired Korean War vet who'd caught her in the tree several evenings ago. Today he was seated at a table in the shade, not far from the restrooms.

Would he recognize her in a crisp, ivory-colored blouse and blue linen walking shorts rather than running gear? She suspected he might.

If she ever decided to get out of her car, she planned to keep a low profile, sit awhile and watch the children from a distance—something she'd been unwilling and unable to do after Erik's death.

She remained behind the wheel a moment longer, then reached across the console and turned the angel picture facedown in the passenger seat. Next she climbed from the car and locked it.

Before heading toward the park grounds, she adjusted her sunglasses. It wasn't as if she was trying to hide or planning to stalk anyone. She was just curious, that's all.

Her gaze drifted to the playground, where several kids laughed and played. When Erik had been a preschooler, she used to bring him to the park whenever possible.

He'd loved the outdoors. She had, too.

Yet now the sight of happy children—even two preschoolers squabbling over the same red plastic bucket—triggered a rumble of grief.

She had the urge to bolt before her eyes filled with tears, but that's what the sunglasses were for. To shield her sadness from the world.

Up ahead, Walter sat at a table, his chess game spread before him. She wondered if he was waiting for a friend.

Perhaps he wouldn't mind having company for a bit. She certainly couldn't very well hover near the playground. If she were still a parent, she'd be concerned about a childless woman hanging out by the swings and slides.

She made her way across the lawn, and when she paused beside Walter, her shadow darkened the chessboard.

As the white-haired old man glanced up, recognition dawned on his craggy face, triggering a crinkled grin. "Come by the park to climb trees again today?"

"I'm afraid not." She pointed to her knee, where a bandage covered another scrape she'd gotten yesterday while retrieving Analisa's picture.

"Oops. Did that happen the day I saw you?"

"No. The time after that."

He let out a little chuckle. "So you really are a treeclimber."

"Not anymore."

"Too bad. A lot of fellows my age take to birdwatching, which I always figured was a boring hobby. But I didn't realize they occasionally spotted pretty chicks."

She offered him the hint of a smile. "Are you waiting for someone?"

"No one in particular."

"Then do you mind if I sit for a minute or so?"

"Not at all." He brightened, a spark in his tired gray eyes hinting at the life still in him.

Claire brushed a few leaves aside from the green fiberglass bench, then sat and studied the playground.

A dark-haired girl with pigtails walked along the wooden beam that bordered the sandbox, her arms outstretched for balance while she tottered along, placing one foot in front of the other.

On top of the slide, another girl perched, ready to shove off. The sides of her hair—white blond—were held back with red barrettes.

That could be her, Claire realized, but there had to be hundreds of other possibilities in a city the size of Fairbrook.

Finally, she voiced her question. "I don't suppose you know a little girl named Analisa?"

"I generally steer clear of the kids, but I do know that one. She comes with her nanny nearly every day. Why do you ask?"

"Just wondered."

Walter lifted a gnarly, liver-spotted hand and pointed toward the slide. "That's her. The little blond tyke who just landed in the sand and is now walking toward the swings."

"Cute kid."

"Yep."

Analisa wore a red cotton blouse, denim shorts with a ruffled hem, and white sandals. She appeared to be clean and well-cared for.

Claire watched as the child backed her bottom into the seat of a swing and began to pump her little legs, soaring toward the sky. "What do you know about her?"

"Not much. She used to live with her parents in a foreign country. I forget which one—Guatemala maybe. Anyway, from what I understand, they were missionaries and died. Now she lives with her father's brother."

Unkel Sam, Claire realized. A man who worked more often than a lonely, grieving child would like him to.

If Claire had a chance to speak to Analisa's uncle, she'd tell him to find more time for the girl. To enjoy her while he had a chance to appreciate all he'd been blessed with.

"Why the interest?" Walter asked.

Claire shrugged. "I . . . uh . . . found a letter she'd written."

"To who?"

Did she dare confide in a virtual stranger and tell him she'd entered a pen-pal relationship with a child who thought she was corresponding with God?

You need to go back and see that doctor again, Ron had told her over and over. *There's other medication they can prescribe.*

If Claire had been able to take a magic pill to make

the overwhelming sadness go away, she would have gladly done so.

People grieve differently, the psychiatrist had told her. *Your husband has put the death behind him, but you're not ready to. And that's okay.*

The doctor had also agreed that married couples ought to support one another, to respect their differences. Instead, Ron had begun to spend more time at the office and less time at home. His absence, along with the emotional distance that separated them even while they were in the same room, pushed her to agree when he finally suggested they divorce.

Claire searched the old man's face. Something decent flickered in his eyes, although she couldn't quite put her finger on exactly what it was.

"Just between you and me?" she asked.

"I'm good at keeping secrets, especially when I don't have anyone to tell."

Sincerity in his tone gave her cause for relief. Sympathy, too. It seemed they had more in common than either would have guessed, and she felt compelled to confide in him. "Analisa wrote a letter to God and placed it in the big mulberry in the center of the park."

He arched a bushy white brow. "So that's what you were doing when I spotted you in that tree."

"Actually, the first letter practically fell in my lap."

"How many has she written?"

"Two. And yesterday she left me a picture she'd drawn." Rather, she'd left it for God and Claire had taken it home and placed it on the refrigerator overnight. Now it sat in her car.

Walter didn't object or accuse Claire of doing anything especially odd, so she added, "I felt sorry for her. She wanted to know if her parents were happy in Heaven. I told her they were, but that they missed her."

"You believe that?" he asked.

Claire shrugged. "Once upon a time I did." And she wanted to now, but somehow it was difficult believing that a loving God had taken her son, leaving her to wallow in grief and trudge through life alone.

As a child, she'd believed angelic choirs sang in the clouds and walked along streets of gold. But the thought of Erik being anywhere other than in a satin-lined box under six feet of sod was hard to imagine, even though she'd tried.

Walter didn't respond, and she was almost sorry he hadn't.

"I suppose you and I are on the same page," he finally admitted. "I've got a lot of friends who've passed on. Too many, actually. And I'd like to believe I'll see them again, but the truth is I'm not so sure."

A part of Claire had hoped for more from him, reassurance or some kind of confirmation. Yet she realized he'd probably had a few faith-busting trials of his own. Somehow, commiserating didn't seem to be anything that would help either of them.

"I used to believe," she told him. "Now I merely hope."

"You'll probably get a few brownie points for renewing a child's faith."

She chuffed. "Maybe so, but taking up a pen and claiming to be God could just as easily trigger a well-aimed lightning bolt."

"Nah. From what I understand, God's big on the Golden Rule." Walter chuckled. "To tell you the truth, I'm not sure what I would have done if those letters had fallen to me. Probably tossed them in the trash."

Claire hadn't even wanted to admit to Erik that Santa and the Easter Bunny weren't real. She fingered the hem of her shorts, then brushed at the edge of the adhesive bandage that protected the scrape on her knee. "I hope I did the right thing."

"Not to worry. In fact, I admire you for what you did."

Claire turned, caught his eye. For a moment they shared some kind of connection, although she'd be darned if she knew what it was.

Walter tossed her a wry grin. "I have no delusions about the Ol' Boy Upstairs being all that proud of me—even though I've straightened out my sorry life in the past couple of years. And I don't pretend to have an inside track."

Claire certainly didn't. She watched the girl for a moment longer. Analisa now had a face. On the outside, she appeared clean and healthy. But if her uncle didn't have time for her, were her emotional needs being met? And if not, to what extent did Claire want to get involved?

Oh, for Pete's sake. She was barely taking care of her own emotional needs. What did she have to offer anyone else?

She got to her feet and excused herself. "It was nice chatting with you, Walter, but I've got to go. I have errands to run."

"I'm here most every day. Anytime you want someone to spot you while you climb trees, I'd be happy to. 'Course, if you tumble, I'm not as strong or quick as I used to be."

"My tree-climbing days are over." She offered him a smile that held more warmth than the last. "Thanks for sharing your table."

"Any time."

She nodded, then headed toward her car. As she retrieved the keys from her bag, an old van pulled into the parking lot, the engine grinding to a halt. She stole a glance at the driver—a Latina who looked familiar.

For a moment, Claire had a difficult time recalling where she'd seen her before. Then she remembered. It was a woman who'd come in for a loan a week or so ago. Maria Somebody. Rodriguez?

Averting her head, Claire aimed her key at the car, clicked the button, and unlocked the door. Then she quickly climbed in and turned the ignition.

There was no need coming face-to-face with the woman she'd been unable to help. Why make either one of them feel uncomfortable?

But as she glanced into the rearview mirror, it wasn't Maria's gaze that she wanted to avoid.

• • •

Maria Rodriguez pulled the twelve-year-old minivan into the parking lot at Mulberry Park. From the sound of the motor, she suspected the transmission was slipping again.

Just what she needed. Another major repair.

"Analisa doesn't always come to the park on Saturdays," Danny said, "so I hope she's here today. She likes the swings, too. And I'm going to show her how to jump out and land in the sand."

"You need to be careful, *mijo*. I saw you do that the last time you were here, and I don't want you to get hurt."

"Don't worry, Mama. I know what I'm doing."

Wasn't that just like a child? To feel invincible? To downplay parental advice?

Maria had said as much to Tía Sofía when she'd been warned about dating the children's father. But did she listen? Oh, no.

"You're very brave and strong," she told her son, "but it's important to be wise, too. Don't confuse courage with stupidity."

"What do you mean?"

"Sometimes, when we have a reason to be cautious and ignore warnings of danger, it's often because we're being foolish, not brave."

Her dark-haired, blue-eyed son flashed her a smile, reminding her of his father. "Don't worry, Mama. I'm brave *and* smart."

"I know you are, *mijo*."

After shutting off the engine, Maria climbed from the maroon Plymouth Caravan, circled to the side door and opened it.

Danny unbuckled his seat belt. "I see Analisa's car, so she's here. Can I run ahead?"

"No, you need to help me." Maria unfastened the harness that secured two-year-old Sara in the car seat. "You carry the lunch and place it on an empty table in the shade."

"Okay. But can we sit next to Analisa and her *abuelita*?"

Actually, Mrs. Richards was Analisa's nanny, not her grandmother, but Maria didn't correct the boy. "You can ask Mrs. Richards if it would be all right if we share their table."

Danny snatched the blue plastic Wal-Mart sack that had been packed with sandwiches, apples, and graham crackers. "Okay."

Sometimes Maria worried that she expected too much from the boy, that she might be pushing him into a more grown-up role than was fair. But following his father's arrest and conviction, she'd been determined to do whatever it took to make sure her children grew up to be more responsible than her husband had been.

"Down," Sara said. "Peese?"

With those expressive blue eyes, Sara also favored her daddy, a handsome man who knew how to lay on the charm when he wanted to. Maria prayed his baby-blues and captivating smile were the only things his daughter and son had inherited from him.

When they'd separated for the final time, she'd taken back her maiden name, and when he'd gone to prison, she'd insisted the children go by Rodriguez, too.

The arrest and trial had been tough on Danny, who'd had to tolerate the whispers in the neighborhood, the taunts of kids who'd heard his father had killed someone. It had been tough on Maria, too. The pointed fingers, the knowing looks, the murmurs.

Maria placed her daughter's feet on the lawn and, as she watched the child toddle after her big brother, rubbed the small of her aching back.

Babies were a blessing, or at least they should be, but it was hard to get excited about the little boy she was carrying and would deliver soon. Not that she wouldn't love him once he arrived, but he'd been unplanned, a mistake she'd made one lonely night, when lust won over wisdom.

It wasn't the child's fault, but she feared this pregnancy would be a penitence she'd be paying for years to come.

While Maria approached the playground, she placed a hand on her swollen stomach, feeling a little bump—a knee or a foot—that moved across her womb. Soon there would be another mouth to feed.

As Maria neared Analisa's nanny, her steps slowed. She and the older woman had chatted a few times, but Mrs. Richards wasn't very friendly. Still, as was her habit, especially with the children present, Maria conjured a happy face. "Hello, there. It's a beautiful day for the park, isn't it?"

Hilda rarely smiled warmly, but there was something especially lackluster today. Her expression seemed drawn, pale.

"Is something wrong?" Maria asked.

"It's just this fool arthritis." Hilda rubbed her knobby-knuckled hands together. "And it's been acting up like old fury today."

Tía Sofía, Maria's aunt, had suffered with aches and pains prior to her death, and it had been sad to watch.

Hilda's gaze swept over Maria, settling upon her belly. "I imagine you're not too comfortable these days, either. I hope your husband helps out around the house."

Maria didn't want to lie, but she didn't want to share the ugly details, either. "I'm divorced, so it's just me and the kids."

"Too bad."

That might be true, but under the circumstances, she was much better off without a man, although that wasn't a subject she wanted to broach.

She reached for the plastic spoons and cups she'd packed in the diaper bag. "Excuse me for a minute. I need to give Sara something to play with."

Moments later, as the toddler plopped down in the sand and began to dig, Maria returned to Hilda and took a seat.

"You know," Hilda said, "that little boy is always here."

The elderly woman hadn't needed to point out a child in particular. Maria knew she was referring to Trevor, who sat alone on the down side of a teeter-totter. "Yes, I've noticed."

He was quiet and tended to keep to himself, although every once in a while, Analisa or Danny managed to draw him out.

Hilda clucked her tongue. "And he's never supervised."

Maria thought he might be a latchkey kid, left on his own each day. "Some children aren't fortunate enough to have parents who look out for them."

"Well, we don't live in the same world as we used to, and there are wicked people who prey on little ones."

Maria found it impossible to argue with her logic or to defend the boy's parents.

They sat quietly for a while, lost in their own thoughts and worries. When Maria's tummy growled, she glanced at her wristwatch, then at Hilda. "Maybe we ought to call the children and have them eat lunch."

"Good idea."

Maria took the kids to the restroom and helped them wash up. When they returned to the table, she passed out sandwiches and apple slices, but something kept her from joining Danny and Sara and opening the baggies that held her own meal.

Her gaze drifted to Trevor, who remained seated on the teeter-totter. He reached into the pocket of his jeans and pulled out a handful of something small and bite-size.

A snack?

Maybe.

The baby moved about in her womb, and her stomach grumbled again. Her blood-sugar levels had been screwy lately, so she shouldn't skip lunch, but she suspected that whatever had been in Trevor's pocket had been his breakfast, too. So there was no way she'd eat in front of him. She'd just have to leave the park early. And next time, she'd make an extra sandwich—just in case.

"Trevor," she called to the boy. "If you like peanut butter and grape jelly, you can join us for lunch. I have plenty."

The boy's eyes, as leery as a stray cat, studied her for a moment. A *long* moment. Then he slowly got up from the sloping wooden plank on which he'd been sitting and trudged to the table.

Maria placed the food she'd packed for herself next to Danny. "I'm glad you're going to join us for lunch." She nodded toward the gray cinder-block structure that housed the bathrooms. "Why don't you wash up first?"

The boy glanced at his dirty palms, then turned over his hands and furrowed his brow as if he'd just noticed how grimy they were.

As he headed for the restroom, Maria wondered what his story was. Yet even though she was curious about who was looking after him and tucking him in at night, she wouldn't ask. After all, there wasn't much she could do, other than offer him scraps of food. She was having a tough enough time looking after her own kids and certainly couldn't afford to take in strays.

Especially since she'd once been—and still felt like—one herself.

After lunch, as Trevor sat in the swing, digging the toe of his tennis shoe into the sand, a shadow settled over him. He looked up and saw Analisa standing beside him.

"Can I talk to you?" she asked. "We're going to be leaving soon, and I need you to do something for me again."

"Climb the tree?" He couldn't believe she was still leaving notes and pictures and stuff for God.

She nodded, then pulled out a folded envelope from her pocket. "I wrote another one last night."

"Why do you keep doing that? He hasn't been answering you."

"He did *once*. You saw it. And the letters we leave are always gone the next day."

"Anyone could've taken them."

Analisa crossed her arms. "*God* took them. And He'll answer every single one of them when He has time."

How was Trevor going to get it through her head that this was a waste of time? God didn't answer prayers. Trevor knew that; he'd prayed a ton of times and nothing had happened.

She stood there, that dumb letter in her hand.

Trevor should have told her no, but he took the note instead. "I'll stick it in the tree, but I hope you're not expecting an answer."

"God's just very busy, that's all. How would you like to be in charge of the whole wide world?"

"If He's *that* busy, why bother Him?"

"You can't bother God, Trevor."

The dumb little girl had an answer for everything.

"I'll prove it to you," she added. "What do you want? I'll ask Him to give it to you."

Trevor, who'd learned to keep his troubles a secret, wouldn't tell her what he really wanted. But there was something else he'd really like to have. It was a long walk to the park, and he'd asked his dad for a bike last Christmas.

Absolutely not, his father had said. *No bicycle*. The way he'd said it made Trevor think no one but God could ever change his dad's mind.

Trevor got off the swing and took her challenge. "Okay. I'd like a bike. A red one."

Analisa grinned as though she and God were best friends. "Okay. Let's pray."

"Here?" Trevor scanned the park. "Are you nuts? No way."

She reached out her hand. "It works best this way."

"What way?" He merely looked at her.

"If we hold hands. A prayer works better when two or more people agree."

So much for the bike. Trevor wasn't going to hold

hands with a girl. And he wasn't going to pray out loud in the park.

"Don't you want a bike?" she asked.

"Not that bad."

Her arms were still crossed, and she shifted her weight to one foot like his mom used to do when Trevor did something to annoy her. "God doesn't like it when people don't believe in Him."

Trevor looked over his shoulder, but didn't see anyone paying attention to him or to Analisa. "Okay, but let's go behind the tree."

Analisa led him to the center of the park, and when he was sure they weren't being watched, he let her take his hand.

This was *so* dumb.

She lowered her head and closed her eyes. "Dear God, please let Trevor have a bike. He needs to know that You love him and want him to have good things. Amen."

As Trevor started to pull his hand away, she held on tight. "You gotta say it, too."

"Say what?"

"*Amen*. It's like saying good-bye to God."

Oh, brother. "Amen. Okay?"

Analisa grinned as though everything was wonderful now.

Yeah. Right.

As Trevor turned to walk away, he shook his head. If a new red bicycle magically appeared on his front porch, then maybe he'd have to change his mind about God.

Of course, there were some things he needed a lot more than a bike.

But God—if He was up there—already knew everything about that.

And He hadn't done anything about it.

Chapter 5

E ven for a Saturday, the park had been pretty quiet. Trevor hung out until after the last kid went home, but why stay by himself here when he could do that at home?

He looked at the sun, saw it slipping lower than the big palm trees near the brick office building. He wasn't all that good at guessing the time unless there were other things making it easy. Like the old guy who'd packed up his chessboard and was heading toward his red pickup.

It had to be way after five o'clock, so it was time to go—especially if Trevor wanted to beat Katie home, which he did. Some nights she worked really late, but this wasn't one of them.

Besides, he was getting hungry even though he'd had more to eat for lunch today than he usually did. It was cool having a mom-made lunch for a change. Mrs. Rodriguez had cut the skin off the apples just like Trevor's mother used to do.

It had been sad, too, and Trevor had gotten pretty quiet while they ate. That happened whenever he thought about his mom. Sometimes he couldn't even remember what she used to look like, and he was afraid that when he got to be old like the chess-guy, he'd forget he even used to have a mom. That her hair had been blond. That she sometimes sang silly songs when she drove him to school. And that she smelled nice and kind of powdery.

Trevor blew out a sigh. Not having a mother sucked. Katie tried hard, but it wasn't the same.

As he headed toward the apartment complex where they'd moved a couple of months ago, he kicked a half-crushed beer can along the edge of the road. His shoelaces flip-flopped from side to side, but he didn't care.

If his dad was here, he'd tell Trevor to stop and tie them. So would Katie. But when Trevor was all by himself, he didn't have to obey anyone or do anything he didn't want to do.

A kid at the park once told him that he was lucky, but that wasn't true. Trevor was probably the unluck-iest kid in the whole world.

As he approached the weeded area near Paddy's Pub, his stomach rumbled in spite of the peanut butter sandwich he'd eaten today, so he considered taking the shortcut home.

"If you go to the park," Katie always told him before she left for work each day, "you can only stay for an hour. And be careful when you walk. Stay on the side-walk and don't cut through that vacant field."

Trevor didn't always listen to Katie, though.

As he took the path that wound through the empty

lot, a noise buzzed in his ears. Some kind of insects, he suspected, but they had a scary, snakelike sound, and it was hard to tell for sure.

The weeds had grown really high, so he couldn't see anything to the right or left of him. For that reason, he stayed on the dirt walkway. Rattlers were deadly, but even pet snakes in an aquarium-like cage scared him.

Once, when Trevor first moved to this side of town, he'd asked a younger kid if they ever spotted rattlesnakes in the area.

"No," the kid had said. "But you gotta be careful of the cobras 'cause they'll spit in your eye."

Trevor knew cobras didn't live in California, so he figured the kid was just dumb.

Still, he watched his step and listened for a rattling sound. He was more than halfway across now, so he kept walking, scanning the field ahead and feeling like Dorothy and her friends in Oz as they chanted, "*Lions and tigers and bears, oh my.*"

There wasn't much Trevor was scared of, so he didn't like the feeling now. Didn't like the pounding of his heart, the sweaty prickle that skittered down his spine.

Off to the right, something red and black and shiny lay almost hidden. He stood at a crossroads, tempted to trek through the knee-high brush and check it out, yet wanting to remain where there were definitely no snakes.

It could be junk.

But what if it wasn't?

He stepped off the path and spotted more and more red. It looked like a . . .

It *was*. A skateboard.

How did it get way out here? Had someone thrown it away? Or maybe hidden it for some reason?

He picked it up and turned it over, studying it carefully. The scarred wood base was kind of dirty and banged up a bit. But not that much.

Josh Ryder, his friend from the old neighborhood, was really into skateboarding and had everything that went with it—the gear, the clothes.

Trevor placed his hand on the wheels and made each one spin. The trucks, the part of the board that the wheels were connected to, seemed a little loose. But at least it worked.

Cool.

For a moment, he wondered if his dad would approve of him having a skateboard. Probably. It wasn't as big as a bike.

Ooh. Wow. That was weird.

Thoughts of the brand-new bicycle he'd always wanted made him remember the prayer he and Analisa had shared earlier today.

Well, this definitely wasn't a bike.

But it *was* red and had wheels. It was also kind of magical how it had just appeared on the very same day they'd asked for a bike.

Maybe God didn't like crossing parents. Maybe He wouldn't give a kid something a kid wasn't allowed to ride. Maybe He'd decided to give Trevor something his dad would approve of instead.

How cool was that?

Trevor would take the skateboard home and hide it under the bed until it was safe to bring it out. And then he'd take it to the park each day and practice until he learned how to ride it like the guys in the skateboard magazines at the grocery store.

A grin tugged at his lips. This was the best thing that had happened to him in a long, long time.

Maybe God was looking out for him after all.

On Wednesday morning, after his appointment with Doc Eldridge and a stop at the drugstore to fill a new prescription to control his cholesterol, Walter drove to the park. Along the way, he passed a kid trying to ride a skateboard while keeping one foot practically tethered to the ground.

No, not just any kid. *The* kid. The one who hung out at the park.

Maybe someone had gotten him a birthday gift or something. That was nice, although Walter hoped the youngster didn't break his neck.

What was he doing? He shouldn't be riding along the sidewalk on a busy street. Not until he learned how to balance on the blasted thing.

For a moment, Walter thought about pulling over and talking to the boy, but he made it a point not to stick his nose in other folks' business.

Besides, what did he know about kids? His own

stepsons had pretty much disowned him, and he couldn't say as he blamed them.

He pulled into the parking lot, next to the car Hilda and Analisa were climbing out of. His lips twisted in a crooked grin at the thought of the blond pixie writing letters to God.

It was kind of cute, if you asked him.

"Good morning." His voice held a friendly tone and boomed as though he was outgoing and had a habit of greeting everyone he ran into. In reality, Walter had always been shy—except when he drank.

Funny thing, though. The other day, after talking to Claire, who hadn't shined him on like most people did, his confidence level had risen.

"Good morning," Hilda said.

"Ought to be a nice day," he added.

She glanced around, as if she hadn't realized the sky was such a pretty shade of blue and the ocean breeze would make it pleasant today.

The sun glistened off strands of silver and platinum in her hair. She'd be an attractive woman if she smiled more. But then again, maybe—like him—she didn't have much to be happy about these days.

"I asked God to find you a friend," the little girl told him. "One who knows how to play *chest*."

"You did?" The fact she'd mispronounced the name of the game didn't faze him, and he'd be darned if he'd correct her. He supposed he ought to thank her. As far as he knew, nobody had ever prayed on his behalf before. Except maybe Margie when she'd been alive. "I appreciate that, young lady."

"You're welcome." She blessed him with a grin that turned his heart to mush, then looked at her nanny. "Can I run ahead to the playground? Please?"

"Sure. Go ahead. But don't you try to jump out of the swing. If something happens and you get hurt, your uncle will tell us we can't come back to the park."

The little cutie pie dashed off, leaving Walter and Hilda to bring up the rear. It was his cue to go his own way, but he didn't. "How's that arthritis?"

"Not too bad today."

"I don't know about you," he quipped, "but I used to be a kid not so long ago. And all these aches and pains are for the birds."

Hilda actually grinned, which took years off her face. "I couldn't agree more."

They walked toward the shaded table near the playground, where she and the girl usually sat. Rather than part ways and move on, Walter stuck around for a moment. Maybe she'd flash him another one of those rare smiles.

"Mind if I sit here for a minute or two?" he asked.

"No. Go ahead."

They didn't speak right away, which wasn't surprising. Right now, they seemed to be two strangers treading on shaky ground.

He finally asked, "How long have you been a nanny?"

"Nearly thirty years. I married just out of high

school, but when my husband Frank died, I had to figure out a way to support myself. And since I always liked children and we'd never had any of our own . . ." She dropped the subject, which made him think she was still dealing with either the loss or the disappointment. Maybe both.

"Ever remarry?"

"No."

That was too bad. The so-called Golden Years were merely gilded without loved ones or friends, and Walter suspected she was nearly as lonely and miserable as he was.

"How about you?" she asked. "Are you married?"

"I was once. She was a pretty gal named Margie, a single mother with two little boys." Hilda didn't ask for details, but Walter rarely had a chance to reminisce out loud. "She was a waitress, and I used to eat most of my meals at that little coffee shop where she worked, just so I could see her."

In fact, when the two of them started dating, he'd curtailed his drinking and settled down, hoping to be the kind of man she and her two sons deserved. And at least while she'd been alive, he'd been able to lay aside his demons and become a family man—for the most part, anyway.

"She was a good woman," he added. "A fine wife and mother. And she made me a better man."

"How did you lose her?"

"She had a heart attack." It had been completely unexpected.

"I'm sorry."

"Me, too." She'd been on life support for a while, and he'd stuck by her side at the hospital, hoping and praying God would spare her.

But He hadn't.

Her death had been devastating, and before long, Walter had fallen back into his old lifestyle, resulting in a blur of bars, booze, and brawls.

"Did you two have any children?"

"Just her boys. None of our own. I don't see much of them anymore."

"That's too bad. Families ought to stick together."

"Yeah. And stepdads shouldn't drink themselves to death, either."

Walter usually kept to himself and never shared personal thoughts and pain like that, so why had he now? He wanted to reel in the words, to smother the confession.

But Hilda didn't seem to be judging him for being either a drunk or a blabbermouth, so he added, "I've been sober three years now."

The tone of his voice, still strong and steady, belied his shaky confidence about staying on the wagon.

"Do the kids know about your sobriety?" Hilda asked.

"No." He doubted that it would make a difference. He'd been a mean drunk for too many years.

In fact, time and again, he'd been a real embarrassment to the boys and later to their families. But he wouldn't tell Hilda that. Nor would he admit that Tyler and Blake had become so disgusted with him and tired of his behavior that they'd both shut him out of their lives.

It had shaken him up, of course, but he'd eventually quit approaching them, realizing it was no use.

How many times could a fellow say he was sorry?

Over the next week, Claire considered coming clean and telling Analisa that God had neither read nor answered her poignant letters. Yet each time she'd finished her daily run and sat under the mulberry, she'd been unable to find the words that wouldn't disappoint the child.

Claire had also thought about just leaving the notes in the branches of the tree so Analisa would grow tired of waiting for an answer that would never come, but she feared someone else might find them, that maybe a predator would take advantage of the little girl. So each time she'd spotted a colorful paper or envelope in the mulberry, she'd taken it home with her.

In addition to the sketch of Erik the Angel, Claire had found a new letter nearly every day.

Monday's had been written on yellow paper with a teal-green crayon and read:

Dear God.
I reely wish you wuld give Unkel Sam a angel.
I herd him on the fone when he sed he was in trubel becuz Juj Rile was sined. Pleez forgive him for the bad word he sed. Thats why he needs the angel.

Claire had no idea what kind of trouble Unkel Sam had gotten into. Nor did she know who Juj Rile was. Whatever he or she had done, Analisa seemed to think it was sinful. Hopefully, it wasn't anything illegal. The orphaned child had been through enough already.

Choosing not to respond to that particular letter hadn't been too hard. Even if she'd wanted to, what words of comfort or advice could she have given?

Then the next day, she'd found another note written on lavender construction paper with a forest-green marker.

Dear God.
I no your buzy. But pleez bless Mrs. Richerdz.
She has panes in her hands and neez. And she
forgits stuff. Can you help her rememer where
she put the neklis her huzbin gave her? And
the box?

Claire suspected Mrs. Richerdz was the elderly woman who accompanied Analisa to the park. The arthritis, if that's what plagued her, was to be expected, as was some memory loss. Even Claire, who was pushing forty, found herself heading upstairs and forgetting why. Or peeking into the refrigerator and unsure of what she'd been looking for.

Hopefully, Mrs. Richerdz wasn't actually losing it, especially if she was supposed to be looking after the child. Of course, that wasn't Claire's concern; it was

Unkel Sam's—whoever he was. Perhaps he should stay home more and keep out of trubel.

Late Wednesday afternoon, Claire found another message written with a red crayon on a lime-green sheet of paper.

Dear God.
Do you no some buddy who can play with Mr.
Klinfelor? I meen someone not in hevin. Can
you tell him to come to the park and talk to an
old man who sits by hiself?

Claire, who'd been so focused on her own misery, had neglected to consider how lonely Walter might be. Not that she was in any position to do much about that, but truthfully? Claire wished she knew something about the game of chess. If she did, she would offer to sit with him one afternoon and play.

Maybe it would do them both some good.

Interestingly enough, she'd begun to see the world through Analisa's eyes and found herself more aware of the people she'd merely seen in passing—those she saw regularly at the park. And she'd begun to feel compelled to put a face to the names Analisa had mentioned.

Yesterday's letter, a pale blue note with brown writing, spoke of a child named Danny. There was no telling who the boy or his mother were, but apparently Analisa had reason to believe the family was strapped for cash and that they'd have to sell their house and move far away if the woman didn't marry a hansum prince who liked kids and had a whole lot of money.

Today, as Claire sat on the concrete bench under the mulberry, her legs still tense and shaky from her run, she read the latest note drawn on pink paper with a green marker.

Dear God.
Trever dint use to beelve in you. He duz now.
Thank you for the skate bord. Maybe you dint
here me good when we prade about it. Trever
reely wanted a red bike. The bord is ok. He is
happy and rides it all the time. Did he thank
you? I told him he shood.

Claire sat in the shade of the tree, just as she had each evening this week, and pondered whether she should answer this letter or not. Every other night she'd taken it with her, but now she was vacillating.

If she did answer, maybe she ought to respond as herself, a woman who'd merely found the letters.

Apparently, the child had a tremendous amount of faith and had been voicing her prayers out loud, too. She'd obviously asked God to give her friend a bike and believed he'd been granted a skateboard instead.

And speaking of skateboards . . .

In the distance, the sound of wheels on rough concrete drew her attention, and she glanced toward the parking lot, where a boy was practicing on a banged-up board—no helmet, no pads.

And no sign of any adult supervision.

As much as she'd like to mind her own business, the former mother in her, as rusty as it had become, couldn't keep still. She folded Analisa's letter and put it into the pocket of her shorts, then strode across the lawn to where the boy tried to balance on the skateboard, stumbling more often than not.

"Excuse me," she said.

The boy, his scruffy brown hair badly in need of a trim, stopped in his tracks and gazed at her, his eyes wide and wary.

"Is your name Trevor?"

His brow furrowed as he nodded. "How'd you know that?"

"Just a lucky guess. I'd heard you had a skateboard."

"Yeah." He glanced down at the board that rested beside his untied shoes, then back at her. "I found it in a field, and I thought . . . Well, whatever. Is it yours?"

"No, but I couldn't help worrying about you. Shouldn't you be wearing protective gear?"

He shrugged. "I guess, but I don't have any. *Yet.*"

Claire and Ron had purchased different safety gear for every sport or activity in which Erik had been involved. They were in the garage now, including the helmet and pads he'd used for his in-line skates.

Ron had packed it all away and told her to give it to the Salvation Army, but she'd been unable to part with anything. Unable to let go.

She opened her mouth to offer them to the boy, but

couldn't seem to utter the words. Instead, she asked, "Do your parents know you're here, riding a skateboard in the park?"

"My mom is dead. And my dad doesn't live with me."

Claire's heart, once stone-cold and buried with Erik, pulsed like a bleep on a hospital monitor. "Who's looking after you?"

"Katie."

Claire wanted to ask more questions, but refrained. It really wasn't any of her business, and she couldn't believe she'd interfered this much already. Of course, the boy was about the age Erik had been when . . .

She cleared the knot of emotion from her throat. "Accidents happen in the blink of an eye, Trevor. People get injured, especially small boys. Please be careful. *For me?*"

He shrugged. "Okay." Then he nibbled on his bottom lip the way Erik used to do when he had something weighing on his mind. "Can I ask you something?"

"Sure."

"What's that smell?"

"Excuse me?" Did she stink? She'd just finished her run and had been perspiring. "What are you talking about?"

"Your perfume. I can just barely smell it, but it's nice. And powdery." His eyes glistened. "Like the kind a mom might wear."

She tried to utter a thank-you, but the words wadded

up in her throat, making it hard to swallow, hard to breathe.

When it became apparent that she wasn't going to answer his question, even though she'd meant to, he turned and walked away. His feet shuffled, his dirty, frayed shoelaces untied and slapping the ground.

"Trevor?" she called.

He stopped and glanced over his shoulder. "Yeah?"

"My perfume is called Everlasting. My mom used to wear it, too."

He nodded.

"One more thing," she said before he went on his way.

She spotted a now-what? in his eyes.

"Tie your shoes, okay?"

Their gazes locked, and a warm whisper blew through her chest like a spring thaw.

Neither of them moved.

"Please?"

A wry grin tugged at his lips. "You even *sound* like a mom." Then he knelt on the ground and grabbed the strings, tying them into a double knot.

She wanted to say, "I *am* a mom." But that wasn't true anymore. Instead, she started for her car. As she reached into her pocket for the keys, her fingers brushed against Analisa's letter. The one she'd found today.

Unable to help herself, she headed back to the mulberry tree to take a seat and pen an answer to the child's letter.

But God only knew what she would say.

Chapter 6

As Analisa stood under the big tree at the park on Saturday morning, her heart zoomed in her chest. God did it! He *finally* did it. He answered another one of her letters.

Where was Trevor?

She looked near the parking lot, where he'd been practicing on the skateboard God had given him. He was still there, so she ran along the sidewalk to talk to him. "Trevor!"

He turned to look at her. Sweat on his forehead made the hair around his face wet. He didn't exactly smile, but he didn't look unhappy to see her, either. That was good because she wanted to be his friend, even if Mrs. Richards thought he was too old for her.

"I need you to climb the tree again."

"Oh, *no*." Trevor, who had one foot on the board and the other on the sidewalk, frowned and crossed his arms. "You're not going to stick another letter up there, are you?"

"I didn't write one last night. But He answered the one from yesterday. Look!" She pointed to the branch where it now rested. "We put it higher, remember?"

Trevor blew out a loud sigh, the kind Uncle Sam blew out when he got a phone call after dinner and wanted to watch TV instead. But he didn't look angry or tell Analisa she was dumb. He just stooped to pick up his skateboard and carried it to the middle of the park, where he rested it against the concrete bench.

Then he glanced around, as though making sure no one could see what he was doing, and climbed up the tree to get her note. He dropped it down to her, and she scooped it up.

The writing wasn't in cursive this time, so she could probably figure it out by herself, but she and Trevor were kind of becoming friends. And since God was listening to both of them now, she thought it would be a good idea if she let Trevor be the first to know what God had said.

When Trevor jumped down, she handed it to him. "Will you please read it to me?"

"Sure." He took the letter and unfolded it.

Dear Analisa,

You're right. God is very busy, so I am answering this for Him. My name is Claire.

I admire your concern for your friends at the park. I would suggest that Mrs. Richards see a doctor. Perhaps she will get some relief for her pain with medication. The doctor may be able to help her memory, too.

The best way for Mr. Klinefelter to have a friend is for him to be one. It's a piece of advice a little birdie once told me. And as far as your friend Danny and his mom are concerned, I'm sure God will work things out for them.

By the way, if I had been blessed with a little girl, I would have wanted her to be just like you.
Love,
Claire
P.S. Please tell Trevor to wear a helmet whenever he rides his skateboard.

"Who's Claire?" Analisa asked.

"How would *I* know?"

" 'Cause she cares about you." The breeze blew a loose strand of hair across Analisa's face, and she brushed it away. "Claire must be an angel like Erik. I'll bet she's probably *your* angel."

Trevor blew out another sigh. "You gotta quit thinking that God is writing you letters and that angels are flying all over the earth trying to spy on people."

"God didn't write *this* one. It was from His helper angel. And they don't spy on us. They take care of us."

"Yeah, right. There's no such thing as helper angels."

"There is, too. Lots of them. And sometimes birdies talk to them, just like Claire said in the letter. Then, when God gets busy, they work for Him, just like the elves who help Santa when it's Christmas."

Trevor clucked his tongue again like he didn't believe her, but after she was walking back to the playground, she glanced over her shoulder and saw him looking for something up in the tree.

For an angel, she suspected.

Dear God, she prayed, *please let Trevor see one. Okay?*

Then he'll really *believe.*

Claire returned to the park late Saturday morning with a contrite heart. She'd tried to make things right with her note to Analisa yesterday, but wasn't convinced that she had. Hopefully, the pen-pal relationship would stop, but if it didn't she'd have to speak to Mrs. Richards about it. Of course, she really should talk to the girl's uncle instead, but she suspected he was too caught up in himself and his work to consider the child—just like her ex-husband had been.

Ron, a workaholic, had spent most weekends at the office or preparing for a business trip. Claire hadn't minded giving him up during the week, but on Saturdays and Sundays she'd wanted more of his time. Her childhood had been neither typical nor happy, and she'd wanted the white-picket-fence dream for her son—a dream that had died with Erik.

A quick scan of the playground told Claire that Analisa was here again today, as she'd suspected, but she sat behind the wheel a moment longer, pondering her reason for coming. She really shouldn't interfere, but she was in too deep already.

She climbed from the car and started toward the rolling blanket of freshly mowed lawn. The sun warmed her face, while a red-breasted bird chirped and chattered in the branches of one of the smaller trees. A robin, she decided.

She couldn't remember the last time she'd been drawn this closely into the world around her.

Yes, she could. It had been three long years ago.

Off to the left, Trevor rode his skateboard on the sidewalk that ran along the perimeter of the park. His balance didn't appear any better than before, and he still wasn't wearing any protective gear.

The boy could really stand a haircut, a bath, and a new pair of shoes. A new outfit, too. The denim jeans he wore sported a frayed hole in the knee, and his blue T-shirt was too small. She wondered who'd chosen his clothing this morning, suspecting he'd dressed himself.

A sense of unfairness crept over her. She'd had a son she'd adored, but lost. And someone else had a child they should appreciate, but apparently didn't. As had become her habit, she struggled to shove the negativity aside. Her life was dark enough without adding more.

As she started down the walkway that led to the playground, the elderly woman who brought Analisa to the park approached with a catch in her gait. Dressed neatly in a pair of pale green polyester slacks and a matching polka-dot blouse, the woman headed toward the parking lot, favoring her right leg.

With Analisa happily climbing onto a teeter-totter with another girl, Claire had a perfect opportunity to speak to the nanny.

"Good morning. My name is Claire," she said, introducing herself.

The silver-haired woman seemed a bit surprised to be stopped by a stranger, but she managed a smile. "I'm Hilda Richards."

"If you have a minute, I'd like to talk to you about Analisa."

Mrs. Richards stiffened, drawing herself up as tall as her barely-five-foot stature would allow. "What about her?"

Before Claire could comment, a skid and a swish ripped through the midsummer morning, followed by a gasp and a hard thump. Both women turned to see Trevor crumpled on the ground, his skateboard upside down in the street. They hurried to his side.

"Are you all right?" Claire asked.

He nodded, sitting up and cradling his arm, his elbow scraped and bloody. He bit his lip and grimaced as he assessed his injury. Tears welled in his eyes, yet he didn't cry.

"Where are your parents?" Hilda asked.

"I don't have any," he said. "Not really."

Claire stooped and helped him to his feet.

"Who's looking after you?" Hilda asked.

"Katie, but she had to work today."

"I keep a first-aid kit in my car," Hilda told Claire. "Why don't you help him wash up while I go get it?"

Trevor glanced down at his skateboard, then stooped to pick it up. "I have to bring this with me. I don't want anyone to steal it."

"You'd be better off if someone did," Hilda quipped. "A boy I used to take care of split his lip, chipped his front teeth, and broke his wrist with one of those fool things. I'd been warning his father, but it took an accident to make the man finally see reason and take it away."

Trevor opened his mouth to object, then clamped it shut instead.

Hilda shook her head as she walked away to retrieve her first-aid kit.

As much as Claire agreed with Hilda on the dangers of skateboards, she sympathized with the child who claimed he didn't *really* have parents, and a plan formed in her mind.

"If you promise not to ride that again until tomorrow afternoon," she told him, "I'll bring you some knee pads and a helmet."

He gazed up at her in disbelief—or perhaps skepticism. His hair, damp from perspiration, was almost as curly as Erik's had been. He managed to muster a grin. "Thanks."

The offer was on the table, and she couldn't very well take it back, even if a battle still waged inside. Yet truthfully, she couldn't live with herself if she was able to prevent a serious injury to the boy and failed to do so.

She supposed Ron would be proud to know she would finally be parting with something of Erik's, but she wouldn't tell him. They rarely spoke anymore; they had no reason to.

As she led Trevor to the restroom, she placed a hand on his shoulder and guided him to the ladies' side.

"Oh, no you don't. No way." He balked, digging in his heels. "I'm not going in the girls' bathroom."

Well, they were in a bit of a quandary. Claire couldn't very well go into the men's room.

Or could she?

"Okay, I'll make the sacrifice. You go in first and make sure the coast is clear, then I'll come in."

"I can do it myself," he said.

She suspected he'd been doing way too much for himself as it was. "Wounds can become infected if they're not cleaned properly, Trevor. Why don't you let me help?"

When he reluctantly agreed and made sure the bathroom was empty, she supervised the cleansing of his elbow. Then they returned to Mrs. Richards, who had a handy-dandy first aid kit of Mary Poppins proportions. Before long, they'd applied antiseptic, an antibacterial salve, and a gauze bandage.

Claire watched Trevor trudge toward the playground carrying his board. She wondered if she should have asked to keep it, just to make sure he didn't break his promise.

"You know," she said to Mrs. Richards, "I'm going to run home and get the helmet and pads for Trevor."

"All right, but before you go, what did you want to talk to me about?"

Claire tore her gaze from the boy. "I had a question to ask you. I wondered if you knew that Analisa has been writing letters to God."

"Yes, I'm aware of it. Her uncle is a bit concerned,

but I'm not. With time, I'm sure she'll grow tired of waiting for a response and stop."

Okay, so maybe Claire shouldn't have answered any of those letters, but she had. Did she dare admit it?

If she did, she'd feel compelled to defend her actions.

Hilda crossed her arms, yet relaxed her pose. "Most children have very active imaginations. Analisa's interest in angels and Heaven is sure to wane. Why, next week, she could easily change her focus to unicorns and fairies."

Claire wasn't a psychologist, but she, better than anyone, understood how a child could turn to fantasy as a coping mechanism. When she'd been a little girl, living with a disabled mother and an alcoholic stepfather, she'd created two imaginary playmates to help fill the days until she was old enough to attend kindergarten.

"I'm not an expert," Claire admitted, "but it might be a good idea if Analisa spent more time with her uncle."

If Hilda wondered how a stranger had come to know about the letters or the child's living situation, she didn't mention it.

"My employer is a very busy man. In fact, his office is nearby." Hilda nodded toward the professional building adjacent to the park. "Mr. Dawson is working today, but he'll be coming soon. He promised to meet us here for lunch."

Realization struck as Claire stared at the building

that housed the law firm she'd recently visited.

Was the attorney Claire had consulted Analisa's uncle? She held her questions at bay, but scanned the nanny's craggy face for answers.

"He's a lawyer." A stray silver curl had plopped onto Hilda's forehead, and she brushed it aside, smiling. "And a very good one."

Claire couldn't argue. Sam Dawson was not only a competent attorney, but he seemed to have it all together—a partnership in a prestigious firm, apparent wealth, professional success.

Yet Analisa thought Sam needed an angel to look after him, and Claire couldn't help but wonder why.

Sam glanced up from the open file spread across his office desk and looked at the clock: 12:49. Uh-oh. He'd promised to take lunch across the street to the park and eat with Hilda and Analisa today, but he'd almost let the time get away from him.

It was usually quiet in the office on Saturdays, which was one reason he'd come in to work. The other was because he was fulfilling his California Bar requirement of fifty pro bono hours per year.

Since he had the telephone number of Dagwood's Deli on speed dial, he quickly placed an order, but before he could hang up, the second line buzzed. He switched from one to the other. "Sam Dawson."

"Hey," Jake Goldstein said. "I had a feeling you'd be at the office today."

"Why's that?"

"You didn't answer at home or on your cell."

Sam patted down the pocket where he usually kept his phone, not finding it. Had he left it in the car? Or on the kitchen counter? No wonder it had been so quiet this morning.

Jake chuckled. "I figured you'd be knee-deep in work today, even though everyone else in Fairbrook is out enjoying the fresh air and sunshine."

"Someday I'll surprise all my friends and take a *real* vacation, away from phones and the Internet."

"*You?* The law-school boy wonder voted as most driven to succeed? *Never.*" When Sam didn't argue, Jake asked, "So what's got you locked in your office on such a beautiful Saturday?"

"A pro bono case."

"Are you still doing criminal defense work down at Legal Aid?"

"Not anymore." Sam didn't mind defending clients who were actually innocent or those who had screwed up and were somewhat remorseful, but his last defendant had been a real sleaze and as guilty as sin. "I got burned out and wanted a change."

"I can understand that. So what are you working on now?"

"A divorce for a domestic violence victim."

"Be careful, you can get burned out on those, too."

Sam knew what Jake meant. It was tough for most people to understand the dynamics at work when a victim remained in an abusive relationship. In this particular case, the battered woman had stayed with the brute she'd married until her oldest son, a nine-year-old, felt obliged to defend her. In his haste to get to her side, the boy "accidentally" fell down some stairs and broke his arm. The cops bought the bogus explanation, but Sam didn't.

James Danrick, the victim's husband, might be an exec dressed in an Armani suit, but he wasn't any better than Sam's old man had been.

"I've taken a personal interest in this case," Sam admitted. "And I want to do the best job I can representing her."

"Is there something making this case any tougher than the norm?"

"The husband comes from money and made a mint himself, but he kept his wife under his thumb and control for years, refusing to let her work or pursue any kind of life outside the home. And her escape to a woman's shelter has pretty much left her penniless."

"Should be a slam dunk," Jake said.

"I thought so, too, until I learned Judge Riley has been assigned to the case."

Jake blew out a whistle. "That's too bad."

It was known in legal circles that the Honorable Alfred Riley had very little sympathy for women. He'd even tap-danced around a sexual harassment suit that had been filed against him a few years back.

Sam had gotten word of the judicial assignment on Sunday evening, just as he'd sat down to dinner, and a profanity had slipped out of his mouth.

Analisa's gasp told him he'd tumbled off any pedestal on which she might have placed him.

"I'm sorry," he'd told her later, knowing her father wouldn't have approved of the inappropriate comment, either. Sam was going to have to watch his Ps and Qs around her from now on. Or rather his damns and hells.

"That's okay," she'd said. "God forgives you, too, Uncle Sam."

Yeah, well it had been Analisa's forgiveness he'd been seeking. He figured God—*if* He was up there, even casually keeping watch on things down here—hadn't been too happy to hear of Judge Riley's assignment either and would have understood Sam's frustration.

"Who were you talking to?" she'd asked. "And why did you get mad?"

"That call was from a woman I work with. And I wasn't angry at her. Just upset about some news she gave me."

"Why?"

Sam had meant to skim over the question, but the innocence in Analisa's eyes had a way of tripping him up sometimes, and he was never sure what to say to her.

The truth, he supposed.

"The lady told me that Judge Riley was assigned to one of the cases I'm working on. And that's not good news for me or my client."

"I'll ask God to fix it for you."

Her faith had merely unleashed another kind of frustration. How far was she going to take all this God stuff?

As far as he was concerned, she was barking up the wrong tree when it came to divine intervention.

"So what's up?" Sam asked Jake.

"I heard that Claire Harper has you on retainer, and I called to ask if you'd talk to her for me."

Sam leaned back in his chair, the leather creaking as he swayed. He knew where this conversation was heading, but asked anyway. "What about?"

"It would be nice if she'd write a letter of recommendation for Russell Meredith's parole hearing."

"You're dreaming. She'll never do that."

"Then maybe you can persuade her not to fight his release."

"That's not going to happen, either."

"If she knew how tough Russell's incarceration has been on his son, she might. Or if she knew how sorry he was that the accident happened."

How could Russell not be sorry? He killed a child and destroyed a family.

"Will you give Mrs. Harper a call as a favor to me?" Jake asked.

"I have reason to believe it's a waste of time."

"But you'll feel her out?"

A part of Sam wouldn't mind having an excuse to contact Claire Harper or meet with her. Yet he feared the compulsion to pick up the phone and dial her number also had something to do with the color of her eyes and the lilt of her voice.

There was something about Claire that tugged on his heartstrings, what few he had, and he found himself sympathizing with her more than he should, more than was wise.

When she'd come to his office the other day, her waiflike smile, as faint as it had been, had touched him in a way that made him feel a bit heroic, which was a little unsettling when he didn't have anything to offer that another attorney couldn't provide. An awkward sense of responsibility had hovered over him, making him wonder whether he should have taken the case.

"So what do you say?" Jake asked.

"I'll give it some thought." But he hadn't given it much.

Twenty minutes later, after walking to the nearby deli and picking up enough sandwiches, chips, and cookies to feed three starving attorneys rather than himself, a child, and an older woman, Sam walked across the parking lot to Mulberry Park. He'd dressed casually today in a light blue golf shirt, khaki slacks, and a pair of loafers he'd chosen for comfort rather than style.

The warmth of the sun and a cool ocean breeze mocked the confinement of his office on a Saturday morning.

How long had it been since he'd spent an entire day outdoors? For the life of him, he couldn't remember.

As he approached the playground, he saw Analisa at

the top of the slide. When he and her father had been kids, they'd spent a lot of time at the park on the weekends. It had been one way to avoid going home and getting yelled at for something they may or may not have done—at least, until they'd gotten to an age and size that would allow them to yell back. To tell their old man that if he laid another hand on them or their mother that the paramedics would have to mop him off the floor.

Sam spotted Mrs. Richards seated at a bench, not far from where an attractive brunette wearing black slacks and a white cotton blouse handed a young boy a helmet and pads. The young woman stood about five-four, her hair swept up into a twist, her eyes hidden behind sunglasses.

As he drew near, the brunette turned and her lips parted.

Claire Harper?

When she lifted the dark lenses and rested them on top of her hair, the answer was clear. To say he was taken aback—albeit pleasantly so—was an understatement. He and Jake had just been talking about her. How had she come to know Hilda?

"Hello, Sam." She reached out her hand, soft and manicured, yet devoid of polish or jewelry.

"What a surprise." The clichéd response thudded in his ears, and he wished he'd come up with something more clever.

When she glanced at the cardboard box of deli food he balanced in one arm, he lifted it and grinned. "I brought lunch. As you can see, there's plenty. Would you like to join us?"

A smile sparked her green eyes and dimpled her cheeks. "Thanks for the offer, but I have some errands to run—clothes to pick up at the dry cleaner, some weekly grocery shopping to do."

"Have you eaten?" he asked.

"No."

Maybe he ought to insist she at least take something with her. She was thinner than she'd been during the civil trial, but he doubted that was because she'd gone on a diet. Instead he imagined that she'd thrown herself into her work and had skipped meals because there was no one around to encourage her to eat.

The weight loss hadn't looked bad on her, though. She was still an attractive woman.

Sam glanced down at the sandwiches wrapped in white butcher paper, at the brightly colored bags of different chips, at the plastic containers of fresh fruit. Then he shrugged a single shoulder and tossed her a playful grin. "I was hungry when I placed the order, and I forgot Analisa couldn't eat as much as some of the attorneys in the firm. There's going to be a ton left over. You'd be helping me out by joining us. Most of it will probably go to waste."

She seemed to ponder the offer, but just for a moment. "All right. Thanks."

With her sable brown hair swept into a neat twist and a calm demeanor, she appeared to be a woman in control, although he suspected that wasn't the case.

Something told him that the pain still lingered and that her life hadn't returned to normal.

He wondered whether it ever would.

It was too bad that her husband had divorced her, leaving her to grieve alone. Couldn't Ron Harper see what Sam could? The loss of her son, first, and then her husband had obviously taken a toll on her.

Her scent was soft and feminine, and he felt compelled to compliment her on it, to mention that he liked the way the sun highlighted strands of gold in her hair. To tell her she looked especially nice today.

Instead, he kept quiet.

If he'd met Claire Harper in a bar, he'd know just what to do, what to say. But this woman who was also a client had him feeling like a freshman geek with a crush on the prom queen.

And Sam, who'd actually kissed the high school prom queen when he'd been in the ninth grade, had never been the least bit self-conscious around women or clients in his entire life.

So now what?

Sam the Geek was in uncharted water.

Chapter 7

It had been ages since Claire had taken part in a family picnic. Ages since she'd wanted to.

As she stood awkwardly beside the fiberglass table, Sam removed the sandwiches, chips, and fruit from his box. In a way, she wished she'd declined his invitation for lunch. In another, it seemed as though it might be time to venture into the world again.

Hilda, who'd gone to retrieve Analisa and take her to the restroom to wash up, returned with the child, whose pastel-colored butterfly barrettes held back the sides of her blond hair.

Yet it was more than Analisa's outward appearance that gripped Claire's heart, it was her sweet spirit, her innocent faith.

"Analisa," Sam said, "I'm not sure if you know Mrs. Harper or not. She's a friend and a client of mine."

Claire smiled, thinking the word "friend" was pushing it a bit, yet the idea touched her in an unexpected way. "I've seen you playing, Analisa. It's nice to finally meet you."

The child, who held a dark-haired doll in her arm, wore a pair of pink shorts, a white eyelet blouse, and a sweet smile. "I saw you before. You were sitting by Mr. Klinefelter. Are you *his* friend, too?"

During the past three years, Claire had burrowed into an emotional fetal position, letting several friendships wither from neglect. She'd known it was wrong, but at the time, she hadn't had the energy to do anything about it.

Perhaps she still didn't.

Vickie had called again yesterday, leaving a message on Claire's answering machine. "Just checking in," Vickie had said. "I miss you and thought we could spend some time together. Maybe at the new spa in Del Mar?"

Claire hadn't returned the call yet, although she knew she should. Vickie might stop reaching out altogether one of these days, and Claire couldn't blame her if she did.

Friends like Vickie didn't come along every day, but the pain of being around a happily married woman with healthy children was a bit too much for Claire to handle.

But Mr. Klinefelter? The old man who hung out at the park?

"I've met him a time or two," Claire admitted to the child. "And we've chatted, but I wouldn't call him a friend."

Analisa nibbled on her bottom lip, then zeroed in on Claire. "But do you know how to play *chest?*"

"No, I'm afraid not."

"That's too bad." The girl's shoulders slumped, and her brow furrowed.

Claire suspected she'd been hoping to find an opponent for Walter. Or, more likely, she'd been expecting God to provide one, and she'd hoped Claire had been duly appointed.

"Ham, turkey, or pastrami on rye?" Sam asked, drawing Claire's attention from her musing.

"Turkey, please. But only half. Maybe someone else can share with me."

"Look at the size of those sandwiches," Hilda said. "We'll be able to feed an army with the leftovers."

"Like I said . . ." Sam tossed Claire a crooked grin. "I forgot who I was ordering for. Besides, I'm hungry." Then he reached into the box for the sodas. "I'm afraid I only purchased three drinks at the deli, but if Hilda has any paper cups, we can make this work."

"I brought herbal tea for myself, so those three sodas will be plenty for you." Hilda slipped her hand into a large canvas tote bag, and her smile soon morphed into a grimace of perplexity. "Oh, dear. Where's my thermos?"

"Did you leave it in the car?" Analisa asked. "Like last time?"

Hilda faltered momentarily, then brightened. "Maybe so." As she got to her feet, she added, "You all go ahead and eat. Please don't wait for me."

After the elderly woman headed for the parking lot, Analisa bent forward and lowered her voice to a whisper. "Sometimes she forgets stuff, and I have to remind her."

Sam didn't seem too concerned about the comment, but Claire, who'd been privy to the child's pleas to God, wasn't so sure. Children didn't always have a grasp on what was going on in the adult world, yet Analisa seemed to be unusually aware of everyone around her, including the grown-ups.

As they sat at the picnic table and began to unwrap sandwiches and pass out chips, fruit bowls, plastic forks, and napkins, Claire couldn't help but steal a glance at the child. The doll she held, a brown-haired baby with tan skin and dark eyes, was a bit tattered and worn, but in a Velveteen Rabbit way.

"You have a nice baby," Claire told the girl. "What's her name?

"Lucita." Analisa carefully propped her doll on the table, so that it sat beside the sandwich. "She used to belong to my friend, Soledad. But when Uncle Sam came to get me at Rio del Oro, and we had to leave, Soledad gave her to me."

"Analisa has plenty of dolls at home," Sam said, "all brand-new. But she prefers that one."

"That's because Soledad loved her so much." Analisa caressed the scraggly brown hair, then offered Claire a smile. "Me and Soledad didn't used to like each other. But when Mommy died, I had to stay with her family for a while, and she was nice. So we made friends. Then, when my daddy died and I had to go with Uncle Sam, we cried and cried. Soledad said that since she still had her parents and I didn't, she wanted me to have Lucita. So I have to take really good care of her."

An ache settled in Claire's chest. Did Sam realize Analisa had lost not only her parents, but a friend, too? A child who'd given up her prized possession to the little girl she'd never see again?

Had he made arrangements for the children to talk on the telephone? To write? To keep in touch somehow?

"Know what, Uncle Sam?" Analisa adjusted the doll, making it face her bowl of fruit.

Sam unwrapped the pastrami on rye, then tore open a bag of tortilla chips. "What's that, honey?"

"Trevor said that dolls are dumb."

Sam popped a chip in his mouth. "Who's Trevor?"

Analisa pointed toward the playground, where the boy sat on the down side of the teeter-totter all by himself. "There he is."

Sam slid a glance at Claire, eyes sparking, a grin tugging at his lips. "Someone needs to teach Trevor a little tact, especially when it comes to dealing with girls."

"What's *tact?*" Analisa asked.

"It's choosing your words carefully," her uncle told her, "so you don't offend someone."

"What's *offend* mean?"

He cleared his throat, glancing at Claire, before returning his attention to the child. "It means to hurt them or upset them."

"Then Trevor really needs to learn it." Analisa lifted the top off her sandwich and removed the slice of tomato.

"Trevor is still a child," Claire said in the boy's defense, "so that means he still has a lot to learn."

"You're a boy, too," Analisa told Sam, "so maybe you can talk to him about it."

"I don't think a stranger ought to tell him about that sort of thing. Besides, it's a lesson his parents should teach him."

"Why don't I talk to him?" Claire said. She had no idea why she'd volunteered, yet now that she'd opened her mouth, she wasn't sure how to backpedal. "I'll explain that Analisa loves Lucita as much or more than he loves his skateboard."

It's the approach Claire would have used if Erik had been the one to make light of a doll that had become much more than a toy.

A shadow of sadness skulked over her again, as it often did whenever she thought about her son, and she tried her best to ignore it.

About that time, Mrs. Richards returned to the table with a thermos, unscrewed the lid, and filled a red plastic cup with herbal tea. Then she looked up and smiled sheepishly. "I knew I'd brought it today. I always do."

Analisa agreed. "Mrs. Richards loves tea. And when she was a little girl like me, she used to have tea parties."

Hilda smiled, then took a dainty sip from the plastic cup.

For the most part, they ate their lunch in silence. When Claire had finished her sandwich and fruit, she excused herself, saying she had to go. "I need to stop by the dry cleaners and the grocery store."

Sam got to his feet. "If it's okay with you, I'll walk you to your car."

"All right."

As Sam began to pick up the used napkins and wrappers, Hilda shooed him away. "You go on back to the office, Mr. Dawson. I'll clear the table. It'll give me something to do."

"All right, Mrs. Richards. Thanks." After saying good-bye to Analisa and telling her he'd see her at home, Sam walked with Claire to the parking lot.

There was a light wind from the west, a salty ocean breeze that stirred the scent of his musky cologne. Their shoulders brushed once, twice.

The first time it happened, she didn't think much of it. She just basked in an awareness of his bulk and his warmth. But the second touch triggered a flutter in her pulse that suggested they could become more than the friends he'd claimed they were.

Not liking the direction her thoughts had drifted and looking for a distraction, Claire glanced up ahead and saw Trevor. When his gaze met hers, he lifted his hand and wiggled his fingers.

She waved back. She'd promised to talk to him about Lucita, and she would—later. After Sam left.

For some reason, she felt compelled to extend her time with Sam, although she refused to ponder why.

"You know," he said, interrupting her thoughts. "I'm not used to dealing with kids, especially girls."

"I'm sure you're doing just fine."

He shrugged. "My home life was crappy when I was growing up, and to be honest, I never really saw myself becoming a parent. So, needless to say, I'm out of my league."

Claire's own early years had left a lot to be desired, too, yet she'd always wanted to be a mother, to have a big family. She'd dreamed of living in the suburbs with a house full of kids and driving a loaded-down minivan to soccer practice or dance lessons.

But Ron hadn't wanted children. "I'm not up for all the drama," he'd said on more than one occasion.

If truth be told, Claire, who'd been an only child, wouldn't have minded the noise, the you-started-it squabbles, or the age-old cootie wars.

"By the way," Sam said, "I received a call from Russell Meredith's attorney today."

As Sam's steps slowed, Claire turned to face him, her wistful reflection fading as quickly as her hackles raised. "What was that about?"

"It seems that Russell has been a model prisoner and has shown a great deal of remorse. There's a good chance he'll be released."

"*Great*. And then what? He just goes back to his six-figure income, his home in the most exclusive neighborhood in town?"

Sam didn't respond.

She crossed her arms. "I'll never believe that he wasn't driving while intoxicated that day, that he didn't know he'd hit my son. And I told you before, I don't want him released before he serves his full sentence."

"I understand where you're coming from and why you'd like to see him punished. I'm fully prepared to represent you and your interests during the hearing in the next couple of weeks. But for what it's worth, Russell has lost a lot in the past three years."

"So have I." Tears welled in Claire's eyes, and a drop slipped down her cheek. Then another.

Sam placed a hand on her shoulder, his grip warm and tender, his gaze intense, his compassion sincere. "I *know*."

She wanted to lean into him, to rest her head against his shoulder, to seek the emotional support that had been missing from her life long before Ron had packed his things and moved out of the house. But she rallied and stood firm, going so far as to step back.

"Words can't express how sorry I am for your loss, Claire, but punishing Russell won't bring Erik back."

As the truth of his words hung over her like a shroud, she gazed at him through watery eyes. "I know. Erik's loss is something I have to live with. Something I'll never be able to shake."

"It's got to be tough, but you're not the only one suffering."

Claire merely looked at him.

"Russell has a boy about the same age as your son was, a boy who hasn't seen his father outside of prison in three years."

For a moment, her resolve waffled—but only temporarily. "At least Russell still *has* a son."

Sam, who probably never had trouble conjuring a counterpoint in court, didn't argue.

"Thanks for lunch." She forced a smile, then turned and walked away. For a while, it had seemed as though she'd joined the world of the living again.

But she hadn't been able to stay.

Claire couldn't remember the last time she'd pulled out her sewing machine or laid fabric on the dining room table in order to pin on a pattern. But that's what she'd done this evening.

On Saturday afternoon, when she'd left the park in a rush, she'd only been thinking about getting away before Sam saw her break down and cry. And when she'd arrived at home, she'd realized she hadn't talked to Trevor like she'd promised Analisa she would. So on Sunday, she'd returned to Mulberry Park, hoping to find the boy, but Trevor hadn't been there. Neither had Analisa.

Rather than go home to an empty house, Claire had wandered over to the mulberry tree and sat on the concrete bench. Out of habit, she'd glanced into the branches, where sometimes there'd been a letter waiting for her.

There hadn't been.

As she'd sat on the cold stone seat, the ocean breeze caressing her face and taunting wisps of her hair, her thoughts settled on the orphan who'd penned the poignant letters to God and her scraggly-haired doll. It hadn't taken long for an idea to form.

On the way home, Claire had stopped by the fabric store, where she spent a surprising amount of time picking out pieces of flannel and cotton, as well as rickrack and lace. Then she chose several patterns for doll clothes.

Now, as she carefully cut a piece of pink cloth that would soon be a romper for Lucita, Claire focused on her task. In the course of the week, after her workdays, her plan was to make a stack of nightgowns, diapers, and receiving blankets for Analisa's doll. Then she'd return to the park on Saturday with her surprise.

As the scissors snipped around the first pattern piece, the telephone rang.

Usually, Claire let the machine answer, since most of her calls at this time of night were from telemarketers, but for some reason, she reached out and took the receiver in hand. "Hello?"

"Hey, I finally caught you at home."

It was Vickie, and there wasn't any way to avoid the call.

"I'm sorry, Vick. I meant to call you back, but I've been pretty busy lately."

"Busy is good. I hadn't talked to you in months, so I thought I ought to give you a call. What have you been up to?"

Claire glanced at the fabric littered table. "Actually, I've been sewing."

"I'm glad to hear it. You've always been a great seamstress. I still have that apron you gave me a few Christmases back, the one with all the intricate appliqués. And I still get tons of compliments on it."

Silence lingered on the line, as Claire scrambled to find some common ground without quizzing her friend about her family or her kids. Vickie's son, Jason, had been only a year older than Erik, and each time Claire thought of the boy, thought of the things he was involved with, the sports he played, she was reminded of all Erik had missed out on. All the activities she, as a mother, hadn't been able to share.

It wasn't as though Vickie had been insensitive to Claire's discomfort in the past. She'd always gone to great lengths to avoid bringing up family stuff, although tiptoeing around it didn't work very well, either.

"So what do you say about having a girls' day?" Vickie said. "I don't know about you, but I could certainly use a day of pampering. And that new spa is supposed to be great."

All right, Claire wanted to say. *Let's grab our Day Planners.* However, Claire's calendar was pretty blank these days, and Vickie's had to be filled to the brim with . . . What sport was Jason playing this time of year? Little League?

"How does this Saturday work for you?" Vickie asked.

Claire glanced down at the pink flannel, ran her finger along the soft fabric. "Actually, I'm busy this weekend." For once, the excuse rang true.

But so did the possibility that Vickie would finally throw in the towel of their friendship. And try as she might, Claire couldn't forget how tight they'd once been.

After all, Vickie had been the first one to arrive at the hospital following the accident, the one to wait while Erik was in ICU, offering to put him on the prayer chain at her church. And during those dark days before and after the funeral, it had been Vickie who'd called the president of the PTA and saw to it that meals were brought in to the Harper home on a regular basis. For the next couple of weeks, when it was all Claire could do to roll out of bed and put one foot in front of the other, Vickie had done the laundry and picked up groceries.

She'd been a godsend, and Claire had told her so many times. But as life and reality began to settle around them, Claire had finally been forced to level with Vickie, admitting that as much as she loved her, as much as she valued her friendship, being around a happy wife and mother hurt too much.

And Vickie, bless her heart, had understood. "I'll continue to call and check on you every couple of months or so," she'd told Claire. "Just let me know when you're ready to pick up where we left off."

They'd had lunch two or three times over the past couple of years, and Claire had called Vickie when Ron had moved out. But they were no longer close. Not like they'd been in the past. And now that Claire thought about it, she realized that Vickie's calls were becoming less frequent.

If Claire didn't snap to pretty soon, she stood to lose the best friend she'd ever had. Something she couldn't let happen.

"You know," she said, "although I'm busy this Saturday, I'm free the next. Are you?"

Vickie cleared her throat. "I . . . uh . . . well, darn it. That won't work for me."

A dance recital maybe? A baseball tournament? A family camping trip?

Claire knew better than to ask, and Vickie was sensitive enough not to explain. But at least Claire had agreed to meet her.

"Why don't I give you a call in a week or so," Vickie said. "Maybe then we'll be able to lock in some time to get together."

"Sounds good." Claire gripped the receiver until her knuckles ached, trying to hold onto the frayed connection. "I know how busy you get, Vick, so I'll call you. And if the spa doesn't work, maybe we can try lunch again."

"That would be great."

When they said their good-byes and the line disconnected, Claire returned to her project.

She realized that she could have altered her plans to take the doll clothes to the park this weekend, going with Vickie instead. But she'd also promised to talk to Trevor on Analisa's behalf.

Hopefully, seeing a smile light up the little blonde's face would be more therapeutic than a massage.

On Monday morning, Walter made his way toward the sidewalk that wove through the park. He walked just steps behind Hilda, who clutched her canvas tote to her side as if it held everything she owned.

Analisa had run ahead to the playground, leaving the elderly nanny to bring up the rear.

"Good morning," Walter called out.

When Hilda turned to face him, he lifted the two folded lawn chairs he carried, one in each hand. "These are a lot more comfortable than the park benches. I had an extra one in the garage, so I thought you might want to use it."

"Why, thank you." She offered him a weary smile. "I believe I'll take you up on the offer. Those fiberglass seats are hard on more than my back. And since I forgot to take my pain medication this morning . . ." Rather than go on to explain, she clucked her tongue instead.

Walter tended to keep to himself these days, yet he had a feeling Hilda was in the same boat he was. Well, maybe not the same one; sometimes he swore his was sinking. "I know you like the shade, as well as being close to the playground to watch Analisa. So what do you say we set your chair here?"

"That'll be just fine."

Moments later, he had the seat open, sturdy and ready for her. "There you go."

When she thanked him, he asked, "Do you mind if I join you for a while?"

"Sure. Go ahead and sit down." Her smile softened the lines in her face and caused her blue-gray eyes to sparkle.

Once he'd set up his own chair, she reached into her tote, withdrew her thermos, and poured herself some tea. "If you happen to have a spare cup, I'll share this with you."

"No need. I'm a coffee drinker anyway. And I've had my fill of it this morning."

They sat for a while, watching Analisa play with a little red-haired girl, a child who wasn't one of the regulars.

"Analisa makes friends easily," Walter said.

"Yes, she does." Hilda took a sip of tea. "Since she's an only child and would spend every spare minute in her bedroom, coloring and playing by herself, I like to get her outdoors as often as I can. Besides, she really enjoys the park."

"How about you?" Walter asked. "What do you enjoy doing? On your day off, I mean."

Hilda shrugged. "I visit the library. Sometimes I go to the museum."

"I take it you live around here," he said.

"I have a small apartment a couple of blocks away." She took another sip of tea.

"My place is nearby, too. It's completely paid for now—thank goodness. I feel sorry for retired folks who have a mortgage or rent to pay on a fixed income. Of course, you're employed, so it's probably not a problem for you."

"Working at my age wasn't part of the plan. I made a foolish mistake, and now I have to face the consequences." Hilda took another drink of tea. "I used to own a home and had a nest egg, too."

"What happened?"

"I made a bad investment. I'm afraid it was the most foolhardy thing I've ever done in my life. And now I'm stuck living in a rundown apartment complex, where the other tenants are young and loud."

"I'm sorry to hear that."

"Well, the hardest part is realizing that it's true what they say: 'There's no fool like an old fool.' "

He wanted to quiz her more, but hated it when

others pried into his business. So instead, he nudged her with his arm. "Don't beat yourself up for the mistakes you made in the past. At least, that's the advice I was given. And believe me, I've made my share, which I'm sure were a lot worse than yours."

Hilda slid a doubtful glance his way.

"Did I ever tell you about the time I went to the market and didn't realize I'd forgotten my dentures at home?"

"That must have been embarrassing."

"You don't know the half of it." Walter chuckled. "They were handing out free samples that day, and I'd skipped lunch. I was starving, so I stopped by a display of trail mix. I threw back one of those little paper cups full of nuts and clumps of oats and all kinds of hard, crunchy things. Once I chomped down on it, I remembered my teeth were still on the nightstand."

"That must have been a real hoot." Hilda slid him a grin. "I would have liked to have seen it."

"We may as well laugh about our follies, huh?" Walter nudged her arm again, as if they'd been friends for years and had grown used to giggling over their antics and mishaps. "It's easier that way."

"Well, I'm afraid my foolishness had a lasting consequence."

"You seem to be making the best of it."

"Am I? I find myself moping around about it, when I used to be a happy person. And I tend to snap and snarl at others."

"You gotta look on the bright side," Walter said.

"That's what my friend Carl used to always tell me."

"I suppose that's true." Hilda drank the last of her tea, then refilled her cup. "The trouble is, I should have known better. After all, I've always prided myself in having a good head on my shoulders. Of course, that's no longer the case."

"What do you mean?"

She didn't answer for the longest time, and when he'd just about decided she wasn't going to, she said, "I've been pretty forgetful lately, and I have reason to believe my mind isn't . . . well, it isn't what it used to be."

"*Tell* me about it." Walter half-snorted, half-sniggered. "The Golden Years aren't what they're cracked up to be, are they?"

"You've got that right. My arthritis is acting up like old fury again today, and you'd think I'd be able to remember to take my medicine." Hilda ran her index finger along the rim of her plastic cup as if it was an expensive goblet and she was hearing the validating sound of crystal ringing. "You know, I haven't shared this with anyone, and I'm not sure why I am now. But I'm really growing concerned about my forgetfulness."

"I have that problem, too. Remember the teeth? And I never can find the darn television remote control, which is a real shame since I'm the only one living in the house."

"A certain amount of that is part of the aging process, I suppose, but my mother and her sister both developed dementia. Or maybe it was Alzheimer's. Who knew for sure back then?"

Walter reached out and placed his hand on top of hers. "I'm sorry. But that doesn't mean you'll get the same thing."

She smiled, although he suspected it was forced. "I can't stand the thought of becoming like Mama and Aunt Rose, and it scares the liver out of me. What if Sam—Mr. Dawson—decides I'm too old to be a nanny? Too negligent, too scattered these days?"

Walter caressed the top of her hand, hoping his touch could warm the chill of her fear. "Don't fret about it. I'm sure he realizes a little memory loss is to be expected at our age."

"Maybe you're right." Her gaze snagged his. "But I truly hope you'll keep what I said to yourself."

"You'll find I'm good at keeping secrets."

She turned her attention back to the playground, and Walter glanced down at his liver-spotted hand, where it covered Hilda's. He slowly removed it, letting it plop back into his lap. He didn't usually reach out to people like that, so the boldness of his touch surprised him. But he'd sensed the fear of senility was more real for her than for most old folks, and his heart had gone out to her.

They both went back to watching the children play, yet he suspected Hilda's mind was miles away— stewing about her forgetfulness, most likely. There wasn't much a person could do about growing older, though.

"You know," he said, unwilling to give up the intimacy they'd been tiptoeing through, "my mind isn't what it used to be, either. But I don't stress too much about losing my memory, probably because there are some things better forgotten."

"Like what?"

"The bad memories." The ones he used to drink to forget. But now that he was on the wagon, it was a constant struggle to keep them at bay.

"What are you trying to forget?" she asked.

"If I spilled my guts, it would stir them all up again."

"What could be that bad?" she asked.

"Killing someone."

"You *killed* someone?" She didn't get up from the chair, but he watched her draw away from him just the same.

"During the war. In Korea." At times the nightmares of bloody battles woke him still. Walter reached over and patted the top of her hand again, enjoying the contact more than he dared admit. "But let's not get into that."

"All right then." She nudged him with her arm in a way that seemed a bit . . . playful, he supposed, although flirty had come to mind.

There were more memories he'd like to forget. And even though he'd broached the subject and it might make him feel better to unload them, he was leery about going on and on about his shortcomings when it came to being a husband and stepfather. Especially when this chat had him thinking that maybe—if he didn't blow it—he and Hilda could become friends. And if that were the case, she didn't need to hear him list his faults.

They sat quietly a bit longer, enjoying the fresh air and the rustle of leaves overhead.

Walter watched little Analisa run up to Hilda and hand her a baby doll. "Mrs. Richards, will you please hold Lucita for me?"

"Yes . . ." Hilda paused for a long moment, then slowly took the doll, ". . . honey."

As the child skipped back to the playground, Walter said, "She sure is a cute little tyke."

Hilda nodded. "I know. But it's unsettling when that happens."

"When what happens?"

"When I can't remember her name."

Chapter 8

Maria stood at the kitchen sink, washing breakfast dishes and humming the tune of a song she'd learned in Spanish as a child. Some women didn't like household chores, but she wasn't one of them.

She loved everything about her home, a three-story Victorian that was one of eight still remaining on Sugar Plum Lane, a quiet street in the heart of Old Town Fairbrook.

The kitchen, with its pale yellow walls and Formica countertops, had been remodeled about twenty years ago and was ready for another renovation. But Maria wouldn't change much—even if she had the money to do so. She wanted it to remain just as she remembered it.

When Tía Sofía had been alive, the warm, cozy interior often bore the hearty aroma of a pot simmering on the stove or something fresh from the oven—cinnamon rolls, pumpkin bread, *pan dulce.* So in keeping with the tradition and hoping to pass on the same pleasant memories to her children, Maria cooked and baked, too. Earlier today she'd made oatmeal cookies. And later this afternoon, she would prepare *albóndigas* soup, a family favorite.

As she rinsed the cast-iron skillet in which she'd scrambled eggs and chorizo for breakfast, she faced the kitchen window which was adorned by a white eyelet valance on top and small potted plants and ferns along the sill.

She peered into the backyard, which was looking more and more like a jungle these days. Her aunt, who'd had a green thumb and loved flowers, had created a garden showcase over the years and would be heartsick to see it now, although Maria suspected she'd understand.

A couple of months ago, while trying to start the lawnmower, Maria had jerked numerous times on the rope to turn over the engine until a pain ripped through her abdomen, causing her to drop to her knees. She'd known enough to stop what she was doing, go into the house and take it easy, but she'd bled some and experienced strong contractions that continued well into the evening.

She hadn't called the doctor, though.

When she'd first learned that she was expecting her third child, she'd considered having an abortion, but hadn't been able to go through with it. At the time, she'd no longer had her *tía* to fall back on, so when it appeared she might lose the baby after all, she'd decided to let nature take its course.

Deep in her womb, the little one kicked, as if letting his mother know he wasn't too happy about the manner in which he'd been conceived, either. And that he thought it was horribly unfair of her to blame him for any of it.

It was enough to make her conscience cringe.

A light rap-rap-rap sounded at the back porch door, and Maria wiped her hands on a yellow-checkered dish towel before answering.

Eleanor Rucker, looking older and more frail than ever, stood on the stoop, her curly gray hair uncombed, her shoulders slumped.

"Good morning, Ellie. Come on in." Maria held open the door and waited as the elderly woman shuffled into the house.

Ellie had been a dear friend and neighbor of Sofía's for years, but at eighty-four, her health was failing. Her grandson had been encouraging her to put her house on the market and move in with him, so, like Maria, she stood to lose her home, too.

Maria certainly could understand Ellie's reluctance

to give up her independence. Still, at her age and with her medical problems, she really ought to be closer to family—an option Maria no longer had.

Ellie, bless her heart, realized that and sympathized. Recently, she'd offered to babysit so Maria could continue to work. But the poor woman had arthritis in her back and a heart condition. So, while touched by the suggestion, Maria thanked her, yet declined. She wasn't comfortable leaving Ellie with two active kids, one of whom was a toddler.

The elderly woman scanned the small kitchen. "Where are Danny and Sara?"

"Watching a cartoon movie on television."

Maria pulled out a chair for her neighbor. "The coffee's decaffeinated, and it's still fresh. Let me pour you a cup."

"Don't bother. I can't stay. My grandson is picking me up shortly. I've got a doctor's appointment later this morning, but to tell you the truth, I think it's a setup."

Maria took a seat beside the older woman. "What do you mean?"

"The doctor and my grandson are probably in cahoots. I figure they plan to team up on me and tell me again that it's time to sell my house and move in with my grandson and his wife."

"How do you feel about that?"

Ellie let out a bone-weary sigh. "Resigned to it, I suppose. I had a scare last night. Woke up and didn't know where I was. As I fumbled around in the dark, I tripped on the cat and fell."

Maria reached across the table and caressed her neighbor's arm. "Are you all right?"

"I got a bruise on my backside and a knot on my head." Ellie lifted a clump of curls, revealing a black-and-blue lump. "It could have been worse, though. At least I didn't break a hip."

"Well, I'm glad you're okay. Maybe you should get a nightlight."

"Maybe so." Ellie clucked her tongue and slowly shook her head. "Poor Pretty Boy. I nearly scared him out of all nine lives. He leapt to the top of the hutch and hasn't come down yet."

Ellie was known on the street as the cat lady, but the only one she had left was a frisky young tabby who was too hyper for his own good.

"And speaking of Pretty Boy," Ellie said. "My grandson's wife is allergic to animal dander, so when the time comes, I'll need to find a home for him. I don't suppose you'd be willing to take him?"

A pesky feline that seemed to have a flying squirrel in his pedigree? Maria could hardly take care of the responsibilities she already had, but she didn't have the heart to tell Ellie no. "Sure. If you need to move, I'll keep your cat."

Ellie's eyes glistened, and as the tears spilled over, she swiped at her cheeks with the back of her hand. "I appreciate that."

"Aw, Ellie. I'm *so* sorry." Maria wished there was something else she could say, something more she could do.

"I know, but that's life." The woman slumped in her seat. "You know what they say, 'There's a time to be born and a time to die.'"

Maria placed her hand on her womb, felt her baby stir. Reality and resignation settled over her, as it had for her neighbor. It was just a matter of time and life as Maria knew it would be changing, too.

Ellie reached into the pocket of her housecoat and withdrew a business card. "I asked for two of these last Sunday. This one's for you."

The small white card, which had blue and gold lettering, also bore the smiling face of William "Billy" Radcliff, a Realtor.

"That fellow attends my church," Ellie said. "I don't know him personally, but the woman who gave it to me assured me he was fair and honest."

Maria wanted to hand the card back, to tell Ellie, *Thanks, but I won't need it.*

Instead, she took it.

"How are you feeling?" the older woman asked. "Your time must be getting near."

"I'm doing all right, I suppose. The doctor said I might go into labor early, but even so, the baby should be fine."

Another wave of anxiety slid over Maria, shoving the budding resignation aside. She couldn't help wishing she weren't pregnant and wondering what she'd done to deserve being backed into a corner like this.

"It must be tough having kids and no husband to support you."

It was. But even if her ex was still in town and not locked up in a prison up north, he wouldn't have been much help.

That boy is trouble, her *tía* used to say. *He'll find a way to break your heart.*

And he had.

"I wish there was something I could do to help you," Ellie said.

Maria reached across the table, took the older woman's hand in hers and gave it a gentle squeeze. "I'll be okay."

"I'm sure you will." Ellie slowly got to her feet. "I won't keep you, dear. I just wanted to make sure Pretty Boy had a home. And to give you that Realtor's card."

Maria watched Ellie walk away through a blur of tears. She'd been trying so hard to hang on, but it was too late. As if on cue, the baby shifted in her womb, reminding her that it would all be over soon.

A time to be born . . .
. . . and a time to die.

Maria suspected Ellie had been quoting the Old Testament, but a golden oldie by The Byrds began to repeat in her mind—*"Turn, turn, turn . . ."*

She studied the card she'd been given, then forced herself to pick up the telephone and make the call she'd been dreading. Several minutes later, she had an appointment on Wednesday morning to meet with

Billy Radcliff and show him the house.

It had been the right thing to do, the only thing to do, yet as she scanned the small, cozy kitchen, she began to weep, first softly, then with gut-wrenching sobs.

Under her breath, she cursed her ex-husband for ruining her life, for dashing her dreams.

Tía Sofía had seemed to think that God would work it all out somehow, but if He'd truly had a part in all of this, Maria couldn't see any evidence of it.

"Mama?" Danny asked from the doorway.

Her back was to him, so she reached into the napkin holder on the dinette table, grabbed a handful to use as tissues, and quickly wiped her eyes. "Yes?"

"Are you okay?"

Maria blinked back her tears the best she could, then turned and forced a smile. "Yes, *mijo.*"

"What's the matter? You're crying." The boy made his way to where she sat at the dinette table and placed his hand on her knee. The worry in his gaze nearly turned her heart on end. She didn't want him to see her like this—broken and feeling sorry for herself.

"These are happy tears," she lied. "I was counting all my blessings."

And she really should have been.

She wrapped him in her arms and kissed his cheek. "Why don't we celebrate our good fortune at the park today?"

His eyes lit, and he relaxed his stance. "Okay."

"If you go help Sara put on her shoes, I'll fix a picnic lunch."

As Danny dashed off to find his sister, Maria snagged another napkin and did her best to wipe the sadness from her face. Then she grabbed the peanut butter from the cupboard, the strawberry jam from the fridge, and a loaf of bread from the pantry.

Tía Sofía used to say that God never gave someone more than he or she could handle, and Maria hoped that wasn't just wishful thinking. Surely she'd reached the end of her rope.

She pulled out the breadboard and laid out the fixings for three lunches, then opted to make one for Trevor, too. She wished there was more she could do for the lonely boy, other than giving him an occasional sandwich and cookies.

But how could she help him when she couldn't even take care of her own kids?

The wheels of Trevor's skateboard swished upon the sidewalk as he made his way to the park. He'd gotten a late start this morning, thanks to Katie's alarm, which didn't go off and made her late to work.

After she'd gone, he'd looked under the bed, where he kept his skateboard and the gear the lady at the park had given him the other day. Then he'd put on the helmet and pads, just the way she'd shown him how. And now he was on his way to the park.

He used his left leg to push off, then rode along for a while, balancing better than ever before. Not that he was Tony Hawk or anyone, but he didn't fall so much anymore.

As he neared the intersection that was only a couple of blocks from the park, a skinny teenager approached. He wore a black T-shirt and baggy cargo pants that hung so low at the waist that the top of his white boxers showed.

Trevor was going to skate around him, but the kid stepped in front of him and blocked his way, causing him to lose his balance when he came to a stop.

The big kid crossed his arms. "Hey, dude."

"What do you want?"

"Where'd you get that skateboard?"

Trevor didn't answer.

The kid narrowed his eyes and frowned. "What'd you do, steal it?"

"No."

"Well, it looks just like the one my friend used to have, but his was stolen."

Blurting out, "Too bad–so sad" or "Finders-keepers" came to mind, but Trevor clamped his mouth shut. No need to make the kid mad, but he wasn't about to give up his skateboard, either. Not without a fight. 'Course he'd probably get his butt kicked.

The kid whipped out a cell phone and made a call. "Tito, it's me. What did Artie's skateboard look like? Wasn't it red and black?"

Trevor's stomach knotted, as he stooped to pick up his board, then pulled it up against his chest like a shield. No way was he going to give it up just 'cause some dumb teenager said so.

The kid lowered the phone from his ear and looked

at Trevor. "Turn it over. I wanna see the bottom. My friend had a decal on his."

Trevor thought about running, but figured the kid would catch him. Besides, his board didn't have a decal on the bottom. Just on the top. So he turned it around and showed the kid.

"I guess it isn't Artie's," the kid said into the phone. "There isn't a flame decal on the bottom."

There *was* one on the top, though. Trevor's heart beat so loud he could hear it thumping in his ears.

Instead of moving, the kid just stood there like a big, dumb brick wall.

So Trevor, his heart still pounding like crazy and his body scrambling to act cool, walked around him, clutching his board instead of riding it. If he needed to get away, it would be better to run.

Just then he heard a cell phone ring and the teenager say, "Yeah."

Trevor picked up his pace.

From behind him, the kid yelled, "Hey, come back here. Let me take a look at the top of that board."

Trevor ran as fast as he could. For a moment, he thought about heading back home and hiding in the apartment until he felt safe again. But there was no one there. Katie had already left. Besides, she still didn't even know he *had* a skateboard.

The park, it seemed, was best. Maybe, with all the people there, one of the adults wouldn't mind if he sort of hung out by them for a while.

He ran through a parking lot, then jumped behind a

hedge, zipping this way and that. When he finally arrived at Mulberry Park, his heart was pounding like a boom box in a lowrider. And even though he was looking for a grown-up, Analisa was the first one to spot him.

Sure enough, she came running, a big smile making her look all happy. As she got closer, she pulled out a folded yellow envelope from her pocket.

Aw, man. Not again.

She was all out of breath when she reached him. "I was hoping you'd come today, Trevor."

As much as he hated the idea of hanging out with a girl, Analisa really wasn't so bad. "What do you need this time?"

"I want you to put this in the tree."

He figured that's what she was up to again. "Aren't you afraid you're bothering God?"

"No one can bother Him, Trevor. He's everywhere and can do everything."

He wanted to tell her that maybe God didn't get bothered, but Trevor did. He kept his mouth shut, though. Analisa had always been nice to him, even if she didn't know as much about God as she thought she did.

She crossed her arms over her chest, the yellow envelope tucked in her fingers, crunching it. "Besides, God wouldn't keep making people if He didn't have time for us."

Trevor wasn't sure she knew what she was talking about, but he hoped it was true because he planned to whisper a prayer of his own later today. When he was alone and no one could see him.

First off, he needed all the help God could give him because he didn't want to get his butt kicked. And second, he didn't want to lose his skateboard. It wouldn't be fair.

He'd lost too much already.

Saturday dawned sunny and bright, and as the morning wore on, the temperature rose steadily.

After pulling into a parking space and cutting the engine, Claire glanced in the rearview mirror and checked her lipstick—something she hadn't stressed about in years. These days, once she put on her makeup in the morning, she rarely freshened it later. Yet she wasn't naïve enough to pretend she didn't know why she'd done so now.

While it seemed likely that she would run into both Analisa and Trevor if she arrived in the middle of the day, that was also true of Sam—should he decide to bring lunch again. And although meeting the attorney hadn't been a part of her strategy, she couldn't shake the idea that she might see him or that, if she did, she wanted to look her best.

She reached across the console for the basket of doll clothes that rested on the passenger seat, grabbed her purse, slipping the strap over her shoulder, and locked the car.

It was warmer than usual today, and what little breeze there was blew from the west. As she walked along the sidewalk, she scanned the playground for Analisa, spotting her on the swings with several other children. Nearby, a pregnant Latina stooped, tending to a toddler. When the woman straightened and spotted Claire, an awkward sense of recognition passed between them.

Claire didn't always run into people on the street who'd applied for loans and been turned down, and it wasn't particularly comfortable when it happened. It was no wonder why they both looked away.

In a shady spot on the grass, Hilda sat in a lawn chair next to Walter. And about ten yards behind them, Trevor, who wore the helmet and pads Claire had given him, had plopped down, his legs crossed, the skateboard resting in his lap. His head was bent as he picked and scratched at a flame decal with his finger-nail.

It might have been three years since she'd been a mother, but she knew most boys didn't sit by them-selves for no reason at all. There were usually miti-gating circumstances, like a time-out punishment or an injury—either physical or emotional.

Unlike other boys, Trevor always seemed to hang out by himself anyway. So why wasn't he practicing on the skateboard?

Unable to help herself, she stopped beside him. "Hey, Trevor. How's it going?"

He looked up, squinting at the midday sun. "Okay."

She stepped to the side, casting her shadow over his face. "I see you're using the pads and helmet."

"Yeah. Thanks again. I have a feeling I would have really got banged up a few times if I hadn't had them."

"What are you doing?" she asked. "Taking a break?"

He nodded, but she wasn't convinced.

"Are you sure you're all right?"

He glanced over his shoulder, toward the parking lot, as though looking for someone. "Yeah. I'm okay."

"I'd like to talk to you. Do you mind if I sit down for a minute or two?"

"No, go ahead."

She took a seat on the grass and placed the basket in her lap. "I wanted to tell you something and fill you in on a secret."

That seemed to perk his attention.

"You know that doll Analisa plays with?" she asked. "The one she calls Lucita?"

He nodded.

Claire tilted the box so he could see inside. "I made her some clothes."

He shot her a what-kind-of-secret-is-*that?* expression, and she supposed she couldn't blame him. Erik wouldn't have been impressed by homemade doll clothes, either.

"Do you know why I made them?" she asked.

Again, he shook his head no.

"Because Analisa's doll is more than a plaything to her. And do you know why?"

He scrunched his face, indicating that he might actually be wondering why, too, and slowly shook his head.

"Because not so long ago, Analisa lived in another country with her mom and dad. And when her parents died, she came to live with her uncle. That doll represents the life she used to have. It's like holding onto a memory. Can you understand that?"

Trevor dropped his gaze into his lap, where the skateboard rested. Then he glanced up, his eyes glistening. "Sort of."

"So even though the doll might seem dumb or ugly to you, it has great value to her. And if someone teases her about her love for the doll, it hurts her feelings."

"So that's why you made clothes for the doll?" Trevor asked. "Because you knew how special she thinks it is?"

"Yes."

He didn't respond right away, then added, "You gave me the helmet and pads, too."

"Well . . . yes." She had, although her reason for doing so had been entirely different.

The boy seemed to study her as if she were some kind of adult anomaly—and a nice one at that. "Is that because you knew how special my skateboard is to me?"

"And how special *you* are," she said, feeling a bit guilty for accepting his unspoken praise. "I didn't want you to get hurt."

A grin started at one side of his face and broke into a full-on smile. "I'll bet Analisa is going to be super happy to see the stuff for her doll."

"I hope so."

He grew silent, and since Claire couldn't very well batter him with questions or lectures, she got to her feet and approached Hilda instead.

"Good morning," she said, as she joined the woman and man seated in lawn chairs.

Both Hilda and Walter turned. Walter grinned, but Hilda, who held Lucita in her lap, appeared . . . distressed. When the older woman lifted a hand to shield the sun from her eyes, Claire noticed beads of sweat had gathered on her upper lip.

"Are you feeling all right?" Claire asked her.

"No," Walter said. "She isn't. She's having stomach pains. I suggested she go home and lie down."

"I . . ." Hilda winced. "I thought it would pass, but it seems to be getting worse. I'm a bit dizzy, too."

"Then you'd better not get behind the wheel," Claire said.

"If you wouldn't mind driving her car and taking her and Analisa home," Walter said, "I'll be happy to pick you up and bring you back here."

"Of course."

"Perhaps a bit of tea will help me feel better," Hilda said, grimacing as she reached for her tote bag.

Claire lowered the basket she held in her arms. "I brought some doll clothes for Analisa. Do you mind if I give them to her?"

"Not at all. That was nice of you." Hilda glanced down at Lucita and shook her head. "It's an ugly old doll, isn't it? But Analisa loves her."

Claire understood why, though. Didn't Hilda?

Of course, the poor woman wasn't feeling well.

"If you don't mind . . ." Claire nodded toward the playground. "I'll take these to Analisa and tell her it's time to go home."

"Thank you." Hilda took a few sips of tea, then grimaced and tossed the rest of the cup onto the grass. She turned to Walter. "This isn't sitting well with me."

Claire carried her box to the playground and motioned for Analisa to join her at the edge of the sand. She suspected Hilda was in a hurry to leave, so even though she wanted to show the doll clothes to the little girl, she decided to do so in the car.

When the child came near, Claire said, "Hilda isn't feeling well, so she asked me to drive the two of you home."

"We have to go now?" Analisa asked.

"I'm afraid so."

Before Claire could continue, the child grew still. "Uh-oh."

"What's the matter?"

Analisa pointed toward the restroom. "I think that big boy is mad at Trevor."

Claire glanced over her shoulder, where a teenager had cornered Trevor against the outside block wall of the men's room. And she quickly surmised Analisa was right. "You wait here."

She jogged toward the boys. "What's going on?"

Relief washed over Trevor's face the moment she appeared on the scene.

The teenager, a sloppy punk dressed in black,

crossed his arms. "This little kid stole my friend's skateboard, and I'm just trying to get it back."

"I did *not,*" Trevor said. "I found it in a field. Someone threw it away."

The teenager stiffened. "That's a lie."

"Why should I believe you over him?" Claire asked. When the boy didn't offer any reason, Claire continued. "If your friend has a claim on this board, you have him come talk to me."

Before the teenager could comment, Walter's voice rang out through the park.

"Somebody help! Call an ambulance!"

Chapter 9

At the sound of Walter's cry, Claire turned to find Hilda crumpled on the grass and Walter on his knees beside her. Claire started to rush to them; then, having second thoughts, grabbed Trevor by the arm. "You come with me."

She wasn't leaving him with a bully.

As they neared Hilda, who was pale and trembling, the boy pulled back. "What happened to her?"

"I'm not sure."

Walter glanced up, his gaze snagging Claire's in a mire of concern. "She's in severe pain."

Claire dropped the box of doll clothes on the grass, then pulled her cell phone out of her purse and dialed 9-1-1. All the while, Trevor stood aside, frozen and unmoving.

The pregnant woman—Maria?—approached, carrying her toddler on her hip. "Is there anything I can do to help?"

"Maybe you can—" Claire stopped in midsentence when her call connected, and she reported the emergency to the dispatcher. "We need an ambulance at Mulberry Park." She went on to explain Hilda's pain and her collapse.

When she'd been assured the paramedics were on their way and the call had ended, she put her cell phone back in her purse. Her adrenaline was pumping, and she scanned the park, hoping that if anything else went wrong, there was someone better prepared to help than she was.

Several looky-loos craned their necks from a distance, but none of them were jumping to the forefront.

Hilda startled. "Cindy? Oh, no. Where's the baby?"

"You mean Lucita?" Claire asked. The doll Hilda had been holding for Analisa now lay on the grass next to her.

"No." Hilda grew agitated, her eyes opened but unfocused. "Where's little Cindy? I'm her nanny. And I need to meet her mother . . ."

"She's talking about Analisa," Walter said. "She's in so much pain that she's confused."

Oh, dear God. Where was that ambulance?

Claire stepped forward and knelt beside the disoriented woman. "Don't worry, Hilda. I'll make sure she gets home safely."

Hilda placed a cool, shaky hand on Claire's forearm

150

and opened her mouth to speak. Instead she moaned and closed her eyes.

Claire got to her feet and took Maria aside. "I'd better find Analisa and talk to her. I don't want her to worry."

"It's too late," Trevor said. "She's running over here now. And she looks pretty scared to me."

Claire feared there was good reason for the little girl to be frightened, but tried to conjure a soothing smile as she strode to meet her.

Panic seized Analisa's voice. "What's wrong with Mrs. Richards?"

Dropping to one knee, Claire slipped an arm around the child. "Mrs. Richards has a pain in her tummy. And since she feels better lying down, we've asked for an ambulance to take her to the hospital. A lot of doctors and nurses work there, and they'll know just what to do to make her better."

"But sometimes they *don't*," the girl said, as she studied the elderly woman lying on the grass.

Claire had meant her words to be comforting, yet began to realize how little truth they held for a child who'd lost both her parents while living in a third-world country. A child whose mother had died from an infection that wasn't treated properly.

So what more could Claire say? Especially when she, too, had faced a life or death situation and been forced to accept the limits of medical intervention, even in a hospital that boasted modern technology and top-notch personnel.

With Trevor and Analisa flanking her, Claire stood and watched as Maria made her way to the stricken nanny.

In spite of the young mother's advancing pregnancy and the toddler still balanced on her hip, she stooped beside Hilda and whispered something. Words of comfort, maybe. Then she reached for the doll that lay abandoned on the grass next to Hilda's tote bag and brought it to Analisa.

But Analisa refused to take it. "No, let Mrs. Richards have Lucita with her when she goes to the hospital. It'll help her feel better."

From somewhere deep in Claire's chest, emotion rose in her throat, nearly strangling her, as she realized the value of Analisa's precious gift. But she couldn't see sending that little doll to the hospital, where it might easily be lost.

Claire took Lucita from Maria. "I have a better idea. Maybe Analisa and I can take the doll to visit Mrs. Richards later. After she gets settled."

"That's a good idea."

Claire held the doll in one arm and Analisa's hand with the other, as a siren sounded in the distance.

It had seemed like ages before the ambulance finally arrived, but it had only been a matter of minutes. Before long, the paramedics began working on Hilda, then placed her on a bright yellow portable gurney and loaded her into the ambulance.

Walter, who'd stayed close to the stricken woman through it all, held Hilda's handbag and tote as he approached Claire. "I'm going to follow the ambulance, then if you'll give me your number, I'll call you once I hear what the doctor has to say."

"All right." Claire reached into her purse for a scrap of paper and pulled out a Starbucks receipt. She scratched out her number on the back side, then handed it to Walter. "I'll let Sam—Mr. Dawson— know what's going on. I can take Analisa to him, if he'd like. Or I can watch her for him this afternoon."

"While you make that phone call," Maria said, "I'll play a game with the children."

Claire gave her an appreciative smile and mouthed, "Thank you."

"Come on, Trevor." Maria placed a hand on the boy's shoulder. "I want you to join in, too. It'll be fun."

The boy scanned the park, then nibbled on his bottom lip for a moment. He glanced at Claire, as worry and indecision welled in his eyes.

"It'll be all right," Claire told him. "I'll keep an eye out for that big boy and won't let him bother you."

"Okay. But when you take Analisa to her uncle, can you give me a ride to my apartment? I don't feel like walking today."

She didn't blame him. "I'd be happy to take you home. Now go play with the others."

Maria slipped her arm around the boy's shoulders, and he ambled off with her, the skateboard still clutched in his arms.

Claire wasn't sure what else might be going on

between Trevor and the teenager. Nor did she know how to keep him safe from harassment in the future.

The thought of simply buying him a new skateboard crossed her mind. That way he could let the teenager have the one in dispute. Normally, she wouldn't even consider giving a child a gift that required parental approval, but Trevor had already been allowed to have a board.

Claire would think more about that later, though. Right now, she had a call to make.

Wanting to get out of the sun, she walked over to the concrete bench under the mulberry and took a seat. Then she dialed 4-1-1 on her cell, requested the number for Sam's law firm, and waited to be connected.

Sam answered on the second ring.

After identifying herself, Claire explained the situation. "I can bring Analisa to you or keep her for a while. Whatever you'd like me to do."

"I'll wrap things up here as quickly as I can, then I think I'd better go by the hospital and check on Hilda. Poor thing. She's a widow and doesn't have any children. I'm afraid I don't know any of her friends, so I haven't got a clue who to call."

For a moment, Claire thought of all the friendships she'd let go by the wayside since Erik's death. If anything happened to her, who would be notified? Would anyone even care?

At this point, Vickie still might, which was a good reason to try and reconnect with her.

Claire cleared her throat, hoping to dislodge a lingering sense of regret. "Let me give you my address. You can pick up Analisa whenever it's convenient."

"I'd sure appreciate that."

"I'm glad I can help."

"You know," Sam said, "while I've got you on the line, I want to apologize for pressing you about that Russell Meredith issue last week. I was out of line."

"That's all right. I'm sorry that I got a bit weepy and emotional over it."

A clumsy silence stretched between them, yet she wasn't sure what to do about it.

"Well," Sam finally said, maybe feeling it, too. "I'd better get busy so I can go to the hospital. I'll see you later this afternoon."

"Take all the time you need."

When the line disconnected, Claire glanced at the playground where Maria had gathered the children on the lawn and was playing Duck, Duck, Goose.

Claire hadn't allowed herself to get involved in anyone else's life in ages—three years to be exact. Maybe even longer than that. And it was a bit discomfiting to allow herself to be drawn in now. Yet on the other hand, the psychiatrist she'd once seen had told her that time would heal.

So each day, she'd placed a big X on her calendar, hoping that if she scratched out enough squares, the pain would ease and life would become normal again. And she'd seen evidence of that today.

I'm glad I can help, she'd told Sam. And for the first

time in what seemed like forever, her words had rung true.

Leaves rustled overhead, and she looked up. There, wedged on one of the lower branches of the mulberry, was a bright yellow envelope.

"Oh, Analisa," she whispered in an exasperated sigh. "What am I going to do about you and your letters to God?"

In spite of a growing reluctance to remain involved in the pen-pal relationship, Claire looked around, then climbed on the bench and tiptoed in order to reach the envelope. Once it was in her hand, she slipped it into her purse to read later. But she had no intention of answering this one.

Claire had responded to the original letter so that Analisa's faith wouldn't be shaken. But now, with Mrs. Richards in an ambulance racing to the hospital, she feared her effort had been a waste of time.

How could Claire continue to nurture the child's faith when God—or Fate—kept bombarding her with the deaths and illnesses of people who cared for her?

Walter carried Hilda's canvas bag and purse into the Emergency Room at Pacifica General, a pale green stucco building that overlooked the city of Fairbrook, and followed the paramedics inside.

He hated hospitals. Just the smell, a hodgepodge of disinfectant, bland food, and medicine permeating the walls, turned his gut inside out. Add that to the pain and misery of patients and visitors walking along the squeaky clean corridors, and . . . well, it wouldn't take much for a man like him to balk and hightail it out of here while he was still healthy enough to escape.

Hospitals might be a place for some people to get better, but for others?

It was merely a waiting room for an elevator ride to the morgue.

Twenty years ago, Walter had sworn he'd never make another visit without kicking and screaming all the way—even if he was strapped to a gurney or manacled by tubes and wires to a monstrous medical apparatus that would keep a head of broccoli alive.

So needless to say, as he dogged behind Hilda's gurney, his stomach clenched and the old fight-or-flight response kicked in. Of course, at his age, there wasn't much fight left in him, nor was there much energy left for a tail-between-the-legs sprint.

He supposed he could have just let the paramedics haul off Hilda and gone on about his business, but that didn't seem right.

When she came to, who would explain what had happened to her? Tell her that Analisa was safe?

Or hold her hand—*if* she needed it?

As the paramedics stopped the gurney before a double door that required a code to enter, a buzzer sounded. The barrier swung open automatically, revealing a middle-age nurse who allowed the gurney inside, but stopped Walter from entering.

"Are you her husband?" she asked.

"No, just her friend." Walter wasn't sure how Hilda

would feel about that claim, but she was the closest thing he had to one these days.

He'd expected to be turned away but was told to take a seat in the waiting room.

"I'll send someone from registration to speak to you," the nurse said, "then you'll be called back to her bedside after she's been examined."

"No problem," he said, but he figured he'd soon bomb the friend test. He and Hilda had been chatting a bit over the past couple of days, but he really didn't know squat about her. Just that she was a widow. And that life hadn't been too good to her the past couple of years. In that sense, they had a lot in common.

He scanned the room, then chose a seat across from a television that had been perched on a shelf in the corner. He didn't remain there very long, though. When the guy next to him started hacking and coughing, he moved across the room. That was the problem with hospitals. If a fellow arrived healthy, he risked going home sick.

Hoping to increase his odds for a healthy getaway, he took a chair near the reception window.

Hilda hadn't been conscious when they'd brought her in, but even if she had been, he wasn't sure if she would have been coherent.

No telling what had caused her to be disoriented at the park. Pain and whatever ailed her, he hoped. Still, he'd known she'd been concerned about forgetfulness; he just hoped it wasn't related to her confusion now. Either way, he doubted she'd want anyone to know about it. For that reason, when Hilda had asked about a baby named Cindy and Claire had looked at him quizzically, he'd attributed the delusion to her illness.

He sure hoped that's what had caused it—for Hilda's sake.

His, too.

Glancing at the purse he held in his lap, he realized there was a wealth of information inside. Trouble was, ever since he'd been a kid, he'd felt funny about getting into a woman's handbag. Once, when he was seven, he'd gotten caught snooping in his foster mother's purse. She'd come unglued and walloped him upside the head and bawled him out until he swore he'd never invade a woman's privacy again. And he hadn't. Not even his wife's, when she'd been alive.

This was different, though. Wasn't it?

Hilda didn't have any family, but surely there was someone he could contact for her. If she had an address book, he could start with the As.

He wouldn't know unless he checked, so he unsnapped the handbag and peered inside.

No address book that he could see, but she had a wallet. He pulled it out and searched for a driver's license.

Yep. Now he could tell the hospital things about Hilda that she hadn't shared with him. Like her middle name was Marlene, and that she lived at 431 Elm Street, Apartment 6B.

Her date of birth was—hey, how about that?—August 12. Three days before his, and it was coming up in less than a month. She'd be seventy-two. Just a spring chicken.

Walter hadn't purchased a gift for a lady in ages and wondered what she might like. That is, if he decided to go that route and surprise her. Some women got kind of fussy about their age. But that didn't mean the day wasn't important.

In one of the side slots of the wallet, he found a Medicare card. Good. They'd need that.

Any other insurance? Yep. She had Blue Cross as a supplement, another good thing to know.

Curiosity got the better of him, and he continued looking in her purse like a kid peering into a bulging Christmas stocking: Butterscotch Life Savers; a small, travel-size package of tissues; a grocery list . . .

Uh-oh. She'd listed bird seed and cat litter. Funny, but she'd never mentioned anything about having pets.

The doctor could—and probably *would*—decide to keep her for a while. Days maybe. What would happen to those little critters?

He spotted her keys on a black leather fob with little silver charms on the ends—a variety of mama cats and kittens.

Yep. She'd *definitely* want him to check her house and feed her pets. Or would that be stepping out of line if he did so without her permission?

"Who's here with Hilda Richards?" a woman called from the reception window.

Walter stood, ready to provide all the information the hospital needed—just as if he'd known Hilda and been her friend for years.

Funny thing, though. It didn't take much effort for him to believe that it was true.

Vista Del Mar was a gated community on the west side of town, where white stucco walls and red-tiled roofs dotted the lush hillside and overlooked the ocean.

Claire had given Sam the security code earlier, along with directions to her place. So at the gate, he was able to let himself into the quiet neighborhood.

Not bad, Sam thought, as he scanned the splashes of brightly colored flower gardens that garnished well-tended lawns. As far as upscale condominiums went, Claire had chosen a nice place to live.

After making a quick right, he took the second left to Bandolero Court, then pulled along the curb and parked. There he double-checked the address she'd given him—number 213, a downstairs, corner unit.

Earlier, while at the hospital seeing about Hilda, he'd called Claire to see how Analisa was doing.

"She's fine," Claire had said. "I'll let you talk to her."

The moment Analisa had gotten on the phone, she'd blurted out, "We're going to make cookies for Mrs. Richards. And then me and Mrs. Harper are going to cook dinner for you, Uncle Sam."

"You are, huh?" A grin tugged at his lips. Claire had stepped in when he'd needed her, but he hadn't figured on getting a dinner invitation, too.

When the phone had been passed back to Claire, she'd said, "Unless you already have plans for the evening?"

He didn't. He'd thought about picking up a pizza or hamburgers, but something homemade sounded a whole lot better. "Actually, dinner would be great. Thanks."

When the call ended, he'd gone back to the office to finish preparing for a trial scheduled to start on Monday morning.

Now the sun was making its descent into the Pacific, and dusk wouldn't be far behind.

Sam walked along the sidewalk until he reached the front door, where two rustic clay pots of red geraniums flanked a woven welcome mat.

He rang the bell, and moments later, Analisa greeted him with a smile. "Guess what, Uncle Sam. We made spaghetti and meatballs and salad and bread and cookies. But we didn't make the ice cream. That came from the store."

"Mmm. That sounds good." He tried to keep his focus on his niece, but as Claire approached from behind, wearing a white sundress and a pale blue apron tied at her waist, their gazes locked and his pulse kicked up a notch.

"Hi, Sam." She swung open the door and stepped aside to allow him in.

For one awkward moment, he found himself at a sudden loss for words, so he focused on his surroundings instead.

The living room, with its hardwood floor, dusty green walls and white crown molding, displayed a rock fireplace and a distressed wood mantel. The sofa and love seat, with coordinating floral and plaid printed upholstery in shades of green, yellow, and beige, were the overstuffed kind. Nice to look at and probably comfortable. She'd done a good job with the décor.

Is this what Ron Harper used to come home to each night? What he'd walked away from?

The aroma of basil, tomatoes, and a hint of sausage wafted through the room, assaulting an empty stomach and reminding Sam he'd worked through lunch again.

"Is there something I can do to help?" he asked.

"No, I've got everything under control." She tucked a strand of hair behind her ear, revealing a single diamond stud. Nothing big or fancy—just classy. "Why don't you have a seat while I put the food on the table. Maybe you can finish reading *The Silly Princess* to Analisa while I get things ready. It'll only take me a couple of minutes."

"Mrs. Harper bought it for me at the store," Analisa added. "It's really a good story, so you should start at the beginning. But I left the book in the kitchen, so I have go and get it. Just wait here. I'll be right back."

When the little girl dashed off, Claire asked, "Have

you heard anything more about Hilda? Walter called me from the hospital earlier and mentioned they were still running tests. He said the doctor mentioned her gallbladder needed to be removed, although surgery was out of the question until they could stabilize her."

Sam wasn't sure what was going on or why. He just hoped the medical professionals would get to the bottom of it soon. "While I was there, I met her friend, Walter. I'm glad she has someone to look out for her. Unfortunately, I don't know Hilda very well." He hoped Claire didn't fault him for that.

"I don't know Hilda very well, either. I've just recently begun to chat with people at the park. But it was nice to see everyone rally around her. I hope she'll be okay."

So did Sam. He hated to see anyone sick or injured, especially women and children, but in this case, his concern was twofold. He wasn't sure what he was going to do with Analisa while he worked. There was always daycare, but he didn't like the idea of putting her in a place where she didn't know anyone, then making her adapt to a brand-new school in September. The poor kid had been forced to make too many changes in her life already.

"How is Analisa doing?" He figured Claire knew what he was getting at. After losing her parents, it had to be scary to see her nanny collapse and watch the paramedics take her away.

"I tried to keep her busy and her mind off everything that happened. She's doing all right now, but I could tell she was worried when we were at the park. I stayed for a while and played Duck, Duck, Goose with her and the other children. I thought it might help."

"I'm glad you were there when it happened." Sam placed a hand on Claire's shoulder as a brief, appreciative gesture, but when her hair sluiced along his fingers, his nerve endings sparked.

Had she felt it, too?

For a moment, another unfamiliar sense of adolescent insecurity settled over him, but he shrugged it off, letting his hand drop to his side.

Still, his pulse remained escalated, his senses on alert.

"Actually," Claire said, "it was good for me to spend the day with Analisa. I enjoyed being with her, and it made the time pass quickly."

Did her Saturdays usually drag?

Before he could give it much thought, Analisa skipped back into the living room, and Claire excused herself and headed for the kitchen.

Yet Sam couldn't quite tear his eyes away from Claire, from the gentle sway of her gait.

"Uncle *Sam*." Analisa gave his shirtsleeve a tug. "Did you hear me?"

"I'm sorry, honey. My mind sort of wandered off for a moment."

"That's okay." She plopped onto the sofa, then patted the spot right next to her. "Sit here, okay? That way, I can see the pictures when you tell me the story."

Normally, Hilda read to Analisa in the evenings. In

fact, Sam had allowed the nanny free rein with a lot of things. After all, what had he known about kids and their needs?

Of course, now there were a lot of things he'd have to do himself, like reading out loud about zany fairies and a princess with strawberry blond hair.

They'd just begun a third reading of the story when Claire called them to dinner and led them to a formal dining room, where silver candlesticks and a daisy-filled crystal vase adorned the table.

"Aren't you going to light the candles?" Analisa asked.

Claire looked at Sam, cocked her head slightly, and shrugged a single shoulder. "I told her it was a special dinner. I haven't cooked for anyone other than myself in a long time."

He didn't ask how long. Didn't need to.

"So," she said, "while we're pulling out all the stops, how about a bottle of chianti? I've got some in the wine cabinet."

"Sounds great."

Minutes later, Sam dug into the best spaghetti sauce he'd eaten in a long time.

"You know," Claire said, while twirling long strands of pasta onto her fork, "I haven't had a vacation in the past couple of years, so if it would help, I can take time off and babysit Analisa while Hilda is in the hospital."

The offer both surprised him and provided a sense of relief. "Are you sure?"

"Actually, I think it would be good for both of us." She shrugged, yet a pink flush slid across her cheeks. "I mean for Analisa and me."

It would be good for Sam, too. At least, temporarily.

Coming home to a beautiful woman, a happy child, and a home-cooked meal was a domestic picture that, after his lousy childhood, he'd never imagined.

Never even considered.

Chapter 10

Claire stood in the kitchen scooping vanilla ice cream from a brand-new carton and placing it into parfait bowls, while Sam and Analisa waited in the dining room.

The meal she'd just eaten, one shared at the table instead of consumed from a take-out container in front of the television, had been one of the nicest she'd had in a long, long time.

There'd been a few awkward moments, though. Not the kind where restless noodles rebelled against a fork or spaghetti sauce splattered on a white cotton dress, but the cheek-warming kind that made a woman feel like . . .

Well . . . like a woman again. And now that dinner was over, Claire was reluctant to see the evening end.

She placed three bowls of ice cream, spoons, and a plate of frosted sugar cookies onto a tray, then returned to the dining room.

As she neared the table, Sam's eyes lit up. "Would

you look at that? Homemade Christmas cookies. And in July."

"But since it's *not* Christmas, these are regular cookies." Analisa pointed to the platter. "See? They're cowbells, pinecone trees, and little fawns like Bambi."

"Don't forget the stars." Claire passed out the ice cream, then offered Analisa her choice from the platter.

The little girl bent her arms, placed her elbows on the table, and propped up her chin in the palms of her hands, studying each cookie carefully. She settled on a yellow deer with red candy sprinkles on its back.

Claire held out the plate to Sam, and he chose a pinecone tree—or maybe, due to the color of the frosting, it was a "blue fir."

The conversation stilled as they dug into the ice cream and munched on sugar cookies made from an old family recipe—a holiday treat that was just as yummy as Claire had remembered. And they'd soon eaten their fill.

"I really appreciate you looking after Analisa for me." Sam reached into his pocket and withdrew a business card. "If you've got a pen handy, I'll jot down my home phone number for you, as well as my address—just in case you need them."

After retrieving a pen from the kitchen, Claire handed it to Sam. She watched him write, his brow furrowed, his expression intense, his profile angular and strong.

When he gave her the card, she flicked her thumb against the edge, then flipped it over to the back, where he'd written his address in firm, decisive letters—15692 Abernathy Place.

"What time would you like me to drop her off on Monday morning?" he asked.

Claire had been thinking about this moment all afternoon. The only toys she had at her house were Erik's. Earlier today, to avoid the discomfort of allowing another child in Erik's room and the questions she might face, Claire had suggested they make cookies and prepare dinner for Sam, a ploy she couldn't use every day. So she'd come up with a better idea. "Why don't I come to your house Monday morning? I think it might be best for Analisa to be in her own environment."

And it would be best for Claire, too.

"All right." Sam stood and began to gather the bowls from the table.

"You don't need to worry about the dishes. I'll clean up after you leave." It would give her something to do as the night grew dark and quiet.

"Then I'll just take these to the sink. It's the least I can do for you. So, if you'll just show me the way . . ."

Claire placed the empty cookie platter on the tray and carried it to the kitchen.

Sam followed. "You know, we haven't talked about money, but I plan to pay you for looking after Analisa."

"That's not necessary." She set the tray near the

sink. "I wouldn't have offered if I hadn't wanted to do it."

"But—"

She placed a hand on his chest. "Hold the argument, counselor." Then, sensing the boldness of her touch, she stepped back and crossed her arms. "I don't need the money."

Silence stretched between them, and so did the memory of the civil suit her ex-husband had insisted upon filing. From the day she received it, Claire's share of the settlement just sat in the bank, racking up interest in a high-yield account, a fund she had no intention of tapping or spending. Even so, her job paid well enough and her vacation time would be compensated. She didn't need a nanny's wage to watch Analisa.

"Besides," she added, "I really enjoyed my afternoon with your niece. Babysitting her won't be a chore. The time together will be good for both of us."

She'd said as much earlier—during dinner. At the time, she'd been thinking of her and Analisa, but as she looked into Sam's eyes and felt a stirring, a longing of some kind, the only "us" she could think of included him.

They stood suspended in a quiet, pensive moment, and their gazes locked.

Sam lifted a hand and ran his knuckles along her cheek. "Nevertheless, I still owe you."

The suggestion in his tone and the warmth of his

touch slid through her, backing her heart so far into a corner that it had no choice but to respond.

"Hey." Analisa's voice sounded from the doorway. "What are you guys doing?"

Sam lowered his hand, then glanced at the child. "We were just talking."

Maybe so, but for a moment, there'd been plenty of other options.

"Are you ready to go home?" he asked his niece.

Analisa nodded, and Sam returned his focus to Claire. "I guess we'd better call it a night. It'll be her bedtime soon."

"Of course."

"Uh-oh," Analisa said. "I'd better go and get Lucita and her new clothes. I left them in the living room by the sofa."

"Lucita has new clothes?" Sam asked.

Claire smiled, as both pride and humility struggled for a foothold in her heart. "I figured the doll needed a makeover."

"You're full of surprises. Pleasant ones. Thanks."

"It was fun. And seeing her happy made it all worth-while."

Claire followed Sam and Analisa to the entry, where he paused. She sensed a push-pull going on, although she might be mistaken. Maybe she was the only one wishing they didn't have to leave so soon.

"Thanks again for watching Analisa," he said. "And for dinner. It was great."

"You're more than welcome."

As Sam and Analisa walked down the steps and headed to his SUV, a black Cadillac Esplanade, Claire stood in the doorway, under the yellow glow of the porch light. She watched them until the engine roared to life and the headlights flicked on. Then she tore herself away from the view and closed the door.

Something had happened today, something nice that, ironically, had sprung from Hilda's misfortune.

Claire had gone hours without thinking about Erik or feeling the brittle ache of grief.

Even now, as she stood in the center of her living room alone, the sorrow no longer clawed in her chest. Instead, a memory-laced sadness lingered where the pain used to be.

Her boss and coworkers had been encouraging her to take some time off, but prior to today, the thought of a vacation held little appeal. So when she'd called her supervisor at home this afternoon, he'd been surprised but had given an immediate okay.

For the first time in what seemed like forever, Claire actually had something other than work to look forward to. And someone who needed her.

Analisa was a sweet little girl and so full of life. Claire had been drawn to her ever since reading that very first letter to God.

Speaking of which . . .

Claire made her way to the dresser in her bedroom, where she kept her purse, and retrieved the yellow envelope that contained the latest note. She studied the familiar script on the front: *To God From Analisa.*

Claire envisioned the little blonde sitting in her bedroom, carefully penning each word in a heartfelt letter meant to reach Heaven.

A letter Claire still intended to read but not answer.

She carried it to her bed and sat on the edge of the mattress, then tore open the flap and withdrew the note inside.

Dear God.
Thank you for Clare the helper angel. Trever told me to stop riting to you cuz your to buzy. But I told him your never to buzy for us. Im glad you lisen and help in lots of difernt ways. Will you help Trever? He is reely sad but wont tell me why. I think its cuz he doznt have a mom or dad. Can you give him new ones?
Love Analisa

With an ache in her heart, Claire continued to sit on the edge of her mattress for the longest time, studying the letter through a watery blur.

She'd sensed Trevor's sadness, too. And she wasn't sure what was causing it. Loneliness, she suspected.

When she'd driven him home today, he'd directed her to the apartment complex in which he lived, a bluish-gray, paint-chipped building not far from Paddy's Pub in the seedy part of town.

As he'd climbed from the backseat with the skateboard in his arms, he'd thanked her.

She hadn't really done anything except to protect

him from a bully and drive him home. Nothing that would make his world or his life any better. Not knowing what else to say, she'd uttered a simple, "You're welcome."

Rather than drive away the moment he was out of her car, she'd waited to make sure he got inside safely, watched as he'd trudged along a sidewalk that needed sweeping and climbed a stairway.

He'd reached into his pocket and withdrawn a key strung through a fuzzy piece of braided red yarn. When he'd turned and lifted his hand in a little wave, raw emotion rushed her chest. She'd felt similar grief before, but this time it was for someone other than Erik, other than herself.

Instead, it was for Trevor and all the lonely little boys and girls in the world.

With one last smile, Trevor gave the term "latchkey kid" a dirt-smudged face that would remain indelibly etched in Claire's mind.

And in her heart.

Trevor was sitting on the sofa in front of the television when Katie got home from work.

"Hey, you're still up." She put her purse on the recliner and kicked off her shoes. "Sorry I'm late. Rhonda called in sick again, so I had to cover her shift until someone else got there."

"That's okay." He was used to being alone, even though he didn't always like it.

He spotted a greasy red stain on the front of the

brown vest the restaurant made all their waitresses wear, which made him think she'd had a hard day. He didn't ask, though. It just made him feel sad when things went bad for her.

She took the rubber band out of her long brown hair, then massaged her scalp with her fingertips. Trevor didn't know why they made her keep her hair fixed like that. It looked prettier when she let it hang down.

"Did you eat?" she asked.

"Yeah. Soup and crackers."

She nodded, then headed to the kitchen. He could hear the cupboards opening and closing. The fridge, too.

The restaurant gave her a free meal each day, and sometimes, when she could, she'd sneak stuff home to him—like day-old donuts or a slice of pie. But he guessed she'd been too busy to get a break today.

When she returned to the living room, she carried a plate of crackers and cheese and a glass of milk. She looked especially tired tonight. Maybe that was because she didn't wear much makeup anymore.

"Did you get the mail today?" she asked.

Uh-oh. After Mrs. Harper had dropped him off, he came inside and stayed there. "Sorry. I forgot."

"I was hoping there might be a letter from your father. It's been awhile since we heard from him."

As much as Trevor wanted news about his dad, he hoped Katie didn't send him to the mailbox. The light overhead wasn't working and it flickered on and off like the kind in a mad scientist's lab.

"Do you want to check the mailbox?" Katie took a seat in the recliner and placed her glass of milk on the lamp stand. "Or should I?"

As spooky as it was out there, Trevor wanted to ask Katie to do it. But he didn't like seeing her go outside at night, either. She was a grown-up, but she wasn't very big or strong.

What if something happened to her? Then where would he be?

"I guess we could go together," he told her.

Trevor never used to get too scared about anything when he was a little kid. And once his dad came home—if he ever *did*—things wouldn't be so scary anymore. Like the voices of angry neighbors that woke him up at night. Or the squeal of tires and sirens.

And if that dumb teenager showed up looking for Trevor and acting all tough, Trevor wouldn't have anything to worry about. He'd just go and get his dad who would kick the kid's butt.

Of course, his father hadn't hung out a whole lot at home before anyway. And even if things changed, like Katie promised they would, his dad might not want to fight anyone over a skateboard. But you know what?

Trevor would gladly trade the skateboard just to have his dad home again.

Sometimes, he forgot what it was even like having a regular family.

When Katie finished her crackers, she slipped on

her shoes again. "Come on. Let's go get the mail."

Trevor stood up and joined her at the door. "Do you think my dad will come home soon?"

"I sure hope so."

So did Trevor.

Not having parents sucked.

Pacifica General Hospital, a sprawling, salmon-colored structure with a brown-tiled roof, sat on a hilltop in Fairbrook, overlooking the ocean. There, in a small blue-walled room located just off the intensive care unit, Walter had waited all afternoon and well into the evening to see Hilda.

He'd had more than his share of medical facilities over the years. His first encounter was at a military hospital in Japan during the Korean War, where he'd been treated for frostbite. After his discharge, he'd visited a couple of his more seriously injured buddies who'd been recuperating from wounds received at the Chosin Reservoir. Guys who'd been braver and more heroic in battle than Walter had been. Soldiers who'd deserved the medals they'd received and hadn't shoved them into an old shoebox and stored them at the back of the closet.

His second experience was during those long, trying days following Margie's heart attack, when he'd camped out in a chair in her room. It had just about choked the life out of him to watch them unhook the tubes and wires that had kept her body going even though her essence had already left.

Yep. Walter hated hospitals and had never expected to go inside another one again.

He would have visited Carl, though—if the call had come in soon enough. As it was, Walter received word of his friend's death and upcoming funeral over the telephone. One of those oh-by-the-way revelations that had knocked him to his knees with the caller being none the wiser.

So now he sat, unsure whether he ought to bolt from his seat and run to his car or if he should pace the floors until someone came and told him Hilda was going to be fine. That all she needed was a pill or a shot to fix her right up.

"Mr. Klinefelter?" a female voice sounded from the doorway.

He stood. "Yes?"

A slight, dark-haired woman wearing a white lab coat reached out to shake his hand. "I'm Dr. Singh."

He tried to read a quick diagnosis in her expression, but failed. "How is Hilda doing?"

"We're still running tests and should have more answers for you in the morning. If her electrolyte levels were stable, we'd be scheduling gallbladder surgery."

The doctor may as well have been speaking in a foreign language. "I'm sorry," Walter said. "I'm not following you."

"We're dealing with two separate issues. First of all, Hilda is in need of surgery to remove her gallbladder, but because her electrolyte level is off, we're unable to operate right now. How much liquid does she consume each day?"

Walter shrugged. "I'm not sure, but she carries a thermos of herbal tea with her. And she's also got a water bottle. I'd say she's plenty hydrated."

"Overly hydrated," the doctor said. "That's the problem, and it's probably adding to the confusion and disorientation she presented with."

Could that—and not Alzheimer's—have contributed to the forgetfulness that had been worrying her? If so, Hilda would be relieved to hear the news. Yet what was the deal with the gallbladder? Was it his place to ask?

"We've given her something for pain," the doctor added. "And she's resting easy. I can let you see her for a moment or two."

Walter nodded, then followed Dr. Singh through the double doors and into the intensive care unit. His gut clenched at the sight of such seriously ill patients, at the bleeps and blips of machines and monitors, so he kept his gaze focused on the route the doctor was taking. The place seemed like a maze, and he just hoped he could find his way out of here if it became necessary to make a quick retreat. Right, left, right, right . . .

They paused at Hilda's bedside, where she lay sleeping. Her coloring was wan, but at least she appeared peaceful and out of pain.

"I won't wake her," Walter said.

The petite doctor nodded as if she understood the

179

complexities of a friendship Walter and Hilda had been tiptoeing around, as well as the medical condition that still seemed uncertain at best.

When Dr. Singh walked away, Walter focused on Hilda, but didn't say a word. He noticed a leaf in her hair, which she'd probably picked up while lying on the grass. It was so small, he almost didn't see it. Still, he plucked it away. He probably could have found a trash can, if he'd been looking, but he tucked it into his shirt pocket instead.

He continued to study the silver-haired woman. Her pulse throbbed in her neck, and her chest rose and fell with each breath she took. He wanted to say, "It'll be all right, Hilda. Don't you worry about anything. I'll be here for you."

Instead, he did as he'd promised the doctor—kept quiet rather than voice futile words like the ones he'd uttered to Margie time and again. The promises he'd made during desperate bargains with God.

I'll quit drinking for good, he'd sworn. *I won't gamble or swear. I'll be a better man, a better husband and father.*

When Margie had died anyway, it had been clear that his pleas and promises had fallen on deaf ears. That God hadn't cared about the man Walter could have been. So at that point, Walter had decided all deals were off.

Whether in outright rebellion or plain old grief, Walter had begun on his self-destructive path, a mindless revolt that had lost him the respect of his stepsons and Margie's extended family. A downward slide he'd only recently been able to escape.

Another overwhelming urge to bolt rose up inside him, but he managed not to panic. Instead, he placed a gentle hand over Hilda's, then slowly turned and walked away.

With each step he took away from her bed, he wanted to pick up the pace, to break into a run and try to escape the scent of disinfectant and medicine, the squeak of rubber-soled shoes upon the polished tile floor, the hollow tap-tap-tap of his own worn leather loafers.

Memories of death and desperation dogged him down the elevator and out the lobby doors, where dusk had streaked the sky in shades of orange and lavender. Too pretty for the kind of day this had been.

Determined to do what he'd told Hilda he would do, Walter made his way to the truck and patted the front pockets of his pants, feeling for the set of keys he'd tucked inside when he'd arrived. He couldn't promise the woman that everything would be okay, but he could pick up the items on her grocery list and check on her pets.

Thirty minutes later, he pulled into the Canterbury Lane Apartments and parked in a visitor's space near the carports, where a couple of teenagers stood near a beat-up, ten-year-old Toyota Celica, with its hood open. The lighting overhead flickered occasionally, but it gave off enough illumination for them to work on the vehicle that appeared to have been driven hard and wild.

The taller one swore out loud, then slammed his hand against the side of the car. "This is going to cost a fortune to fix."

Walter grabbed the two plastic grocery bags resting on the passenger seat of his pickup, opting not to ask for directions to 6B and hoping he'd find it on his own.

Near the laundry room, two skateboarders had set up a makeshift ramp and were practicing some fancy moves—without helmets, of course, and wearing baggy pants sure to trip 'em up. Fool kids.

Walter glanced at his wristwatch. Where were their parents? Wasn't it time for them to be doing something constructive, like reading a book or doing their chores?

From an open window in apartment 9B, a male voice—loud enough for the whole complex to hear—berated a woman then lapsed into an onslaught of curses that would make a chain gang proud.

Hilda had been right. Her neighbors were young and noisy.

Walter found building six and made his way up the steps to her front door. If anyone wondered who he was or why he was here, they didn't say anything.

He fiddled with the key in the lock until he finally got it open. He'd have to tell Hilda that she ought to notify someone in maintenance about it.

Once inside the apartment, he ran a hand along the

wall until he found the light switch, then slowly closed the door and scanned the small, cozy living room. An autumn-colored afghan lay over the back of a brown tweed sofa, and two matching throw pillows lay at the sides.

The scent of furniture polish and cleaning products told him the place was spic-and-span in spots a man wouldn't even think to look. And the scent of aged cigarette smoke suggested that a good paint job wasn't enough to rid a place of the habits of old tenants.

He placed the two plastic bags he carried on a gray dinette table and removed the items he'd purchased. He stacked the box of cat litter on the floor and the bird seed and other dry goods—a jar of honey, bottled water, and dish soap—on the counter. The tea bags had been his own contribution. A little surprise for her, he supposed.

Next he removed the quart of milk, the margarine, and the nonfat yogurt into a small refrigerator, where an open box of baking soda had a prominent place on the neat and tidy top shelf.

Margie used to do that. "It's to soak up the bad smells," she'd told him.

Walter wondered if Hilda's fridge always looked this way, as clean as the hospital room in which she now lay, or if she'd recently given it a good scrubbing. He suspected she was the neat and orderly type.

A chirp sounded to his right, and he spotted a bird-cage with two little parakeets—one blue, the other yellow.

"Hey, birdies. Are you hungry?" Walter made his way toward the cage that was lined with the sports page of *The Fairbrook Tribune*. When he noticed the headline, "Padres Shut Out the Dodgers," he realized Hilda had used this morning's edition.

"What did you two think about that homerun in the seventh?" he asked the parakeets, chuckling to himself.

He didn't know much about birds, but he suspected they had enough food to keep them going for another day. Still, maybe he'd better replenish their little tubs with new seeds and give them some fresh water. He figured Hilda would be pleased if he did, so he unhooked the wire door and reached inside, which really set off the blue one.

"Hush, now. Keep it down. You don't want to wake the cat, do you?"

After the birds had been taken care of, he scanned the small living room. "Here, kitty, kitty. I know you've got to be in here somewhere."

No response.

Not that he expected one.

He found the litter box in the bathroom, which convinced him that there was indeed a cat living in here—somewhere. He eventually found the pesky feline in the bedroom when he'd got on his hands and knees and peered under the pale blue dust ruffle. The big, fat gray tabby, which looked more like a raccoon than a house cat, hissed at him from where it hid under the bed.

After replenishing the dry food and water, Walter did his best to change the litter box. He'd never been big on pets, and disposing of cat poop wasn't his cup of tea, but he figured Hilda, who hadn't had children, looked on these critters as her pride and joy. So he did the job he'd come here to do, then washed his hands in the bathroom.

As he reentered the living room, he took time to pause before a desk near a window that looked out to the carport. Beside a brass lamp, he spotted her telephone and a small calendar bearing a photograph of a lighthouse. Walter didn't like snoopy people, but he couldn't help checking Hilda's plans for the month.

No bridge club, no church group. No meetings with a friend.

Next Thursday at seven o'clock in the evening, she had a dental appointment, though. Walter's dentist did that. Stayed open late one night each week for his patients who worked nine-to-five.

Beside the phone, she kept a pad and pencil, where she'd made notes for herself.

Pay the utility bill.
Pick up prescription at pharmacy.
Woman at the park's name is Maria.

Tucked next to a lamp was a bright, glossy advertisement of some kind. He probably ought to leave it be, but curiosity got the better of him. He picked it up, recognizing the snowcapped Alps in the background and realizing he held a colorful travel brochure of Austria and Switzerland.

Was she planning a trip? He hoped so.

Margie never did get the chance to chase her dreams before she died. Not even that second honeymoon in Hawaii that Walter had promised her.

"We'll do it next year," he'd told her, not knowing there wouldn't be one.

Folks ought to travel before their time ran out.

And, hopefully, it wasn't too late for Hilda.

Chapter 11

On Monday morning, Sam had just put on a pot of coffee when the doorbell rang. So as he made his way from the kitchen to the Spanish-tile entry, the aroma of the fresh-ground morning brew followed him to the foyer.

He swung open the front door and found Claire on the stoop wearing a pair of jeans, a black cotton top, and a daisy-fresh smile.

Her scent, something different than before, something soft and tropical, caught him by surprise. He couldn't help taking a second whiff.

"Am I too early?" she asked.

"No, not at all." He stepped aside to allow her in. "Analisa is still asleep, but she should be waking up soon."

"Hmmm. The coffee smells good."

"It's almost ready." He closed the door and led her

to the kitchen, where the sputters and gurgles coming from the pot validated his claim. "Can I get you a cup?"

"Please. I'd love some."

He removed two black ceramic mugs from the cupboard and filled them without waiting for the rest of the water to filter through the grounds. "How do you take yours?"

"With cream and sugar if you have it."

When he turned, two steaming mugs in his hands, he spotted her staring at the front of the refrigerator, where Hilda had displayed several of Analisa's pictures.

"I love children's artwork," Claire said, her back to him. "This one's interesting. It has two suns in the sky."

"Actually, the big one with the smiley face is God watching over us."

Claire turned away from the colorful sketches, crossed her arms and grinned. "I've never met a child as spiritual as your niece."

"Neither have I, but her dad was the same way."

"Your brother?" she asked.

Sam nodded. "His name was Greg. He and his wife were missionaries."

"No wonder Analisa has so much faith."

"I suppose. Greg went through what I thought was a God stage when we were in high school, but he never kicked it. In fact, his beliefs only grew stronger. And as a result, we grew further apart and no longer saw eye to eye on anything."

"I never had any brothers or sisters, which I'd always longed for. So it's sad that you two didn't get along."

"Actually, when we were younger, we did. And now that he's gone, I'm sorry I didn't try harder to respect our differences. Greg was the only family I had."

"At least you have Analisa."

Yes, he did. "She's a great kid, and I'll do my best to raise her to be a happy, well-adjusted, college-bound young woman. I owe it to her father." Not a day went by that Sam didn't regret his inability to change the past or to make amends with Greg, but at least he had a chance to do right by Analisa.

He placed the steaming mugs on the table, and as he approached the fridge to get the milk, Claire stepped aside.

"I'm sure you'll be a good father to her."

"I hope you're right. My old man didn't set any kind of example, so I'm afraid I'm out of my element and feel inept more often than not."

"I think all parents experience that feeling at times." She slid him a wistful grin. "And you're still pretty new at this, aren't you? How long have you had her?"

"Her parents died a couple of months ago—within three weeks of each other. I flew down to get her the day I received word of Greg's accident."

"That's not very long for you to get the hang of parenting or for her to adjust to being orphaned. I'm sure the idea of Heaven and a loving God is a comfort to her."

"You're probably right, but she seems to be a bit

obsessed, and that concerns me." Sam glanced to the doorway, just to make sure Analisa hadn't snuck up on him, which happened sometimes. "She seems to be taking the faith bit too far."

"What do you mean?" Claire asked.

"She talks about Heaven and God a lot. And she's not only drawn pictures of Him, she's gone so far as to write Him a letter."

Claire leaned a shoulder against the fridge. "I'm afraid she's written more than one, Sam."

"How do you know? Did she tell you?"

"Actually, I've read them." She straightened, then strode to the table. "Sit down. I need to tell you something."

Sam pulled out a chair for her, then took the seat beside it. He pushed the sugar bowl and milk toward her, but she didn't reach for it right away.

Instead, she gripped her mug with both hands, as though needing to hang on to something. "Each day after work, I drive to Mulberry Park, where I begin and end a five-mile run."

He took a sip of his coffee, savored the caffeine-laden brew and waited for her to continue. But for some reason, she studied her cup and seemed to ponder her words.

When she glanced up, her gaze locked on his. "A couple of weeks ago, while I was sitting on a bench, cooling down from my run, a letter dropped out of the big tree in the center of the park. It was from Analisa and addressed to God."

"How did she get it up there?" Sam asked. "Hilda never mentioned anything about it. And even if she'd known, I doubt she could have put it in a tree."

"It would have been quite a climb for Analisa, so I suspect she asked someone for help."

Sam didn't like the idea of Analisa roping people—maybe even strangers—into helping her put letters meant for God in trees. His concern deepened.

Claire dribbled a dab of milk into her coffee, then added a spoonful of sugar and stirred. "From the letter, it was apparent that she was an orphan, so I felt sorry for her and responded."

"You talked to her?"

"No, I wrote back to her. And I went so far as to sign it from God."

Sam's brow furrowed. "You pretended to be God?"

Claire lifted her mug with both hands. "I only meant to give her the answers she needed in order to move on."

"The answers?"

"She asked me—or rather God—about Heaven and wanted to know if her parents were happy there. As a mother . . ." She cleared her throat. "Well, as a woman who'd once been a mother, my heart went out to her. And I wanted her to believe that her parents were happy, that they hadn't meant to abandon her."

Sam could see where that explanation might help Analisa, although he wouldn't have gone that far. A part of him wanted to argue that Analisa needed to face reality, but losing her parents, especially at her age, had to have been heartbreaking.

"For what it's worth," Claire added, "I've decided not to answer any more of her letters."

"How many did you respond to?" he asked, hoping it hadn't gone on long.

"Two. But I've been removing them from the tree so that some sicko doesn't find them and stalk her."

His gut clenched into a fist-size knot. "I'll tell her to stop writing them."

"Yes, but faith can be fragile. So I hope you'll be careful not to shatter hers." Claire tucked a strand of hair behind her ear. "Children are resilient, but Analisa's belief in God and Heaven has probably helped her accept her loss and go on. So if you cause her to doubt . . . Well, I'm not sure that's going to be in her best interests. Or yours."

The truth of Claire's statement leveled him with a cold, hard uppercut to the chin.

At the age of seven, Analisa had been through more than was fair, and just recently she'd begun to bounce back. When he'd gone to Rio del Oro to bring her home, her brokenhearted sobs had just about torn him in two.

"So what do you suggest?"

Claire lifted the mug and took a sip. "In my second letter—my last response—I told her that God was busy and introduced myself to her. I assumed she would know I was human, but she's concluded that I'm a 'helper angel.' "

Sam furrowed his brow. "She thinks you're an angel?"

"Well, not *me*. In the letter, I told her my name was Claire. But she calls me Mrs. Harper. I don't think she realizes I'm one and the same."

"We've got to set her straight."

"You're right."

Sam was glad to have Claire's support, but he still wasn't exactly sure how to handle the situation. "Should I take her to a child psychologist?"

"Maybe. But how about a clergyman? Your brother might have wanted you to go that route."

"I'm sure he would have." Sam fought the urge to glance skyward, where he imagined Greg looking down at him, chuffing and shaking his head. "But I don't attend church and wouldn't know who to call."

"Do you believe in God?" she asked.

The question caught him a little off guard. "I used to tell my brother I didn't, just to see him get all fired up. But to be honest, I've always found it hard to believe that the earth and its inhabitants were created by some cosmic hiccup."

"So you don't believe in the Big Bang?"

"That could have happened when God said, *'Let there be light.'*"

"So you *do* have faith," Claire concluded.

"Faith? I don't know about that. I believe in a creator, but I'm not religious. I don't see a need for church attendance. Nor do I go around praying or asking for things I can't provide for myself."

Yet if truth be told, there was something refreshing and innocent about Analisa's faith, and Sam hated to see her lose it completely.

Deciding upon the right way to handle the situation would take some careful thought.

"Good morning," a familiar little voice said from the doorway.

Sam and Claire turned to see Analisa standing barefoot in the kitchen. She wore pink pajamas and held Lucita in her arms.

Claire offered her a cheerful smile. "Hello, Analisa. Did you sleep well?"

The child nodded, then yawned, as she made her way to Claire. "Mrs. Harper, are you still going to be my babysitter?"

"Yes, I am."

"Good. After Uncle Sam goes to the office, are you and me going someplace in a car today?"

"Well, we can go to the park if you want. But there's a story time at the library on Mondays. And the Heritage Museum in Old Town is always fun."

"Maybe we should go to visit Mrs. Richards at the hospital," the child said. "I want to tell her that God is going to make her better. I prayed about it, and He told me He would."

Claire glanced at Sam, and all he could do was shrug.

When it came to dealing with Analisa's faith, they had their work cut out for them.

• • •

On Monday morning at nine, Walter pushed through the revolving doors at Pacifica General and strode through the lobby. He nodded at the pink-smocked, gray-haired hospital volunteer who sat near the entrance to direct visitors and answer questions.

But he knew where he was going. The third floor, room 311. Hilda's electrolyte levels were stabilizing, and they'd removed her from ICU and put her in a regular room. She'd come to, and he'd talked to her briefly, but she'd been pretty doped up.

Walter had spoken to another one of her doctors last night, a young man who reminded him of Doogie Howser—the medical boy wonder on that old TV series.

Dr. Whitehall seemed to be on his toes. If all had gone well during the night, as they'd expected, Hilda would have surgery later this afternoon.

Walter felt only slightly better about being at the hospital again today, but he figured that was because they'd moved Hilda out of intensive care and there was hope for a full recovery. After his Margie had suffered her heart attack, she'd never even rallied.

He stood before the elevator doors, along with a young man carrying a bud vase with three red roses. When the doors opened, they stepped inside.

"Going up?" Walter asked.

"Fourth floor."

Walter hit the buttons for both of them, realizing that, according to the floors listed on the inside of the elevator, the guy was heading to Maternity. Normally, Walter kept assumptions and suppositions to himself, figuring he shouldn't feed his curiosity when it irritated him to be quizzed by others, especially strangers. But for some reason, he couldn't help asking. "Someone you know having a baby?"

"Me," the dark-haired young man said, breaking into a grin. "Well, my wife and I. It's our first. A little girl."

Walter nodded. "Congratulations."

When the door opened at the third floor, Walter stepped out into the hall, then made his way to Hilda's room. Maybe he should have purchased flowers for her. They had some in the lobby gift shop. He'd seen them when he stopped to pick up a soda on his way out last night.

But then again, he wasn't sure how she would feel about his visit. She really hadn't been coherent before.

An RN at the nurses' station glanced up as he walked by, but she didn't say anything, so neither did he. When he reached Hilda's room, he paused in the open doorway and peered inside, his feet growing colder by the minute.

She lay on the bed nearest the door, her eyes closed. Sleeping again?

She turned her head, recognition dawning. She didn't smile, so he wasn't sure if his visit pleased her or not.

He took a step into the room. "How are you feeling?"

"Better, I suppose. A little fuzzy-headed from the pain medication they've been giving me."

"I was here yesterday," he admitted, inching a bit more into the room.

"One of my doctors told me. She said you followed the ambulance and stayed until dark."

He'd been here on Sunday, too, but didn't figure it was all that important to mention. He somehow made his feet move until he was standing at the foot of her bed. "You had me worried for a while."

"They say, after I have surgery, I'll be okay."

He nodded. "From what I understand, all that water and tea you've been drinking created a problem for you and may have played a part in some of that forgetfulness you were concerned about."

"I suppose that's good news."

"Yep." For a guy who'd been determined to avoid hospitals at all costs, he kept racking his brain to come up with more things to say and a reason to stay, which made no sense at all.

How had he gotten himself into such an awkward situation?

She fingered the edge of the blanket that lay across her waist. "Thanks for calling the ambulance and for accompanying me to the hospital."

"You're welcome."

She turned to the side, facing him, and grimaced. "I have a bit of a problem, Walter. And as much as I hate to ask, I need your help."

"Of course. What do you want me to do?"

"I have two birds and a cat at home, and I'm afraid they'll die with no one to care for them."

He cleared his throat. "I . . . uh . . . took care of them yesterday. And I went back to check on them this morning."

"You went to my apartment?"

"Only because I saw your grocery list and was afraid your pets might be out of food completely." Walter stroked his chin, felt a small swatch of stubble his razor had missed this morning. "I hope you don't mind me doing that without your permission. But when I was trying to give the hospital your information so they could admit you, I went through your purse. Your address was on your driver's license."

"You'd make a good PI." She didn't exactly smile, but her lips turned upward. "I suppose you now know my age and weight, too."

She'd be seventy-two on her next birthday, which wasn't far away. She also stood five-feet-two and weighed a hundred and ten pounds. But Walter knew some women were fussy about folks knowing that kind of information, so he blew off his knowledge with the snap of his fingers. "Darn. I should have paid it more mind. Of course, I suspect most women lie about that stuff anyway."

"Not me. That paperwork at the Department of Motor Vehicles makes it clear that you sign under penalty of perjury."

Even though Margie had hated to admit she'd put on weight and was pushing a hundred and sixty-five pounds, which she'd thought was too much for her petite frame, she'd been truthful, too. "You remind me of my late wife."

"How so?"

"Margie was so honest she didn't feel right about taking a shortcut home."

Hilda managed a full-on grin. "I probably would have liked her."

"Without a doubt." Everyone had. "By the way, while I was at the market, I picked up everything else on your list, too. Now you won't have to worry about anything other than getting well."

"You're a good man, Walter."

He didn't know about that, so he shrugged off the compliment.

"How were my pets?" she asked.

"They were fine, although the cat didn't much like me being there."

"Her name is Precious, and I'm afraid she's a bit old and crotchety."

"Like us, huh?" Walter shot Hilda a grin, and she lobbed it right back.

"Yes, I'm afraid so." Her smile didn't last long, although he suspected that was due to the medication she was on and the pain she was in. "Thanks for all you've done for me, Walter. I really appreciate it."

"Yeah, well . . ." He cleared his throat. "If there's anything else I can do, just let me know."

"All right."

He took a seat in the chair next to her bed, wondering whether she'd tell him to skedaddle. She didn't, although she soon lapsed into silence. He tried to think up something clever to say, but couldn't come up with anything. So instead, he turned toward her with a smile, only to see that she'd dozed off.

For a while, he just sat there, waiting for her to wake up. When she didn't, he slipped out of her room, planning to return before they took her to surgery.

There were some things a body shouldn't have to face alone.

After Sam left for work, Claire took Analisa to Pacifica General Hospital to visit Hilda.

"There's a good chance they won't let you in," Claire had told the child before they'd left home.

"But I want to give her the card I made."

When Analisa had looked at her with those puppy-dog eyes, Claire had found it tough to say no. So she'd agreed to drive her to the hospital.

Once inside the lobby, they stopped at the information desk, which was manned by a pink-smocked hospital volunteer.

"We'd like to see Hilda Richards," Claire said.

The silver-haired woman smiled, then, when she spotted Analisa, said, "I'm afraid the hospital doesn't allow children under the age of thirteen to visit unless it's in the maternity ward. The rule is for the protection of our patients, as well as our visitors."

Analisa handed the homemade card to the woman. "Then could you give this to her?"

"Of course." The volunteer carefully studied the child's artwork, a folded sheet of yellow construction paper adorned with glitter and glue. "How beautiful. And so thoughtful. I'm sure she'll feel much better when she sees this."

Claire certainly hoped so. She took Analisa by the hand and led her out of the hospital. "Why don't I take you to the playground while we're out and about?"

Ten minutes later, they pulled into the entrance of Mulberry Park.

Walter wasn't there today, but Trevor was. He had on the safety gear, which made Claire glad she'd given it to him. He also sported a red T-shirt that was at least one size too small, a shirt she'd seen him wear several other times this week.

Was his wardrobe limited to just a few outfits? Or did he, like Erik, have favorites that he chose time and again?

While Claire took her purse from the car and locked the doors, Analisa joined Trevor on the sidewalk. Another vehicle pulled into the lot, and at the sound of a grinding engine, she turned and watched Maria park her minivan a couple of spaces away.

Rather than continue toward a shady spot near the playground, Claire waited for the pregnant woman. The little boy—Danny, if she remembered correctly—was the first to open the door and exit the van. As Maria proceeded to remove the toddler from the car seat in the rear, the boy joined Analisa and Trevor.

"Good morning," Claire said.

Maria glanced over her shoulder and smiled. "Hi. I see you still have Analisa. How is Hilda doing?"

"She's a bit better. From what I understand, her gall-bladder surgery has been scheduled for this afternoon, barring any unexpected complications."

Maria reached for two plastic grocery bags, both chockfull, then took the toddler by the hand. "I'd really like to visit her, but my sitter options are limited these days."

Claire wasn't sure how to respond. For a woman who'd been avoiding kids for the past three years, volunteering to watch Analisa had been a big step in itself. She certainly couldn't offer to babysit for everyone in town. Nor was she up to the task.

As the adults began the short walk to the playground, Maria's breath caught, and she stopped.

Claire slowed her steps, too. "Are you okay?"

"Yes. The last month or so can be pretty uncomfortable."

Claire remembered. She stole another glance at Maria, who'd furrowed her brow and stroked her distended womb.

"Are you sure you're all right?" Claire asked.

"Yes. It's just a cramp. It'll pass."

The toddler pulled her hand free of her mother's and ran toward the playground. Apparently focused on the "little cramp" that made her breathe as though she was in labor, Maria let the girl go.

"How often have you been having those?"

"For several months, actually. Nothing regular. Just

a painful twinge now and again." Maria straightened. "Like I said, it'll pass."

One of these days, it wouldn't. "When are you due?"

"In about six weeks."

That was still considered too early. If it had been Claire, she would have been worried. But then again, Maria had been through this sort of thing twice already. She probably knew whether she should be concerned or not.

"Who's going to help you when you have the baby?" Claire asked.

"I have a cousin who lives up in the Los Angeles area. She agreed to come down and stay with me for a few days. I'm supposed to give her a call when I go into labor."

From what Claire had heard, second and third babies came a lot quicker than the first. And that was a long trip on short notice. She hoped this baby gave Maria fair warning.

Still, a woman needed someone to hold her hand through that sort of thing. A husband, a mother, a friend.

Claire could find fault in Ron for a lot of things, but he'd been a great expectant father. She remembered him standing beside the commode as she'd heaved and heaved each morning until the only thing left was that awful yellow bile. Then, afterward, he'd stood ready to wipe her brow with a cool, damp washcloth.

Ron had been as excited about the first heartbeat and the ultrasound image of Erik as Claire had been. And he'd stuck by her side all during labor. She didn't know what she would have done without him.

Once they reached the playground, Maria pulled some plastic toys from one of the bags so her toddler could dig in the sand. While she did so, Claire turned to check on Analisa, who was no longer chatting with Trevor. Instead, she and Danny were making their way toward the playground, leaving Trevor to practice on his skateboard.

But instead of turning her attention to the child she was supposed to be watching, she couldn't take her eyes off Trevor. There was an aura of sadness surrounding him, and it didn't take a bleeding heart to sense it.

Maybe she ought to offer to drive him home again when it came time to leave. If she did, she might invite him over to play with Analisa. That way, she'd get a chance to talk to his guardian, to meet the woman and learn more about the boy who was too young to be a loner.

So several hours later, while Maria rounded up her children to take them home, that's exactly what Claire did.

If Trevor knew what she was really up to, he didn't let on. Instead, he rode in the backseat next to Analisa.

"Has that big boy bothered you any more lately?" she asked, as she turned onto Applewood.

"No. I've been going another way home. It takes longer, but I don't care."

The fact that he'd been avoiding the kid didn't make

Claire feel any better about his safety. "Promise me that you'll give him the skateboard if he ever finds you alone and starts harassing you."

"But it's mine."

"I realize that, and if you have to give it up, I'll buy you a new one."

"Really? How come?"

Because she felt sorry for him, that's why. "Because I'd rather buy you a new skateboard than see you tangle with someone bigger than you."

Trevor didn't have an answer to that, so she let it drop while she maneuvered the car through the traffic on Main, took a right near Paddy's Pub and headed toward the apartment complex where the boy lived.

"I hope your nanny lets you come over and play at my house," Analisa said.

"She will. But Katie's not a nanny. She's my guardian."

"What's the difference?" Analisa asked.

Trevor paused for a moment, as though not entirely sure.

Claire could have easily jumped in and helped with the explanation, but she thought she might learn more about his home and his situation if she kept still.

"People pay a nanny to take care of you," the boy said. "But your parents can always fire her and get you a new one."

"And parents can't fire a guardian?" Analisa asked.

"No. The court says guardians get to tell you what to do, and only the judge can change that."

"What's a judge?" Analisa asked.

"It's a guy who wears a black robe."

"Oh," she said. "You mean a priest or a pastor?"

"No, a judge is more like God."

"*No one* is like God, Trevor."

Claire glanced in the rearview mirror and decided the boy's scowl was evidence of his disagreement.

Was he unhappy with a judge? Disappointed by the person chosen to be his guardian?

After they arrived at the apartment complex where Trevor lived, Claire parked along the curb in front of his unit. "Is Katie home?"

He scanned the carport. "No, not yet. This is her early day, but that doesn't mean much. There's always a reason why they make her work late."

"Then why don't you give me your telephone number. That way I can give her a call later and invite you to come over and play with Analisa someday soon."

"Okay. But I can just come over. Katie won't care."

That was too bad. Claire had been fussy about who Erik went to play with, whose car he rode in.

She reached into her purse and withdrew a notepad and pen. After she'd done so, Trevor recited his number, and she made note of it.

"I was just wondering," Claire said. "Why do you have a guardian?"

"Because my mom died and my dad works in another country."

"Oh," Claire said, as if that made all the sense in the

world. It did, she supposed, but people who worked out of the country usually made good money. And Katie and Trevor didn't seem to be reaping any of the benefits.

Something didn't ring true.

But how involved did Claire want to get?

Chapter 12

Claire stopped by the market on the way home and picked up everything she needed to make tacos for dinner. Sam hadn't asked her to, but it didn't make sense for them to eat separately when it was no trouble at all to prepare a meal they could share.

Now she stood in the middle of Sam's kitchen, making herself at home amidst the forest-green walls, mahogany cabinets, and black granite countertops. Once upon a time, she'd enjoyed cooking, so she had to admit, working in a modern and functional room that had to have been designed by someone who loved to cook was a real treat.

While Claire grated cheese, Analisa sat at the table in the nook, coloring a picture. Her back was to a big bay window that looked out into a spacious backyard.

The meal was coming together nicely as Spanish rice, beans, and meat simmered in three different pots on the stove. As a result, the blended aromas of tomato sauce, onions, chili, and cilantro wafted through Sam's house.

Claire hoped he liked Mexican food.

Just minutes ago, she'd taken a seat at the built-in desk in the kitchen and called the number Trevor had given her. The boy had answered on the second ring, and when Claire had asked to speak to Katie, she'd learned the woman hadn't gotten home yet.

"I'll call back another time," she'd told Trevor. But she couldn't help feeling uneasy about his lack of supervision.

Outside, a car engine sounded, alerting her to someone's arrival. As doors began to open and close, she realized Sam was home. Once he entered the kitchen, his gaze lit on Claire and a smile broke across his face. "You're going to spoil me."

"Didn't Hilda ever cook for you?"

"Sometimes. When she knew I'd be late. But I hated to ask more of her than was expected." Sam made his way to the stove and lifted the lid off the pot of meat. Then he glanced at the package of corn tortillas resting on the countertop. "Mmm. I love tacos."

"Do you ever fix them yourself?"

"No, I'm not much of a cook."

"With a kitchen like this? That's surprising."

He chuckled. "Not really. I bought this house from a guy who used to be a prep chef at Antoine's before getting a better position at a restaurant in Sonoma."

Before Claire could respond, the telephone rang. Sam strode to the desk and answered.

"You're kidding." His brow furrowed, and his expression sobered. "All I can say is 'Wow.' But I'm not surprised. Thanks for letting me know."

After hanging up, he turned and slowly shook his head. "I'm sorry about that. You know, even when I do my best to leave my work at the office, it seems to follow me home."

"Good news?" she asked.

"Yes and no. That was one of my law clerks. The judge assigned to one of my cases had a heart attack and is in the hospital." Sam walked to the kitchen table, pulled out a chair, and sat next to Analisa.

"That's too bad," Claire said.

"For the judge it is. But since he's a real . . ." Sam glanced at Analisa, who was bent over a picture of a rainbow and a puppy dog in a field of flowers. "Let's just say he's not the least bit sympathetic toward women. And since I'm representing a victim of domestic violence in divorce proceedings, I'd been worried about an unfair ruling. So I'm glad to hear that we'll be getting another judge."

Analisa looked up from her drawing. "What's a heart attack?"

"It means his heart wasn't working very well," Sam told her.

The child's eyes grew wide, apprehensive. "I didn't mean for him to get sick. Is he going to get better?"

Sam cocked his head to the side. "What are you talking about, honey?"

"Don't you remember? I told you I would pray about it."

Sam raked a hand through his hair, then glanced at Claire before returning his gaze to his niece. "You didn't have anything to do with the man's heart attack, Analisa. He had a health problem because he's over-weight, doesn't exercise, and drinks too much. And God didn't have anything to do with it, either."

Analisa nibbled her lip. "But it's not good that he's sick."

"Actually, maybe it is. Now the judge is under medical care. He's been told he'll have to change his bad habits and make healthier choices from here on out. So that part's good. And since another judge is going to understand my client's side in this case a whole lot better, then that's good, too."

She pushed her picture to the center of the table, then picked up her crayons. "I'm going to put these away in my room."

When she walked out the door, Claire turned to Sam and crossed her arms. "What just happened?"

"Analisa overheard a conversation I was having with a law clerk in my office and picked up on my frustration with the judge who'd been assigned to one of my cases."

"And so she offered to pray about it for you?"

"She told me she would ask God to 'fix things.' And now, she's apparently worried that she might have been responsible for Judge Riley's heart attack." Sam raked a hand through his hair again. "I would have never guessed that such a cute, sweet little kid could be so . . . challenging."

"All children can be a challenge at times." Claire's thoughts drifted to the letter she'd received that mentioned Juj Rile. Analisa had come to believe her uncle was in trubel, and now Claire understood why. "But I have to admit, her faith is becoming worrisome."

"Tell me about it."

Claire studied the man seated across from her. He appeared to be burdened by something. And she suspected Analisa's belief in God and in the power of prayer was only part of it.

She leaned her hip against the counter and crossed her arms. "Attorneys sometimes get a bad rap. I didn't realize some of you take your cases to heart."

"I try not to."

"But this one is different?"

He nodded.

"How so?"

Sam glanced down at the table, where his clasped hands rested, then looked up and snagged her gaze. "My client, Deanna Danrick, has a nine-year-old son. He's the one who won my sympathy."

"Because he's close in age to Analisa?" she asked.

"No." Sam studied his hands, but Claire didn't think he was actually looking at them. Instead, his mind seemed to drift far away.

About the time she suspected he wasn't going to explain, he continued. "It's because I know what it feels like to watch your father morph into an ogre who is three times your size, to be scared spitless, to feel your gut turn inside out in fear. And to feel compelled to defend your mother no matter what the cost."

Claire remembered him saying his father hadn't set

a good example, but she wouldn't have guessed he'd been raised in an abusive home. She had the urge to reach out to him, to question him about it. Yet because she also knew how it felt to wrestle painful memories, she decided not to press him.

When silence was his only follow-up response, her heart not only went out to the little boy he'd once been, but to the man he'd become.

After dinner, Sam helped Claire wash the dishes and put the kitchen back in order. He hadn't meant to allude to the past earlier in the evening and had to give her credit for not quizzing him further.

"Thanks for watching Analisa for me and for making such a great meal."

"You're welcome."

"I'm going to owe you—*big time.*" Maybe he'd offer to take her to dinner some time. To Antoine's, a fancy steakhouse located on the top floor of the Fair-brook Inn. She'd probably enjoy a five-star meal with a view of the city at night.

"You don't owe me anything. I used to enjoy cooking, so it was nice to have a reason to be in a kitchen again."

Sam knew that was his cue to extend an invitation or to say good night and start walking her toward the door, but for some reason, he couldn't bring himself to do either. "It's nice outside this evening. Would you like to have a cup of coffee or a glass of wine on the deck?"

Her movements stilled, and he wondered if he ought to figure out a way to renege on the invitation, but then she surprised him with a smile. "Sure. I don't have any reason to hurry home. And wine sounds good. But just pour me half a glass since I have to drive."

"All right. I'll open a bottle of pinot grigio. Why don't you let Analisa know where she can find us."

Ten minutes later, under a starry sky, they sat at a glass-topped, wrought-iron table, wineglasses in hand.

The scent of night-blooming jasmine laced the evening air, and a couple of crickets chirped near the pond Sam had stocked with goldfish.

"I'm going to take Analisa to the library tomorrow," Claire said. "They're having a puppet show during story hour."

"Good. She ought to like that." Sam took a drink of the chilled white wine.

"Do you mind if, one of these days, she and I invite a little boy over to play?"

"Of course not. I'm glad she's making friends. What's his name?"

"Trevor. He's older than she is, and normally I wouldn't encourage it, but I feel sorry for him."

"Why?"

"I'm not sure." She fingered the stem of her glass, but had yet to take a sip. "He gave me his phone number so I could talk to Katie, his guardian. But when I called not long ago, she hadn't gotten home from work yet. I get the feeling that she's never with him, and it makes me wonder who fixes his dinner and tucks him into bed at night."

"Maybe no one. Not all kids have the kind of homes they deserve." Sam, more than anyone, knew that.

"You're right. And it doesn't seem fair."

"Sometimes life isn't."

She paused for a moment, then lifted her glass and took a drink. "Are you thinking about your client and her son?"

He could have been. Instead he'd been thinking about the home in which he'd grown up—something he was loath to admit. "I'm glad my client finally moved out of the house, but it's not enough. Hopefully, I can get her fair compensation in terms of alimony and child support. Then maybe she and her son can begin to heal."

"With a different judge, that ought to be easier."

"I hope so. Her husband comes from money and has done well with his investments, so she'll be okay—financially, anyway. But that kind of abuse, physical as well as psychological, can take a toll on a woman and her family."

"I can't imagine the horror of living in a violent home."

Sam could, and it had been a nightmare.

Claire looked up at the night sky, at the expanse of twinkling stars and a silver-edged three-quarter moon.

He couldn't help but follow her gaze.

"Do you believe in Heaven?" she asked.

"I'm not sure. I've thought about it. And I've often wondered if my brother is now with my mom."

"When did you lose your mother?"

"When I was sixteen."

"I'm sorry to hear that."

Sam shrugged. It was a reality he'd had to live with.

For a moment, he tossed around the idea of changing the subject to something more upbeat, but the memory had been festering inside him for so long that he hoped purging it might help him put it to rest for good.

"My old man was a Vietnam vet," he said. "And an alcoholic who struggled on and off with a heroin addiction. Whenever he was drunk or coming down from being high, he had a nasty temper, and so for as long as I can remember, he used to take things out on my mom. Time and again, my brother and I encouraged her to leave him, but even though each beating became more and more severe, she refused."

Sam scanned the doorway to make sure Analisa hadn't crept up on them, and when he was convinced she hadn't, he lowered his voice and continued the ugly story. "Greg and I took turns hanging around the house, just to remind our old man that he'd have to answer to one of us if he laid another hand on our mother again. At least that had been our strategy until one night nearly twenty years ago.

"I'd gone out to Potter's Pond that afternoon with some friends, expecting Greg to be home that evening. So when a couple of the guys broke open a case of beer and asked me to join them, I did." Sam sat back in his seat, wondering if he was making the right decision, if he ought to go all the way and reveal the dark secret he'd lived with for years.

In the past, he'd never opened up to a woman, especially one he found attractive. He'd never even gone into detail with the social worker who'd been assigned to him after his mother's death and his father's trial.

As an adult who still struggled with guilt and grief on occasion, he wondered if that had been wise.

Maybe it was the passage of time and the development of wisdom that made him lower his guard now. Or maybe it was just something about Claire.

"I didn't know it at the time," he admitted, "but Greg hadn't been home that night, either. He'd gone to a church youth group meeting. In fact, he swore up and down that he'd told me about it earlier."

"So no one was at home to watch over your mom."

"No. And when my dad flipped out because I'd forgotten to change a lightbulb in the closet, something he blamed my mom for not enforcing, things got ugly."

Guilt, as ragged and sharp as it had ever been, ripped into Sam, and he found it difficult to form the words. To say his mother's last beating had been fatal.

Claire leaned forward and placed a hand on his arm, as though he didn't need to reveal any more than he had. As though she understood every bit of emotion he'd been dealing with over the years.

The press of her fingers, the warmth of her touch, was a balm to a raw, guilt-weary soul.

"You can't blame yourself, Sam."

Sure he could. He'd been doing that for years. If he'd only changed that lightbulb . . .

If he'd only told his friends he needed to get home . . .

He cleared the lump from his throat. "Needless to say, that's the day my relationship with my brother unraveled."

And there was nothing Sam could do about healing that rift now. Over the years, he'd told himself that he and Greg would reconcile someday. That they'd eventually put their anger and grief behind them. But Greg had died before that could happen.

Sam studied his hands, particularly the white, jagged scars on his knuckles.

When he'd gotten home that night and found police cars in front of the house—their lights flashing, radios blaring—Greg had run to meet him, tears streaming down his face. He swore in both anger and frustration, then took a swing at Sam.

Too stunned to react at first, Sam had merely stood in shock, watching as the police cuffed his drunken father and the paramedics made a valiant effort to rush his dying mother to the hospital. Then he'd slammed his fist into the garage door. But the throbbing pain in his body couldn't lessen the pain in his heart.

For a while, he'd thought he'd busted a couple of bones, but he'd refused to see a doctor. In his adolescent mind, he'd hoped that being crippled and hurting was a form of penitence that would somehow make things right. Yet in the end, the swelling had gone down and the scrapes had healed.

Sam rubbed his left hand over his right, then stole a glance at Claire. The compassion in her eyes turned him every which way but loose.

"You've got to stop blaming yourself. It *wasn't* your fault, Sam."

"In my heart, I know that."

"Your father is the only one responsible for her death."

He nodded, as if accepting the truth. But it wasn't Claire who could offer him absolution. It was his brother.

And Greg hadn't uttered a word.

Hilda's surgery had gotten off to a late start, so it was nearing eight o'clock when Dr. Singh had come by the waiting room to talk to Walter. "Everything went as well as could be expected. Barring any unexpected complications, she can expect to make a full recovery, but we'll need to keep her here a few more days."

Walter nodded. "Thanks, Doc."

"We'll let you know when she's headed back to her room."

"I'd appreciate that." Walter would pop in just long enough to say hello to her, then he'd head home and get some sleep. In the meantime, he would call Sam Dawson and let him know that Hilda was going to be all right. Of course, no telling when she would be able to go back to work. So even though her health issues had been solved, he suspected finances would be a new concern.

Walter didn't know for sure, but he had an idea that she was having a hard time making ends meet, even when she was receiving a full paycheck. So being on disability would put her in a real crunch.

He could offer to help her out, although he wasn't sure if that would ruffle her pride or not. Maybe he'd have to feel her out about it first. He'd hate to put a strain on their friendship before it even had a chance to get off the ground.

After reaching into his pocket and pulling out a couple of quarters and the business card Sam Dawson had given him, Walter dialed the home number the attorney had written on the back.

Sam answered on the third ring, and Walter introduced himself. Then he shared the news the doctor had given him, which Sam relayed to someone else.

Claire, Walter realized. Good. That would save him a call.

Walter had also promised to keep Maria updated, too. So when the line disconnected, he slid his hand back into his slacks pocket and poked around, hoping to find the slip of paper on which Maria had written her number.

He patted down several pockets, including the one that held his wallet, but didn't have any luck. Where'd he put it?

A few days ago, when they'd been chatting at the park, Hilda had mentioned that Maria lived in the old historical district of Fairbrook, which had caused Walter to sit up straight. "Oh yeah? Which street?"

"Sugar Plum Lane. She owns one of those old Victorian homes. Do you know where that is?"

"Sure do." Even if Walter had been new in town, and he wasn't, he would have known about *that* neighborhood. Each year, the folks who lived on Sugar Plum Lane got all caught up in the Christmas spirit and practically illuminated the entire town with their light displays of Santa Claus, the nativity, and scenes from the *Nutcracker*. Why, people from miles around made the trek during the holidays, just to see how pretty it was.

Walter wondered if Maria went to the same trouble. Probably. He suspected the others in the neighborhood would be up in arms if she didn't.

Still, the cost of the December electricity bill would put a real crunch on anyone living within a budget. And hadn't Hilda mentioned that Maria had been divorced recently? Of course, he didn't know anything about her situation or her finances. Maybe her ex-husband was paying through the nose for his kids.

Not that it was any of Walter's business.

He supposed he could drive by Sugar Plum Lane on the way home and try to spot the minivan she drove.

What else did he have to do tonight?

Fifteen minutes later, as Walter turned down the quiet, tree-lined street, a sense of nostalgia wrapped around him like a soft flannel quilt on a dark winter night. It was easy to imagine he was a boy again, playing stickball or kick-the-can with the neighbor kids. Or sitting by the radio listening to *The Green Hornet* or *Jack Armstrong, The All-American Boy.*

Sure enough, just as he reached the cul-de-sac, he recognized Maria's minivan in front of a pale blue house with white gingerbread trim. So he parked the truck and strode up the walk. The doorbell didn't sound when he pushed on the button, so he assumed it wasn't working properly and rapped sharply.

"Who is it?" a woman—Maria—asked from behind the closed door.

"It's Walter Klinefelter, ma'am. I lost your phone number and wanted to let you know that Hilda came through her surgery okay."

"That's wonderful news." Maria opened the door wearing a blousy maternity top and a pair of shorts. She was a pretty little thing, with long dark hair and big brown eyes. "Would you like to come in?"

He didn't want to be a bother, but truth was he'd always been curious about the houses in this particular neighborhood. "For a minute, I suppose."

She stepped aside, and he entered the quaint and cozy living room, with pink, floral-print wallpaper he suspected had adorned the walls for years.

The hardwood floor, polished and clean, had been darkened by age and scarred from use. If anything, Walter thought it added to the charm, as did the antique furnishings.

"I really like your house," he said. "It's warm and homey. Reminds me of the place I used to live in when I was just a boy."

"In Fairbrook?"

"No. In Escondido. It's about thirty minutes north of here."

Maria's breath caught, and her hand went to her belly.

"You okay?" Walter asked.

She nodded, but rubbed her stomach and made funny breathing noises.

Dang. She wasn't going into labor, was she? If so, he'd better hightail it home.

She arched her back and blew out a bone-weary sigh. "Sorry. I keep having those."

"Pains?" he asked.

"They're called Braxton Hicks contractions."

As far as he was concerned, she might as well have been speaking a foreign language. When he squinted at the term, she added, "It's just false labor."

Since she already had two little ones, she ought to know. So Walter continued his trek into the living room, slowing next to an upright piano.

"That used to belong to my great-grandmother," Maria said. "It's nearly a hundred years old."

Her breath caught again, and he froze in his tracks. Then he slowly turned to face her, slipping his hands knuckle-deep into the front pockets of his slacks. "You're making me nervous, Maria."

"I'm sorry. I still have nearly six weeks to go. And I've been having these off and on for quite a while. I'm sure they're . . ."

She started that fool breathing again, which couldn't be a good sign.

Walter combed his hand through his hair. "Maybe you ought to have someone come and stay with you tonight."

"If I thought I was going into labor, I'd give my cousin a call. She lives in L.A. and promised she'd come and look after the kids when I go to the hospital."

That was all well and good. But who was going to stay with Maria?

Having a baby, no matter how experienced a woman was, couldn't be easy. Not that Walter knew squat about that sort of thing.

"Are you sure this is nothing?" he asked.

"I'm sure. I've had a lot of aches and pains with this pregnancy. Probably because of all the stress I've been under. My husband . . ." She grimaced, then started rubbing her stomach again.

Walter might not be an expert, but he'd seen this sort of thing in movies. And he didn't like it when she stopped talking and started panting. Nope. He didn't like it one little bit.

Surely this was a joke. The Ol' Boy Upstairs must be having quite a laugh at Walter's expense, but this wasn't funny.

"Well," she said, "let's just say that after all the stuff

I've been through I would have lost this poor kid months ago. And I didn't."

Maybe Walter ought to make an excuse and go home.

Why in blazes had he agreed to come inside the house anyway? It only made leaving more awkward.

"You know," he said, "if you're not feeling well, it might be best if I went home. You could probably stand to get a little sleep."

"Maybe you're right."

Good. He began to make his way toward the door. Just a few more steps and he'd be free.

"Oh!" she said to his back.

His steps faltered, his heart rumbled in his chest, and his adrenaline kicked into high gear. He wouldn't bolt, but he was afraid to face her.

"I almost forgot," she said. "I need to give you my phone number so you don't have to drive all the way over here next time."

Oh, yeah.

Relieved, Walter slowly turned and smiled. "Good idea."

She walked to the lamp table nearest the sofa, then opened the drawer. As she fumbled around inside, she suddenly froze.

Oh, no. Not another one. This was *not* Walter's night. He was going to suggest she call the doctor. Or maybe her cousin. Someone female and far more capable than he was.

After all, who was he? Some reluctant patron saint of women in pain?

God, who was probably still enjoying a hearty chuckle, knew Walter was way over his head with this sort of thing.

But Walter hadn't realized how much so, until Maria cried out, "Uh-oh," and he followed her gaze to the floor.

There, a puddle of water pooled at her feet.

Chapter 13

By the time Claire drove home after having dinner with Sam and Analisa, it was nearly nine o'clock. She parked in the garage, but rather than close the automatic door, go inside and secure the house for the evening, she walked to the front yard.

Each night, the sprinklers kicked on just after dark but didn't get enough water on the rosebushes that lined the walkway. Since it had been exceptionally warm the past couple of days, she suspected the plants were thirsty.

She took the end of the garden hose from the spindle on which it had been neatly wound and turned the faucet until a steady stream flowed.

Ron had known how much she loved roses, so he'd gone to the nursery on each of their anniversaries and purchased a plant. After he'd brought home the first, he'd smiled and said, "Any man can buy his wife flowers, but it takes a real romantic to tend a full-on garden."

The bushes numbered ten now, and since he'd

moved out, she'd had to hire a landscape service to look after them.

Her favorite was a hearty plant that produced blood-red flowers with a strong, mesmerizing fragrance. And tonight, it bore several new buds, one of which was opening beautifully.

When she finished watering, she retrieved the clippers from the garage, carefully cut the thorny stem and carried the flower into the house. Unable to help herself, she inhaled deeply, relishing the heady scent.

How long had it been since she'd taken time to literally stop and smell the roses? Or to notice the birds chirping in their nests, the splashes of color along the walkways at Mulberry Park?

She carried the rose into the kitchen, where she placed it in a single bud vase and left it on the counter—right where Ron used to leave them after he'd tended the plants. She hated to admit it, but sometimes she missed Ron. Or maybe she just missed having someone to talk to. Either way, he was dating someone now—a tall blonde named Dana.

The other day, Claire had run into them at the grocery store—one in which she didn't normally shop. She'd turned the corner only to almost bang her empty cart into his.

"Claire," he'd said.

That was it. Just "Claire."

They'd studied each other for a moment, then her gaze had traveled to his companion. He'd introduced the two women, which had been a bit awkward.

"How've you been?" he asked.

"Fine. And you?"

"All right."

Then they'd gone their own ways, just as they had the day they finalized their divorce settlement.

She'd thought about Ron earlier tonight, while she'd sat across the dinner table from Sam. And she'd been unable to refrain from comparing the men.

Sam was the better looking of the two.

That, of course, didn't mean anything. Men and women needed to connect on an emotional level. Like she and Sam had done this evening.

As she turned away from the sink, she spotted the front of the refrigerator where Analisa's picture of Erik the Angel and the blue-and-gray robot her son had drawn three years ago now graced the door. Completely different pictures and styles—just like the two children.

There was no reason to compare the drawings or the kids, as she'd done earlier with Sam and Ron, but while she studied the artwork, Trevor came to mind. Although she had no intention of comparing the boys, either, she couldn't help thinking about the dissimilarities of their homes and upbringing.

She thought about her plan to take Analisa to the library tomorrow. Should she include Trevor, too?

Of course, she hadn't spoken to Katie yet. Was it too late to do so now?

She glanced at the clock over the stove: 9:12. Whenever she'd had to make calls for the school, Cub

Scouts, or sports, she'd tried to do so early. But if she wanted to talk to Trevor's guardian, she'd have to find the woman at home.

Claire reached for her purse, which rested on the countertop. Then she searched inside until she found the number Trevor had given her.

The phone rang three times before the boy answered. "Hello?"

"Hi, Trevor. It's Mrs. Harper. Can I speak to Katie?"

"She's still not home."

Claire's stomach lurched. "I thought this was her early day at work."

"It is. But she called a while ago and said she was going out with some friends."

Leaving Trevor alone yet again?

Claire glanced out the kitchen window, where the trees in the backyard darkened the night with Halloween shadows.

"Are you okay with that?" she asked.

"It's no big deal. I'm just watching television."

Something appropriate for a child his age, she hoped. "Have you eaten yet?"

"Yeah. Chicken noodle soup and crackers."

What kind of meal was that? Claire wrapped the curly phone cord around the length of her index finger. "Does Katie go out very often after work?"

"No. But I think it's good that she has friends and all."

And what about Trevor? Did he have friends? Was Katie concerned about him getting a chance to socialize with children his age?

"You don't mind being alone?" Claire asked.

"No, I'm used to it."

She feared that was all too true, and her heart ached for him.

"Besides," he added, "I got the door locked. And I don't answer it, even if someone bangs on it and says to open up."

"Does that happen very often?"

"No. But it has."

The tip of Claire's index finger turned a dark red, and she slowly unwrapped the cord that hampered the circulation. "How old are you, Trevor?"

"Nine and a half."

The age Erik had been when he died. Claire's stomach, already knotted, twisted into a clump. "I was just wondering something. You said your father worked out of the country."

"Uh-huh."

"Which country?"

"Uhh . . ." He paused. "Colorado."

"That's a state, Trevor."

"Yeah." Another pause. "I mean Colorado, Canada."

Claire knew a boy's lie when she heard one. "I see. Will he be home soon?"

"I don't know. He said he might."

She again asked herself how involved she wanted to get in this child's life, yet she didn't have a ready answer. "Well, I'd better let you go. Will you be at the park tomorrow?"

"I guess so. There isn't anything to do around here."

"All right. I'll see you then." After disconnecting the phone, Claire held onto the receiver until the dial tone kicked into alert-mode.

What was with the whale's tale about his father working in another country?

Her imagination took a couple of flying leaps, making her ponder all kinds of possibilities, most of them suggesting child protective services ought to be contacted.

Instead, she dialed her friend Vickie.

They made small talk for a while, which came easier than she'd expected. And before ending the call, they scheduled a day at the spa—but not until after the Little League season ended, of course.

Under normal circumstances, Claire would have thought about how much Erik had liked baseball and wondered if he and Vickie's son would have been rivals or teammates. But her thoughts took another turn this time.

Had Trevor ever considered going out for sports? Would Katie make sure he got back and forth to practice or to games?

"August third works for me," Vickie said.

"Good." Claire made a note on her calendar, which was pretty bare on weekends. "I'll call and make the appointments tomorrow. Assuming I can get them scheduled around the lunch hour, why don't we plan to eat at Café Giovanni that day, too?"

"Sounds fun. I'm looking forward to it. We have a lot of catching up to do."

They did, but again Claire's thoughts returned to Trevor. "Hey, Vick. Does your cousin still work for the Department of Social Services?"

"Yes, why?"

"Because I wanted to talk to her about this little boy I know."

"What about him?"

"I don't think he's being cared for properly. And I thought she'd know who I should contact if I wanted to make a report."

Vickie recited Marti Stephenson's number, and Claire jotted it down on the notepad beside the phone.

She still didn't know how far she wanted to take this. But at least she could learn her options.

Maria looked at Walter, her big brown eyes glistening with unshed tears. "I'm scared."

She wasn't the only one. Walter was darn near shaking in his lucky argyle socks, which were quickly proving to be not so lucky tonight. And why wouldn't he be scared?

Times may have changed, but he was from an era when men were sent to boil water or to wait in the barn while women gave birth.

He ran a hand through his hair. "Maybe we ought to call an ambulance."

"My insurance isn't all that good, although it's better than nothing. And since I'm not sure if they'll pay for an ambulance—especially if this isn't technically considered an imminent emergency—I don't want to risk it."

Great. "I don't suppose your doctor makes house calls?"

"I'm afraid not." She glanced at the liquid pooled on the floor. "If you'll excuse me, I'll be right back."

He watched her disappear through a doorway, and when she returned, she carried a big, yellow towel and dropped it onto the wet hardwood floor. Then she attempted to mop up the puddle using her foot.

"Let me get that for you." Walter gently guided her away from the mess.

"Thank you." Maria arched her back, then rubbed her belly.

As he proceeded to mop up the floor, Walter felt as though he ought to say something. But what? When it came to childbirth, he was completely out of his league. Not that he was any more competent with bigger children. His stepsons had been eight and ten years old when he'd met their mother, and he'd always let her handle their day-to-day care.

He could offer to babysit, he supposed, although he wasn't comfortable doing so. He glanced at his watch. It was already after nine, and he hadn't heard a peep out of the kids. Maybe they were asleep, which would make it a whole lot easier. Of course, with Walter's luck, the kids would sense something was wrong and wake up. Then he'd be hard-pressed to know what to do with them.

"You know," he said, "you might want to get a hold

of that cousin of yours. If she leaves now, she'll get here just after midnight."

"I'd better call my obstetrician first."

"Of course." Why hadn't Walter suggested that?

She picked up the phone and dialed the number by rote. While she waited, she covered the mouthpiece and whispered, "A triage nurse will take the call."

Okay. Whatever. At least a medical professional would be in charge from here on out.

Apparently the nurse answered, because Maria began to recite her name and the fact the baby was more than five weeks early.

"My water just broke," she added, "and I've been having irregular contractions."

She listened intently for a moment, which meant the nurse was giving her some direction—thank goodness.

After she hung up the phone, Walter asked, "Would you like me to watch the kids until your cousin gets here?"

"No, I think I'll ask my neighbor to come over. She's eighty-four and doesn't get around too well, but she's responsible. And she'll do all right if the kids are asleep. The only one who might give her any trouble is Sara, but fortunately, she's always been a sound sleeper and shouldn't even stir until morning." Maria glanced at the stairway that undoubtedly led to the bedrooms, then returned her gaze to Walter. "But would you mind driving me to the hospital?"

Who? *Him?*

There she went looking at him with those big brown peepers again.

"I'd sure appreciate it."

Aw, man. He'd been afraid she was going to ask him to do something like that. What if she was one of those women who delivered in the car on the side of the road?

Walter glanced at his wristwatch again, noting just a couple of minutes had passed. And the hospital was only nine or ten miles away. Surely, it would take a lot longer than that for her to deliver the baby.

"Well?" she asked. "What do you say?"

Walter cleared his throat. "Sure. I don't mind driving you." He did, of course. But who else was going to help her out? "How soon can you be ready to go?"

"I'll pack some things. Then once Ellie gets here, we can leave."

As Maria headed for the stairs, her water dribbled again, leaving a wet trail.

Walter cleaned it up using the soiled towel he'd left on the floor.

Before she reached the landing, he asked, "Where do you put the dirty laundry?"

"I try to keep it done up all the time. Just drop the towel in the washer. If you go into the kitchen, you'll see the doorway that leads to the service porch. You can't miss it."

She was right. He found it.

Moments later, a soft knock sounded at the front door, and Walter answered. An elderly woman, stooped with osteoporosis, stood on the porch wearing slippers and a pale blue housecoat. Her gray hair sported spongy pink curlers on top.

"Who are *you?*" she asked.

"Walter Klinefelter, a friend of Maria's. You must be her neighbor."

"Yes. I'm Eleanor Rucker, but call me Ellie. Everyone else does."

He stepped aside, and she slowly shuffled into the living room, a tote bag clutched at her side.

"Where's Maria?" she asked.

"Packing."

"Poor thing." Ellie clucked her tongue. "It's a shame she has to go through this all by herself."

"She has a cousin coming from L.A."

"Yes, I know. To watch the children." Eleanor took a seat on the sofa, setting the beige bag on the cushion beside her. "But she's been through so much this past year—death, divorce. This pregnancy. It just doesn't seem fair for her to suffer through childbirth alone."

Walter quit expecting things to be fair a long time ago, but he held his tongue.

About that time, Maria entered the living room carrying an overnight bag in one hand and a pale green towel in the other.

Walter nodded at the cloth. "I already got the mess cleaned up for you."

"I know, but this is for me to sit on in the truck."

Great. Walter hadn't thought about that. Not that he was fussy about his pickup. But it just reminded him of the possibilities that could occur in the next fifteen minutes.

"Thanks for coming over," Maria told the neighbor.

"You're lucky I'm still here. There'll be a FOR SALE sign in front of my house before you know it."

Maria strode to the elderly woman and took her hand, giving it a gentle squeeze. "I *am* fortunate that you're still here, Ellie. You've been a wonderful neighbor. It's a real comfort knowing you're just a few steps away." Then Maria turned to Walter. "I'm sure glad you stopped by tonight."

He supposed she was, but he didn't feel especially noble. All he wanted to do was get her to the hospital, where someone knew which end was up.

"I called Rita while I was in the bedroom," Maria said. "She's leaving now, but it will take her a few hours to get here."

"That's okay." Ellie patted her tote bag. "I brought some reading material."

Maria walked to a bookshelf near the television, removed a videotape and put it into the player. "Just in case Sara wakes up, and I really doubt she will, she loves this cartoon. If you'll sit beside her on the sofa, she'll watch it over and over. All you have to do is turn the TV on and press Play on the remote."

"All right," Ellie said. "That's easy enough. Now you go on. And don't worry about a thing."

Yeah, right, Walter thought. He figured Maria had plenty to worry about. But he wouldn't mention that. "Ellie's right. We probably ought to get going."

Maria agreed, but before she could take a step, her breath caught and she nearly doubled over—another pain gripping her.

Walter stood by, frozen and completely helpless.

A minute or two later, Maria blew out a long, staggering breath, then straightened. "That was a bad one. Maybe we'd better get out of here."

As Walter escorted her outside, he wondered what the chances were of her giving birth before they got to the hospital. Slim to none, he hoped.

But then again, what were the odds that he would wind up escorting two different women to Pacifica General within days of each other?

No wonder he felt like the butt of some big, celestial practical joke.

Maria had expected Walter to drop her off at the hospital, then go about his business. Instead, he'd parked and gone inside with her. She had to admit that she was glad he had and told him as much.

Maybe that's why he'd hung out while she'd registered, saying he'd become an old hand at this.

She'd had a couple of contractions during the wait for the clerk, a tall young man with spiky red hair and a splash of freckles, to input her information in the computer, which seemed to be processing incredibly slowly. The clerk studied the computer screen intently, yet was typing with hunt-and-peck strokes.

"Can't you see she's in pain?" Walter asked.

"Yes, sir. If you'll just wait a moment, I'll get one of the other clerks to help me. I've only been working here for two days."

Walter stiffened as though he wanted to voice a complaint, yet kept still.

"Uh-oh." Maria braced herself for another contraction, this one harder and more vicious than the others. As the tearing pain eased, she glanced at Walter, who was watching her with apprehension. She appreciated the fact that he'd stuck by her side for so long, but when she opened her mouth to tell him so, tears welled in her eyes and emotion clogged her throat before any words could form.

"Hey." He placed a hand on her shoulder. "It'll be all right."

She wanted to believe him. She really did. But it was all so overwhelming, and she wasn't just talking about the pain.

"I'm sorry," she managed to say.

"Don't think anything of it."

"I'm really glad you're here, but I realize this can't be much fun for you. So I understand if you want to go."

"Are you sure you'll be okay?" Walter asked.

"I'll be all right." A tear slid down her cheek, followed by a second and a third. *"Really."*

He studied her face, as though looking for evidence of the lie and spotting it dead center.

The clerk returned with an older woman at his side. "Did you preregister?" the woman asked.

Maria nodded. "My doctor gave me forms to fill out, and I sent them in last week."

"That's what I thought." The woman sat in the clerk's seat, then clicked on the keyboard. "Name?"

"Maria Rodriguez."

"You're in here already." She pointed out something to the newbie clerk, then called for an orderly. "We'll get you upstairs to Maternity. They're expecting you."

When a dark-haired man in blue scrubs offered Maria a wheelchair, she carefully got to her feet, then took a seat.

"Come this way," the orderly told Walter.

Maria expected him to balk, and although he didn't immediately jump, he did tag along.

"I'll just wait and make sure they decide to keep you," he said.

Three hours later, Walter was still sitting at her bedside. And she was in no hurry to see him leave.

The last time the nurse had checked, Maria was four centimeters dilated and the baby's head was right where it was supposed to be.

She was in active labor, and the contractions were coming hard and strong. The last one was incredibly rough, and when it had passed, Walter reached over and pushed the red button that would call the nurse.

"What are you doing?" Maria asked.

"Getting you some relief from this torture."

The nurse, a petite blonde in her late forties, responded to the call. "Can I help you?"

Walter stood. "She's in terrible pain. Can't you give her something for it?"

"We can give her an epidural, but her paperwork stated that she didn't want one."

"It's not covered by my insurance plan," Maria said, as another contraction began to rip her apart.

"Don't worry about the cost. If it'll help and you want it, I'll pay for it." Walter reached into his pocket, pulled out a small roll of bills held together by a red rubber band and flashed it at the nurse. "I may not have enough cash on me, but I've got a credit card."

"You can settle up with the hospital when she's discharged," the nurse said. "In the meantime, I'll call in an anesthesiologist."

When she left the room, her shoes squeaking upon the tile floor, Walter turned to Maria and waited until the last pain had subsided.

"Will they knock you out?" he asked.

"No. I'll be awake."

"If it were me, I think I'd rather take a blow to the head with a baseball bat than suffer those pains. Are you sure you don't want them to put you to sleep until it's all over? I'll be happy to pay if it's an additional charge."

"Even if I wanted to be put out, they don't want the baby to be drugged when he comes into the world. And since he's coming early, he'll have enough to struggle with."

"Oh." Walter took his seat. "Poor little guy."

Maria had to agree. "You know, I've really been

stressed about being pregnant. And now that the baby is almost here . . ."

"Being single with three kids to support would be stressful for anyone. But don't worry. You're a good mother. I've seen you at the park. And not just with your own little ones. You're good to Trevor and Analisa, too."

She blew out a sigh. "It's not that I don't love my children or care about their friends. It's just that I've . . ." It was tough to admit. And she wasn't sure if she could. "It's just that there were times, months ago, when I wouldn't have cared if I'd miscarried. Isn't that terrible? And I'm afraid the baby will somehow know that."

"I wouldn't worry. His brain can't be developed enough to know anything other than hunger or pain."

"I hope you're right. But he was unplanned, and I may lose my house because of the financial burden having another baby has created. I hate his father for doing this to me and I just can't seem to find it in my heart to love this poor helpless baby who didn't ask to be born." She glanced at Walter, wondering what he thought of her now that she'd told him the awful truth, the secret that darkened her heart.

He merely stared at the monitor. "Get ready. Here we go again."

Oh, no. Not another one. As the pain gripped her, she couldn't have said more if she'd wanted to, and she struggled not to cry out and chase Walter away.

When the contraction finally ended and she was

granted an all-too-brief reprieve, she decided to keep the rest of her thoughts and feelings to herself. Walter didn't need to know about the guilt she carried, the fear she had that this unfortunate child would grow up feeling unloved and unwanted. That he'd eventually become a hoodlum or worse. And that it would be her fault if he did.

No matter how hard she tried, she couldn't seem to shake the feeling of doom and despair that plagued her.

"So what's his name?" Walter asked.

The question shouldn't have blindsided her, but it did. "I don't know. Isn't that sad? It's like a part of me wants to pretend this isn't happening."

"I hate to be the one to blow the whistle on your fantasy . . ." He half-chuckled, then leaned back in his seat, threading his fingers together and resting his hands on his belly. "You know, under the circumstances, I think this little fellow deserves a strong name, something he can grow into and live up to."

He was right, of course. "What do you suggest?"

"Well, let me think on it some."

After several more contractions, the anesthesiologist walked in, promising the pain would soon be a thing of the past. Maria just hoped that, along with the epidural, the doctor would inject a flood of maternal hormones into her, something that would make everything fall into place and ensure that she would love her baby once she held him in her arms.

The anesthesiologist had introduced himself, but

she'd been so wrapped up in her pain and her pitiful situation, that she couldn't remember his name. It didn't matter, she supposed. He lapsed into a short speech about the possible complications, but at this point, Maria didn't care.

Walter, on the other hand, appeared pale and hesitant.

Someone—the short, blond nurse?—pulled the screen, and Walter, as he'd done whenever Maria had been examined, stepped behind it to allow her privacy. Each time he'd gotten to his feet, she'd expected him to excuse himself and leave her to have the baby alone. But he'd waited—bless his heart.

Before long, Maria, who'd been curled up like a roly-poly to receive the shot in her spine, was allowed to ease back onto the bed. And as the pain finally lifted, the doctor left and Walter returned to his seat.

"You have no idea how much I appreciate you," Maria told Walter. "And to repay your kindness, I'll fix you dinner every night for a year."

He chuckled. "Be careful, now. You're all doped up, so you might want to think that over. I'm not a very good cook and would probably take you up on that offer."

Maria studied the kindly old man seated at her bedside, noting that the blue of his eyes softened the craggy lines of his face. "Maybe you ought to volunteer to work here, Walter. You'd be a real blessing to someone going through this kind of thing alone."

"No way. I hate hospitals."

"You could have fooled me."

He didn't return her smile. Instead, he stared at the fetal monitor.

"You feeling that?" he asked.

"Just some pressure. No pain."

"Amazing. I guess we should have asked for that epidural sooner, huh?"

We. A grin tickled her lips. Who would have thought that the old man at the park would have stepped in to be her labor coach?

"Thanks for being here, Walter. I was prepared to do this on my own, but it's nice having someone with me."

"Mind if I ask where your husband is? It doesn't seem right that he isn't being supportive. After all, it's his baby, too."

"My husband couldn't be here, even if he wanted to."

"Why not?"

"Two reasons. First of all, I wouldn't allow him in this room. And secondly because he's in prison."

Other than a deepening of the furrowed lines in his brow, Walter didn't react immediately. Finally, he turned to her. "What'd he do?"

Besides being a liar and a cheating husband?

"He killed someone."

Chapter 14

He *killed* someone?"

Walter hadn't exactly asked for details, but his brow twitched, and Maria knew he was curious, so she explained. "He was found guilty of voluntary manslaughter, but it should have been murder. A man died because of his actions."

For some reason, Maria felt compelled to tell Walter the whole sordid mess. And why shouldn't she? She wasn't going anywhere. And apparently, neither was Walter.

"His name is Ray Huddleston, and I met him one summer in Los Angeles while visiting my cousin, Rita. He was a hunk and the heartthrob of every girl in the neighborhood. So when he chose me, I was . . . flattered. And after a whirlwind courtship that lasted less than two months, he asked me to marry him." She fingered the edge of the sheet that covered the bulk of her belly, then turned her head, saw that Walter was listening intently. "Tía Sofía, the aunt who raised me, warned me to stay away from him, but I was in love."

"How old were you?"

"Seventeen. And at an age where I thought I was as smart as I'd ever get. You know what I mean?"

Walter nodded.

"Ray had family and friends in the Los Angeles area, so he wanted to live there. And I, of course, agreed, thinking we were in love and that I was the luckiest girl in the world. That is, until I learned Ray didn't take marriage vows seriously—his own or anyone else's."

"He cheated on you?"

"More times than I probably even knew about." She chuffed, still amazed at her own naïveté. "I was so starry-eyed that I couldn't see reality. And when I got pregnant with Danny, I thought nothing of all those late nights Ray worked, believing he was trying to be a good provider."

"But he wasn't always working?"

"No. I started hearing rumors, and when I confronted him, he admitted to having an affair. But he swore the woman meant nothing to him, that he loved me. And I believed him. When Sara was only six weeks old, I asked one of the neighbors to babysit so I could pick up something for a special dinner. It was our anniversary, and Ray was working late. Or so he'd told me. On the way to the market, I spotted his truck parked in front of the Starlight Motor Inn.

"I couldn't believe he'd do that to me again. Not after begging for another chance the time before. So I made a U-turn and parked near his truck. Then I began to bang on doors until he answered. A half-dressed blonde stood behind him."

"It's a shame you had to find him like that."

"It wasn't even the first time I'd caught him with another woman, but I swore it would be the last. Sofía was actually relieved when I left him. So she invited me and the kids to move back home with her in Fair-

245

brook. I took her up on it, and shortly after arriving, she quitclaimed the house to me."

"The one you live in now?"

Maria nodded. "It's where I grew up. Anyway, about six months later, my aunt died in her sleep."

"I'm sorry to hear that."

"I was devastated. Sofía was actually my father's aunt, and she was the only family I had. So when Ray came to Fairbrook eight months ago, apologizing and offering me the moon and all that glittered, I should have known better, but I was lonely. And he promised we'd make a fresh start in a new town. So I welcomed him into the house and into my life again."

"So that's when the baby was conceived."

Maria nodded. "I can't believe I was that stupid. But because I desperately wanted our family to be whole again, I believed him. He went on to swear that he'd seen the light. And he promised to change, saying he wanted to be the kind of man the kids and I deserved. And for three days, it was a dream come true."

She should have known better, though. Men like Ray Huddleston might make babies, but they didn't know the first thing about being a father.

Or a loyal husband.

"On the fourth day, the police showed up at the front door with a warrant and found Ray playing the part of a loving family man. But it had only been an act."

"What'd he do?"

"He'd gotten involved in a confrontation with his lover's husband. Things escalated until Ray pulled a gun and shot the man. He claimed it had been in self-defense, although he couldn't explain why he had a gun on him. It hadn't taken me long to realize why he'd come looking for me. He was hoping he could sweet-talk me into providing him with an alibi for the night of the shooting."

"I hope you didn't."

"No way. His ditzy blond lover might not have had a problem lying for him, but I refused to, and now he's facing the next twenty years in prison."

"Did your testimony put him away?"

"I'm sure it helped. But they had his fingerprints and his gun. He'd been the one who'd pulled the trigger."

"At least it's all behind you now."

"I hope so. When I was summoned back to L.A. to testify, I stayed with friends in the old neighborhood. The trial and resulting publicity were a nightmare, especially for Danny, who had to tolerate the whispers and taunts of kids who knew his father had killed someone."

"I'm sure it was tough on you, too."

"At times, it still is. I'll never forget the embarrassment, the pointed fingers, the knowing looks, the whispers . . ." She blew out a heart-weary sigh. "After the trial, I couldn't get back to Fairbrook fast enough."

"When did you find out you were pregnant?"

"Believe it or not, I lived in denial for months. I thought the stress caused me to skip my . . ." She turned her head, caught his gaze. "Well, that it caused some irregularity, and that, under the circumstances, a little bloating was to be expected. And now look at me. Still hoping this is just a bad dream and that I'll wake up."

Before Walter could comment on her stupidity or maybe even offer words of sympathy or some sage advice, the nurse returned.

"Let's see how you're progressing." The nurse, who'd introduced herself earlier as Mandy, pulled the privacy screen and slipped on a pair of gloves.

Walter, as had become his habit, ducked behind the curtain.

"Good." Mandy removed her hand, then peeled off her gloves and disposed of them. "You're nearly nine centimeters now. It shouldn't be much longer. I'll call Dr. Overstreet and set up the room for delivery."

This was it. Maria would just have to get used to the idea of having a new baby and make the best of it.

Mandy pulled back the curtain and smiled at Walter. "You can have your seat back, if you'd like. Or you can stay behind the screen."

Walter merely stood there.

"Sir?" Mandy asked. "Are you going to stay or go?"

Trevor lay in bed listening to Katie, who was in the bathroom that separated their bedrooms. It was almost six o'clock in the morning, and she'd already thrown up about a hundred times since she got home last night.

"I think I've got food poisoning," she'd told him around midnight.

After that, she mostly groaned.

But now she mumbled, just loud enough for him to hear through the closed door. "I think I'm gonna die."

He sure hoped she wasn't serious. "Do you want me to call 9-1-1 or something?"

"No. I . . ." She cleared her throat, then made that gasping, coughlike sound and . . . There she went again, puking her guts out.

If rotten food had made her sick, Trevor figured she should have barfed it all out by now.

He threw off the covers, climbed out of bed and made his way to the bathroom, where he stood before the closed door. "Are you *sure* you're okay?"

"I . . . just . . . need to . . . lie down."

"Don't you have to go to work today?" He hoped not, but the first of the month was coming pretty soon, and she always got stressed about her paycheck and bills when the rent was due.

Once he caught her crying about it, and she said, "Don't worry. It's just a little PMS."

When he asked what that was, she'd told him it was "girl stuff," so he dropped it. But she did go on to say that it sucked for the rent and PMS to both hit at the same time of the month.

And now she had to deal with *this.*

"I'm supposed to work today," she said, the bathroom door still shut. "But I can't. I need to call in . . ." She started gagging again.

Oh, man. The puke hit the toilet water like a kid cannonballing into the deep end of a pool. Just the sound was enough to make Trevor sick. So he backed away a few steps.

There was only one bathroom in the apartment—and Katie was locked in it. So if he suddenly had to throw up, he wasn't sure where he'd go.

At the house where he used to live, it wouldn't have been a problem. There'd been lots of bathrooms to choose from—upstairs and down.

"Do you want me to call someone at the diner and tell them you can't come in to work today?" he asked.

"Would you? *Please?*"

He could hear water running from the faucet, which was a good sign that the barfing was over for a while. And that she hadn't passed out or anything.

"Just ask to talk to Marlene," she added.

"Okay. Should I tell her why you're not coming in?"

The faucet shut off, and he heard the squeak of the metal bar as she pulled a towel from the rack. "Yeah. Tell her that I ate something bad last night. All I had was a bowl of clam chowder, but it didn't taste right. But then again, maybe I have the flu. I think it's going around."

"Do you know anyone who's sick?"

"I served an old man yesterday afternoon, and then he decided to leave without eating. He had me box up his food to take home and said he was coming down with something. If so, maybe I caught it from him. Who knows?"

"Okay. Should I call now?"

"Yeah, the diner's already open. Thanks, Trevor. You're the best."

The door opened, and Katie came out wearing her blue nightgown. Her hair was damp around her forehead, and her face was almost the same color as those ghosts in that movie he'd watched while he'd waited for her to get home last night. Of course, he'd turned the TV off before it was over because he got freaked out and thought he heard noises coming from the upstairs apartment, like chains rattling and stuff.

As Katie walked slowly to her room, shuffling her bare feet, Trevor thought about Mrs. Harper calling yesterday—twice. But he knew Katie wouldn't want to talk to anyone right now. Maybe not for the rest of the day.

"Hey, Katie." He followed her as far as the doorway to the bedroom. "A girl at the park asked if I could go to her house, and I wondered if that would be okay with you."

"You met a new friend?"

"Not exactly. She's just a girl. And she's only going to be in second grade. But she's okay for a little kid."

Katie paused by the dresser long enough to look at her alarm clock and turn it off. "What's her name?"

"Analisa. The lady babysitting her is pretty nice, and I told her you wouldn't mind if I went to play." Trevor watched Katie climb back into bed, kind of like a wounded soldier dragging himself into the safety of his trench.

"I'm glad you're making friends, Trev. But I probably should talk to the lady first, although I'm not up for it now."

"That's all right. Maybe I better hang out here with you instead. I could take care of you. Get you food and stuff."

"Thanks. That's really sweet, but I plan to sleep the rest of the day—*if* I can." She rolled to her side and pulled the sheet up to her chin. "Just in case this is a virus or something I picked up, I'd hate for you to catch it. So maybe it's best if you don't stay around the house too much."

"Okay." He leaned against the doorjamb for a while, watching her. Listening to her moan.

She sure sounded as if she was gonna die, but she would have let him call an ambulance if she was afraid of that happening. So he wasn't going to worry too much.

He just hoped she got better fast. Maybe that would happen if it was quiet and she could get some rest. "You want me to get you anything?"

"No. Not now."

Too bad he ate the last of the chicken noodle soup last night. That was supposed to be good food for sick people, wasn't it?

There were a couple of cans of chili beans still in the cupboard, though. Maybe that would work just as good.

Trevor yawned, and for a moment, he thought about going back to bed himself, since he was pretty tired and had woken up each time Katie had last night. But he hadn't eaten much for dinner, and a bowl of cereal sounded pretty good right now.

He also had to call Marlene at the diner.

Maybe afterward, he'd take his skateboard and go to the park early—just so he wouldn't accidentally make noise and wake Katie up.

No one would be at the park yet, but that was okay. He'd just practice by himself.

He was getting pretty good. Well, not like Danny Way or Tony Hawk or some of the other guys in the skateboarding magazines, but he didn't fall all that much anymore.

Hey, maybe Analisa would show up and invite him over to her house again. Katie hadn't exactly said he could go, but she didn't want to talk to anyone on the phone today. And she thought it was best if he stayed away from the house.

What would it hurt?

Besides, it's not like she ever got mad at him. Why would she?

They didn't have anyone else in the world but each other.

When Mandy had asked Walter whether he was going to stay during the delivery or leave, he didn't really answer. Heck, he didn't really *know*.

Funny thing about Maria's room. It was kind of homey, with floral window coverings and matching chairs—not at all like Hilda's, which had a real hospital feel to it.

Maybe that's one reason Walter had ended up staying the night.

And why he was still here.

While the medical personnel focused on Maria and the baby, he stayed behind the scenes. He expected someone to pull the curtain, but they didn't, so he stood near the door and out of the way.

He didn't have a bird's-eye view by any means, but the whole scene unfolding was surreal. Of course, that was probably because the lack of sleep had made him fuzzy-headed. Yet even though he had the urge to skedaddle when the excitement started and the homey setting was suddenly transformed into a delivery room, he couldn't quite bring himself to leave.

In a way, he suspected taking off now would be like cutting out of a movie theater during the last ten minutes of a blockbuster action flick—just as reinforcements arrived to help the good guys.

As Mandy encouraged Maria to push, he remained near the door and watched in awe as a scrawny, dark-haired baby, its body streaked with white, cheesy goo and blood, entered the world.

He'd seen puppies born a couple of times, and a quarter horse foal once at his uncle's ranch, but he'd never experienced anything like this. It was pretty amazing, actually.

Of course, the poor kid was kind of a mess. He was an odd color, too, which was too bad. Walter had hoped Maria would get attached to the little guy as soon as she laid eyes on him, but that might not be so easy.

The silence in the room was unsettling, though. And so was the blue tinge to the baby's skin.

Walter expected Dr. Overstreet to grab the baby by the heels, dangle him upside down and whack his little butt, but he didn't.

Instead, the doctor, a hulk of a man with beefy hands that appeared better suited for handling a football than a newborn, turned the kid this way and that while using a small rubber bulb to suction out his mouth.

Weren't babies supposed to make a fuss?

"Is everything okay?" Maria asked. "He's not crying."

"We're working on that," Mandy said, as the medical personnel in the room seemed to kick into ER-mode.

Walter backed up against the wall, then stopped, as immobile and useless as a statue in the middle of a town square.

"Oh, God," Maria cried. "No. *No.*"

Walter picked up the chant in his own mind. *No, no.*

Time stretched out, the seconds reverberating in his head.

Aw, come on, he thought. *If you're up there, God, let this little guy breathe, okay? His mom didn't really mean it. She wants him. And she's been through more than her share already. Don't leave her to wallow in a slew of guilt and grief.*

A small gasp tore into the silence, followed by an

all-out wail. Well, not really a wail, but the kid had lungs. And they were working.

The sound was music to an old man's ears and almost enough to make Walter drop to his knees, if he were inclined to be religious and believe his silent plea actually had an effect on anything.

Or had it?

"Is he okay?" Maria asked.

"It looks and sounds like it to me," Dr. Overstreet said. "But Dr. Crandall, the neonatalogist, is going to take him to NICU for a better exam. So Mandy, bundle up that little guy and let his mom take a quick peek before he goes."

Mandy swaddled the kid up like a burrito and stretched a little pink-and-blue cap onto his head. Then she stopped briefly at Maria's bedside and held the baby close to her face. Walter watched as the mother brushed a kiss on her new son's cheek and heard her whisper, "Hang in there, buddy. Mommy loves you."

A look so warm, so tender, crossed her face. And Walter knew it was all going to be okay. Maybe not the financial stuff, but he saw love in her eyes.

He'd seen that same look on Margie's face many times, particularly that day Blake had climbed the umbrella tree in the front yard, even though Walter had warned him time and again about brittle branches.

And sure enough. Snap.

The poor kid had taken a hard fall and was knocked unconscious. When he'd finally come to and started squawking, Margie had gotten all teary-eyed and mushy. Yep, Walter knew the look. And Maria had it, too.

"Don't worry. Sending the baby to the NICU for an exam is just a precaution," Dr. Overstreet said, as he continued to tend to Maria. "What're you going to name him?"

"I don't know. I hadn't given it a whole lot of thought." Maria looked at Walter. "Any suggestions?"

Just one. So he tossed it out. "Carl Witherspoon was the finest man I ever knew."

Maria's gaze locked on Walter, and her smile nearly squeezed the heart right out of him. "I'm looking at the finest man I ever met, so I think I'd better call him Walter Carl."

Emotion snaked inside Walter's throat, making it impossible to tell her he wasn't worthy, yet was honored just the same. But he hoped the tears welling in his eyes conveyed it all.

"Thanks for sticking it out with me." Her gaze glimmered with emotion.

"The pleasure was mine."

She slid him a smile. "After staying up all night, you probably need to go home and take a nap."

"Yep. I need a shower and could use something to eat, too. But I'm not in that big of a hurry."

He'd stay a tad longer, just to make sure little Walter Carl was really going to be okay.

Chapter 15

It was late in the morning when Mrs. Harper and Analisa arrived at the park—or maybe it just seemed that way since Trevor had been here for so long.

He stooped to pick up his skateboard, then met them as the car doors opened. "Hey."

Mrs. Harper smiled as though she was happy to see him, which was cool. "Good morning, Trevor."

He watched as she slid out of the car, and when she was locking the door, he figured he'd better let her know that he was good at taking messages. "I told Katie you called last night, but she got home late. So I asked if it was okay if I went to play with Analisa, and she said it was."

Analisa clapped her hands. "Oh, good! Now I can show you my room and my dollhouse and everything."

"I don't know about that." Mrs. Harper crossed her arms.

"Why not?" Analisa asked.

"Because I can't take a child anywhere without talking to an adult and making sure I have permission first."

"Well, you can't talk to Katie this morning," Trevor said. "Her stomach is all messed up, and she was throwing up when I left. She called in sick to work so she can sleep all day."

Mrs. Harper scrunched her eyebrows, looking a lot like Mrs. Banister had last year when she announced a surprise math quiz and realized she'd left the test at home.

"But Trevor already asked," Analisa said. "And Katie told him it was okay. Besides, the other day you gave him a ride home without talking to her first."

Mrs. Harper made a click sound with her tongue, just like Mrs. Banister did when Cody Melville let out a happy "whoo-hoo" about them not having to take the test.

"Katie doesn't care," Trevor said.

Mrs. Harper's face got all soft, like she was going to give in. "You might be right about that."

"I *am*."

Okay, so Katie hadn't exactly said he could go to Analisa's, but she would have—if she hadn't been too sick to talk to Mrs. Harper on the telephone.

Maybe it's best if you don't stay around the house too much, Katie had said. She'd known he would go to the park like he always did. So what was wrong with going to Analisa's? Trevor never got to go any-where anymore. Not even to school, since it was summer.

"Well, all right." Mrs. Harper lifted her hand to shield her eyes from the sun and glanced at the play-ground. "But since we're already here, we may as well stay for a while."

"Do we have to?" Trevor didn't want to stick around

any longer. "I've been here since about seven o'clock."

Mrs. Harper kind of stiffened, like she was surprised Trevor got up that early. He didn't usually, but he let her think he did.

"Well," she said. "I suppose we don't have to stay."

When Analisa got all happy about leaving, Mrs. Harper told them to climb into the car and buckle their seat belts. Once they did, Trevor took off his helmet and pads.

About five or ten minutes later, they arrived at a white two-story house on a street lined with trees, although they weren't very big ones.

Mrs. Harper parked the car along the curb, then led them to the front door and used a key to let them in.

"Come on," Analisa told Trevor. "I'll show you my room. It used to have green walls and a sofa, but when Uncle Sam brought me home to live with him, he had a man come over and paint it special—just for me. Now, it's my favorite color."

Trevor carried his skateboard into the house and left it, along with his gear, in the tiled entry. Then he followed Analisa through the living room. All their furniture, like the beige leather sofa and glass-topped tables, looked brand-new. So did the books and bowls and things on the shelves of a bookcase that lined one whole wall.

"We used to have a big house like this," Trevor said, as Analisa led him down a hall. "But not anymore."

"Why not?"

He didn't tell her.

She led him to a bedroom that was pink, with white wooden shutters and trim. He couldn't help but look around. She had a lot of toys and dolls—all girl stuff.

"It's cool your uncle fixed a room up for you." Katie had done that when they'd moved to the apartment—tried to make his new room special, even though it wasn't very big and didn't have the race-car wallpaper that matched his bedspread. His old bedroom had a window with a little ledge he could kneel on and look out into the backyard where his swing set and batting cage used to be. Now all he saw when he looked out his window was the backside of the Laundromat and a green Dumpster.

"Uncle Sam isn't used to having kids around," Analisa said, "especially girls, so he tries hard to be good to me, even though he's not home very much."

"At least he's *home*. Sometimes people have to work a lot just so you can have a house to live in and food to eat."

"Do you miss your dad?"

That wasn't what Trevor meant, but yeah. "I miss him a lot."

"It's too bad you can't live with him. When my mommy and daddy went to Guatemala, I got to go with them." She plopped down on a pink vinyl beanbag chair that sat next to a white bookshelf. "Do you know where Guatemala is?"

"Nope."

"It's far away. And we had to take a plane to get there."

Trevor's dad was about four hours away and you could go by car, but he might as well have lived in another country.

"Is your daddy a missionary, too?" Analisa asked.

Trevor didn't know what a missionary was, but he didn't think his dad was one. "He used to own a company that made computer software."

"But not anymore?"

Trevor shook his head. "Nope."

"What does he do now?"

"He doesn't do anything."

"Then how come he lives far away?"

"You sure ask a lot of questions." Trevor walked toward the bed. It had a white headboard and footboard, and it was covered with a fluffy comforter with pink flowers. He trailed his finger along the curve of the wood, then looked at Analisa.

Her lips formed a frown—or maybe it was a pout. "I just wanted to know. That's all."

He leaned his hip against the mattress. "Yeah, well, *no one* knows, okay? It's a secret."

"No one knows where your dad is?"

"Just some people. Not everyone. And Katie thinks it's better if we don't tell."

"I'm good at keeping secrets. Once Soledad told me that she . . ." Analisa paused and bit her bottom lip. "Well, she told me a secret, and I never ever told anyone. I won't even tell you if you poke me with red-hot needles."

Trevor knew better than to say anything to anyone about his dad or where he was, especially to a little kid, but sometimes it was hard keeping it inside. "If I tell you, you'll have to promise not to say a word to *anyone*. And if you do, I'll never climb any trees for you again."

Analisa sat up straight and traced a cross over her chest with her finger. "I promise."

Trevor glanced at the door, then strode toward it. When he'd closed it, he turned and faced her. "My dad's in prison."

"You mean *jail?*"

Trevor nodded. "Yeah."

"How come? Did he do something bad?"

"He got in an accident and killed somebody."

"My dad was in an accident, too. In Guatemala. The Jeep he was driving got wrecked and he died. But the other man didn't go to jail. Just to a hospital."

"Yeah, well, my dad hit a kid riding a bicycle. And even though he told them it was an accident, they didn't believe him."

Her eyes opened wide. "They thought he did it on *purpose?*"

"I guess so."

Analisa bent forward and rested her hands on her knees. "When does he get to come home?"

"I don't know. There's some people he has to meet

pretty soon, and if they believe he's sorry, they might let him out sooner."

"Is he? Sorry about what happened?"

"Yeah. *Super* sorry."

For once, Analisa didn't have anything to say. After a while, she asked, "When did it happen?"

"A long time ago. When I was in the first grade."

"And you've been telling people he lives in another country all that time?"

"Katie thinks it's better that way. She's big on privacy."

"Even if she has to tell a *lie?*"

"Yeah. That's because she's afraid of snoopy neighbors who say mean things and reporters and guys with cameras. She doesn't want to have to answer questions and stuff."

"Did they bother you before? When it happened?"

"No. My dad made my babysitter keep me inside a lot, and his attorney said reporters would be in big trouble if they bothered me about it since I'm a kid."

"Uncle Sam is an attorney. Maybe he can help."

"We already got one of those. And my dad still had to go to prison." Sadness rolled through him again. His eyes began to water, and he swiped at them with the back of his hand. "Katie said there's nothing anyone can do."

"That's when you should ask *God* to do something, Trevor. His biggest job is making miracles, like walking on water and healing people. All you got to do is believe and ask Him."

That's *all*? She made it sound easy, when it wasn't.

How was Trevor supposed to believe in something he couldn't see? Or believe that God loved him and everything would be okay, especially when there wasn't much food in the cupboard and Katie's paycheck didn't come for another three days?

Or when Trevor's dad had to sell almost everything they had because he had to pay a whole lot of money to a dead kid's family?

The kids had a pleasant playtime, and at three o'clock, Claire drove Trevor home. Rather than drop him off at the curb, though, as she'd done before, she parked and got out of the car.

"I'll just make sure you get in okay," she told him.

"You don't have to." He started up the steps that led to his door. "I'll be okay."

"I know, but I'd like to meet Katie."

"Oh, yeah." He tried to turn the knob, but found it locked. "That's weird." He reached into his pocket and pulled out his key, which was tied to a braided piece of red yarn. Once the door swung open, he called Katie's name.

No answer.

"I guess she's gone."

"Are you sure?" Claire asked.

He shrugged, then went inside.

Claire remained in the doorway, holding Analisa's hand. She didn't want to appear nosy, but she couldn't help peering into the sparse living room of a nondescript apartment with pea-green carpet that needed to be replaced. The sofa, however, was either leather or an expensive imitation. And the furniture—a coffee table and lamp stands—appeared to be fairly new.

"Sorry," Trevor said, as he made his way back to the door. "She's not here. I didn't look for her car, but I guess she went somewhere. Maybe to work."

"Well, *that's* good news." Claire forced a smile. "It's not fun to be sick."

As much as she would have liked to push for an invitation to go inside, to be allowed to check out the home in which Trevor lived, and try to evaluate the quality of his care, she refrained.

"I'm sorry we missed her," Claire said. "Maybe next time."

Trevor nodded, and Claire led Analisa to the car. Once back at Sam's house, Claire made a pressing phone call that took longer than she expected, then fixed dinner again—barbecued chicken, baked potatoes, and coleslaw.

She'd no more than popped the chicken and potatoes into the oven when Sam arrived home from work—earlier today than he had yesterday. So when he suggested they go out on the deck for a glass of wine, she agreed.

They sat at the glass-top table on padded, wrought-iron chairs. They were close enough to touch, if they wanted to.

The sun had lowered into the west, streaking the horizon with shades of pink and orange. In the waning light, Claire was able to bask in the beauty of the sunset, as well as the parklike landscape: emerald green lawns, colorful gardens, and a custom-built swimming pool, its water blue and pristine.

Considering the time Sam spent at the office, she assumed he hired someone to keep up with all the work. Yet she wondered if he ever rolled up his sleeves and puttered around himself.

"Do you work in the yard?" she asked.

"I probably *would*—if I were home more. As it is, I have a gardener and a pool maintenance company to handle the upkeep, but at least I can enjoy the fruits of their labors when I come outdoors."

"Do you get to do that very often?"

"I usually have my morning coffee and read the newspaper on the deck. If I get home early enough, I sit out here and unwind. Either way, I bought this place because of the yard, so I try to enjoy it when I can."

"I can see why. It's beautiful. If this were my home, sitting out here could easily become a habit." So could spending the end of each day with Sam.

She stole a glance at him, studied his profile. The aquiline nose, the square jaw, the bristled shadow of the beard he'd shave tomorrow. It wasn't just his home and yard that could become habit-forming. She could easily grow to enjoy his presence, his ready smile.

As though aware of her assessment, he turned to face her. The color of his eyes—a springtime green—

was striking at close range. Yet it was more than that setting her heart on edge. It was the intensity in his gaze, connecting them in some way.

Unsure if she was ready to deal with the hormones or pheromones or whatever was buzzing between them, she broke eye contact and studied her wineglass instead. She fingered the stem, but didn't lift it to her lips.

Why should she? She found it a bit intoxicating just to be near Sam.

How long had it been since she'd felt the stir of sexual attraction? The heated curiosity it evoked?

Forever, it seemed. Yet she wasn't sure she was up for it to begin anew.

In the early years, she and Ron used to have a cocktail hour before dinner. It was a time to shed the cares of the outside world and to catch up on the happenings in each other's day. The practice had stopped along the way, although she wasn't sure when. After she got pregnant with Erik, she supposed.

"How was your day?" Sam asked, drawing her from her musing.

"It was all right. I brought Trevor home to play with Analisa today."

"Good. Did the visit go well?"

"It was fine." She bit her lip, wondering how he'd feel about what she'd done and whether she should even bring it up.

"Your words say one thing, but your tone and demeanor suggest something else. What happened?"

"Nothing out of the ordinary—at least as far as the kids and their playtime went. Trevor is a little older than Analisa and not as impressed with dollhouses as she'd hoped he would be, but when I suggested a board game, they ended up having fun. Actually, so did I. It's just that I feel sorry for the kid and think he's being neglected."

"Why?"

"For one thing, he lives with a guardian who isn't ever home, so consequently, he's at the park from dawn until dusk. And since he rarely has a lunch with him, some of the others have been bringing extra to feed him."

"My brother and I had a lot of freedom as kids. And a sandwich made by someone else usually tasted better to me than one I threw together. Maybe he's learned to leave his lunch at home. Are you sure he's neglected?"

"There's a sadness about him, and he's never supervised, which worries me. There are so many dangers, not to mention predators, waiting to take advantage of a lone child. And I'm not just talking about molesters. Trevor's had a couple of run-ins with a teenage punk and was afraid to walk home on occasion. Then last night, after he'd been alone most of the day, his guardian left him to fend for himself and went out drinking with friends. From what I understand, she got in late and had a hangover this morning."

"That's too bad."

"Yes, it is. So I decided that if I didn't do something about it, no one would."

Sam's expression softened, and his eyes zeroed in on hers. "What did you do?"

"I made a report to child protective services."

"Hey. At least someone's looking out for him."

She shrugged. "It just seems so unfair that some parents have children they don't appreciate, while others adore their kids and lose them."

Sam placed his hand over hers, warming her from the inside out, then slowly removed it. "Sometimes life isn't fair."

"Isn't that the truth?"

They both fell silent for a while. Lost in their thoughts. Claire finally took a sip of her wine, hoping to shed her concern for Trevor, but she was having no such luck.

What would happen to the boy if the court removed him from his guardian's care? Where would he go?

For the briefest of moments, she wondered if she would be able to offer him a home. But to be honest, she wasn't sure. Her heart might not be up to it.

Sam lifted his glass and studied the straw-colored liquid, then took a drink. "I had lunch with a friend and colleague today—Jake Goldstein."

"Oh?"

"He represents Russell."

Claire stiffened.

"The parole board meets with him on Thursday."

She'd known July twenty-fourth was coming up, but since she wasn't at work with a calendar prominently displayed on her desk and a schedule to keep, she hadn't realized it was so soon.

Sam took a sip of wine. "I know we talked about this before, so when Jake asked me to talk to you on Russell's behalf again, I refused. But I see you have a real heart for kids. And I think you need to know something about Russell's son."

She didn't want to know anything about the man or his little boy. She wanted Russell to remain distant—locked away, not only in real life, but in some shadowed part of her mind, as well.

And although she felt compelled to stand and turn her back on Sam, to grab her purse and head for the door, she couldn't seem to move or speak.

"Russell's wife died of cancer a year or two before the accident, and he was left to raise their only child, a boy who's about nine or ten now. I have no idea where he is or who's taking care of him while his father is in prison, but according to Jake, Russell believes the boy is depressed and suffering from the loss of both parents."

Claire didn't want to see any child hurt, but what did Sam expect *her* to do? If the parole board released every incarcerated parent who'd left a grieving family at home, they'd have to free half the prison population—if not more.

"Maybe you should visit Russell," Sam said. "Talk to him in person."

"At the state *prison?*" How could he suggest such a thing?

He shrugged. "You could decide whether he's truly sorry and if he's paid his debt to society."

"I can't do that."

"Maybe if you talked to him in person, you might be able to put the past behind you."

Tears welled in her eyes, as Sam's voice morphed into Ron's: *Dwelling in the past is making me crazy, Claire, not to mention what it's doing to* you.

The echo of her ex-husband's accusations slammed into her, making it hard to breathe, let alone think. For some reason, Ron had insisted she was hanging onto Erik. He'd wanted her to "let go," but she couldn't. How was she supposed to pretend her happy, dark-haired son had never lived, never laughed? Never loved?

Erik's death and their different coping mechanisms had strained a frayed marital bond until it could no longer hold two grieving parents together.

And now, Sam was implying the same things Ron had.

Emotions—too varied to name—swam in her eyes until she could barely see, and an ache the size of a boulder filled her chest.

If Claire didn't keep Erik's memory alive, who would?

And what about justice? Why shouldn't the man responsible for Erik's tragic and senseless death pay for his negligence?

Yet none of it would bring her son back. Or put her broken heart and spirit to rights. She was torn. Scattered. And she needed to pull herself together.

Pushing aside her wineglass, she blinked back the tears and stood. "I really need to go."

"I'm sorry, Claire." Sam slid his chair back and got to his feet. "I just don't want to see you hurt anymore. The pain is going to kill you, if you let it. I've had to deal with guilt and anger, too. And now, even though I'd like to bury the hatchet and make things right, I can't."

She understood where he was coming from, yet she wanted to lash out at him. To ask where his father was right now. And ask whether Sam had ever gone to visit, whether the man was truly sorry and had paid *his* debt to society. It was a retort she might have unleashed on Ron, if it had fit. But she didn't want to fight. Didn't want to strain the fragile connection she and Sam had forged.

If she didn't get out of this house, she was going to break down and cry, and she didn't want to show him her pain, her weakness. Didn't want to lose control in front of him.

Was she really as unbalanced as Ron had suggested?

Her heart threatened to explode, and she fought the urge to hurl the wineglass from the deck, to upend the table and throw it to the floor. To scream at the heavens and demand justice. Relief. Peace.

Anything other than pain.

"Did you hear me?" Sam slipped an arm around her waist and drew her to him. "I'm sorry, Claire."

For a moment, she leaned into him, rested her cheek against his chest, gripped the lapel of his jacket and held on tight. She breathed in the faint scent of man and musk, accepting both Sam's strength and support.

Then she rallied.

She didn't want Sam to see her like this, which she feared would lead him to feel sorry for her. To see her as a victim.

You're not the only one in the world who's lost a child, Ron had said. *Give me a break, okay? See a priest or a rabbi, go to a counselor, take some medication. Just get over it so we can get on with life.*

She wasn't sure what she wanted out of Sam. But not that. Not *this*.

She cleared her throat, drawing away. "I'll call you later this evening—about tomorrow." She would return to watch Analisa, if he still wanted her to.

But right now, she had to go.

Trevor lay on his back on the top of his bed, his hands tucked under his head. He stared at the ceiling, where somebody who used to live here had stuck a bunch of stars—little yellow ones. They were supposed to glow in the dark, but they really didn't work very good anymore.

He wished he could go outside and look at the real stars, but he was grounded.

After Mrs. Harper had dropped him off this afternoon and driven away, he'd found a note that Katie had left for him on the kitchen counter. It said,

Trevor, you're in BIG trouble! Call me at the diner as soon as you get home.

He did and found out that Katie had started feeling a little better around noon and had decided to go to work after all.

"We need the tip money for groceries," she'd told him.

He'd felt bad knowing she was probably still sick and had to work anyway. But there wasn't much he could do to help. Last month, he'd asked a guy at Paddy's Pub if there was any work he could do, like sweeping and doing dishes and stuff. But the guy had only laughed. "Are you nuts, kid? Beat it."

That left the job of earning money on Katie, so he couldn't blame her for being mad at him when he called her at the diner.

"So where did you go?" she'd asked—and not very nice. "I assumed you were either hanging out at our complex or at Mulberry Park, but when I went looking for you, I couldn't find you."

"I was at Analisa's house."

"We talked about that this morning, Trevor, but I didn't give you permission to go anywhere."

"Well, I thought you *sort* of did . . ."

"Your dad would shoot me if I turned you loose all day long. It's bad enough I can't afford a sitter and

275

you have to spend the whole summer at home in front of the TV."

Trevor didn't say anything. Katie didn't know he wasn't home all that much.

"I'm supposed to be watching you while your father's gone, and he's worried sick about you. I don't think he'd even like you going to the park for a little while each day, but I tried to be nice by letting you get out of the house some. Now I'm not sure I can trust you to follow the rules."

"You can. I didn't mean to do anything wrong. I just wanted to have a little fun. You don't know what it's like."

"I *don't?*" Katie's voice got loud, letting him know he'd blown it by saying the wrong thing. "I'm twenty-four years old, Trevor. And that may sound ancient to you, but I'm still young. Some would say I'm too young to take on the responsibility of a child your age, but I love your father—and *you*. So I don't mind working my butt off to pay the rent, but keep in mind that I've given up a lot, too. My friends, my social life . . ."

"At least you got to go out last night."

"I went out to dinner with a friend who just found out she has a 'suspicious' spot on her lung. And instead of eating a meal, which would have been nice, I chose the soup, okay? It's not like I was wasting money. Or having a party."

"That's not what I meant." And it wasn't.

She didn't say anything for a minute. Then she

made a huffy sound. "Just go to your room, okay? And stay there until I get home. It shouldn't be long. I'm really dragging. That food poisoning took a lot out of me."

Trevor glanced at the clock on the dresser: 8:07. Katie had gotten home about an hour ago and let him come out to eat. She'd fixed chili beans, although she didn't make herself a bowl.

"I'm kind of nervous," she told him as she munched on a saltine.

"How come?"

"Because the parole board meets Thursday."

He stuck his spoon into his bowl, but left it there. "What do you think will happen?"

"I have no idea."

"Maybe we should . . . you know, pray about it."

"It wouldn't hurt." But she made no move to take his hand or talk to God out loud like Analisa had done, which Trevor was kind of hoping she'd do. He wouldn't suggest it, though. What if she thought he was dumb?

He finished his chili, and she picked up his bowl and put it in the sink.

"Can I watch TV?" he asked.

"No, not tonight. You're still grounded."

Still?

She was being all nice, like she'd gotten over being mad, but now here he was—back in his room again. He'd probably end up in here forever. And when his dad finally got out of prison and came home looking for Trevor, he'd find a shriveled-up corpse with big, black eyeholes just staring at the dumb glow-in-the-dark stars.

Life really sucked. And there was no one in the whole wide world who could do anything to make it better. *No one.*

His thoughts drifted to Analisa.

That's when you should ask God to do something, she'd told him the other day. *All you got to do is believe and ask.*

Then today, while he and Analisa ate turkey sandwiches and orange slices for lunch, Mrs. Harper went looking for a game for them to play together, and Analisa had started in on him again. "Just like I did with my letters. You have to ask God to fix things, then believe He's going to do it. Remember when you and I prayed for the bike?"

"Yeah, and I got a *skateboard* instead."

Analisa had slapped her hands on her hips and frowned. "Sometimes you have to let Him do it *His* way, Trevor."

"Okay, so maybe I believe He *can* help. What makes you think He *will?*"

"Because He loves you and doesn't want you to be unhappy. But you have to believe in Him. That's the way it works. You have to have *faith,* and if you don't, you can't expect miracles."

He'd thought about that for a while.

"You know what faith is, don't you?"

Not really. But he didn't want her to think that she

was smarter than him, so he didn't answer, which was okay. She told him anyway.

"It's when you see a new little baby that used to be inside its mommy's tummy. And when you see a butterfly come out of a cocoon. And when you look up in the sky and see a shooting star. You don't understand *how* God did it, but you know that He did. 'Cause stuff like that doesn't happen by accident."

He hadn't wanted to keep talking about it, so he'd pointed to the swimming pool and asked if she ever went into the deep end.

But now that he was lying here, looking at dumb little stars some guy in Hong Kong probably made, Trevor realized that the real ones couldn't be made in a factory. And he sort of got the idea.

He wished Analisa was here so she could pray for him, like she'd done the day at the park—the day God had given him the skateboard. He felt funny praying out loud.

Maybe he could just write it all down, just like she'd done. He could tell God how bad he hurt, how much he missed not having a mom and dad. And he could ask God to fix things for his dad.

Trevor rolled out of bed, went to his desk and pulled out a pen and paper. Then he sat down and wrote a letter to God. It took two whole pages. But leaving it out on his desk or shoving it in a drawer wasn't going to work. He had to make sure God got it as soon as possible, or else it might be too late.

That meant he'd have to disobey Katie one more time.

So he tiptoed into the hall, where he saw that her bedroom door was open. The light was on and she was wearing her work clothes, even her restaurant vest, so it seemed like she was awake. But her head was drooped to the side, her eyes were closed, and her mouth was kind of open.

No wonder she hadn't let him come out yet. She'd fallen asleep.

Cool. That would give him time to do what he had to do.

He returned to his bedroom and pulled his skateboard out from under the bed, where he kept it hidden so Katie wouldn't know he even had it. For a moment, he thought about taking the helmet and pads, too, but it would take a while to put them on. And if Katie caught him . . .

No, he couldn't risk it. He had to get to the park and back before Katie woke up and realized he was gone.

As he walked softly through the living room, he spotted the telephone. Uh-oh. That could be a problem. He picked it up and turned down the sound, just like he'd seen Katie do that day those dumb telesales guys kept calling and waking her up from a nap.

When he was sure he'd taken care of everything, he snuck out of the house like a Navy SEAL on a dangerous mission, making sure to lock the door behind him so Katie would be safe. Then he hurried to the sidewalk, where he kicked off, setting his board in motion.

It was a little scary being out after dark, but it seemed like someone was watching over him tonight. But not just anyone: *God.*

"See?" he whispered. "I believe in you."

Trevor turned down Second Street and zipped along for a block or two. He didn't usually go to the park this way, but he thought it might be faster. At the intersection, he turned left on Applewood. The cool thing about this road was that it sloped downward, right into the park.

As he picked up speed, the night air cooled his face. For once in his life, or at least for the first time since he was a little kid, he believed that everything was going to be okay. He was right where he needed to be, doing just what he needed to do.

And look at him now. He was bombing a hill, just like one of the Z-Boys.

As he neared the streetlight, he spotted something dark and jagged on the sidewalk ahead. A crack in the concrete maybe?

He probably ought to slow up and go around it. That's what he would have done before. But tonight was different. So deciding to jump it, he stepped back to lift the front wheels. Just then, the trucks underneath the board began to wobble, and the next thing he knew, he was flying up in the air.

For a second, it seemed like he might zoom up to

Heaven—until he fell back to earth and slammed into the street with a thud.

Then everything went dark.

Chapter 16

Claire managed to keep her tears at bay until she arrived at home, then allowed herself a good cry.

Yet this time, instead of falling into one of those prolonged jags that threw her into a blue funk for days, she actually felt better afterward.

Now, as she climbed from the bathtub, reached for a towel and began to dry off, she regretted running out on Sam, especially with dinner baking in the oven. She'd been worried about what he would think if she'd broken down in front of him, yet she suspected he probably thought worse of her for having left abruptly and teary-eyed.

Of course, she took personal responsibility for her knee-gut reaction, but she blamed Ron for it, too.

In the early months after Erik's death, Ron had been brokenhearted, too, so her crying hadn't bothered him. Then, as time went on and he moved through his grief, he'd wanted her to move along with him, but she hadn't been able to. The smallest thing—a Lego she'd found under a sofa cushion, a Popsicle stick on the back porch, a baseball card in a drawer—would set her off and she'd fall apart all over again.

Ron hadn't even needed to say anything. He'd just get that twitch near his eye and that crease between his brows, letting her know her sadness was dragging him down. So she'd hid her feelings the best she could.

As a result, this evening, when facing tears, she'd been afraid to let Sam see them. Afraid he'd think less of her.

During her lavender-scented soak in the tub—aromatherapy, they called it—she'd thought about the way Sam had slipped an arm around her and offered her comfort. Why hadn't she been able to accept it?

Fear of getting too close to Sam? Of facing romantic yearnings again?

That must have been the case, since Sam's presence had set her more on edge than what he'd said about Russell Meredith.

His comments about Russell's late wife and son had bothered her more than she cared to admit, though.

Claire had known the woman who'd supported Russell throughout the trial had been his girlfriend, Kathryn somebody. Jones or Johnson maybe?

Either way, the petite brunette, who couldn't have been much more than twenty years old at the time of the trial, had testified for the defense, swearing under oath that Russell hadn't been drinking before the accident. But Kathryn hadn't been a credible witness. The assistant district attorney had brought her to tears on the stand, accusing her of lying to protect her rich lover and asking if she knew the penalty of perjury.

When she'd left the courthouse after her testimony, she'd been swarmed by cameras and the media.

They'd quizzed her about her years in foster care, followed by a Cinderella relationship with Russell, and she'd broken down again. At that point, Russell's attorney had to step in and help her get away from the reporters.

Claire had almost felt sorry for the woman, but at the time, grief and anger had been the only emotions she'd been able to process.

Sam had been right, though. She really did want to put all of that behind her. It was over, and nothing could bring Erik back.

"Oh, God," Claire uttered more in exasperation than in prayer. "What should I do?"

Would it hurt to do nothing? an inner voice asked.

No, she supposed it wouldn't.

Sam had suggested she talk to Russell, a thought too bizarre to contemplate. She would never make a drive to the state prison to see the man who'd killed her son, but neither did she need to fight his release.

Stepping back was a fair concession to make. That way, whatever the boy was going through would be his father's own doing.

She glanced at the clock on her dresser. It wasn't much after eight and certainly not too late to call Sam. So she took a seat on the side of the bed, picked up the phone, and dialed his number.

He answered on the third ring.

"Hi. It's Claire. I'm sorry for taking off in such a rush. I was afraid I'd have a meltdown, and I didn't want you to see it."

"Russell Meredith is a touchy subject, and I should have known better than to have brought him up."

"No, I'm glad you did. It needed to be said." Silence stretched between them, and she pressed herself to continue. "You were right, Sam. I need to let go of this obsession to see Russell punished. It won't bring Erik back, and it won't help me heal. So I've decided to back off. I won't object to his release."

"I'm glad to hear it. Not necessarily for Russell's sake, but for yours. And for the boy's."

They were at a point where she could wrap up the conversation —if she wanted to. Yet she clutched the receiver as though she could hold on to whatever connection she and Sam had. "I'm not a mean, vengeful person."

"I know you aren't. The thought never crossed my mind."

That was good. His opinion of her mattered more than anything else had in a long time, and she wanted to make sure he understood where she was coming from. "It's just that Erik was my life. And losing him . . ."

"I *know*."

Unspoken words and emotion filled the line again, and she forced herself out on a limb. To ease toward the truth. "I wrapped myself into a cocoon, hoping to insulate myself from any more sorrow than I could handle. But being with Analisa these past few days has helped me come to grips with my loss. Life goes on, and to be honest, I'm finally beginning to feel human again. So, if you don't mind, I'd like to continue babysitting until Hilda can come back to work."

"Does that mean that I still get dinner out of this arrangement? Having you around has its perks, Claire."

She couldn't help but grin. "You mean my grandmother was right? The way to a man's heart really is through his stomach?"

"That's *one* way."

A peace-filled hush—sweet and tentative—swept over them again. While she'd like to bask in it, she also wanted to confront it, but wasn't sure how.

The comment she'd made about the way to his heart had been a slip of the tongue, and his response had been a loaded innuendo.

Or had it been?

"One of these nights," Sam said, "I'd like to hire a babysitter and take you out to dinner and the theater. Just let me know when you're ready."

When she was *ready?* Her pulse spiked, and she fingered the hem along the neckline of her tank-shirt. "What do you mean?"

"I'm asking you for a date and giving you an out at the same time."

A full-on smile broke across her face. "Now *that's* an interesting ploy."

"I thought so. Is it working?"

"Actually, I think it *is*."

Sam laughed. "Good."

Another silence filled the line, this one loaded with possibilities.

"You left without eating," he said. "Are you still hungry?"

She placed a hand on her stomach, realizing she hadn't given food any thought since returning home. "Actually, I'll probably make a sandwich."

"You know, I fed Analisa after you left, but I haven't fixed my own plate yet. Why don't you come back? We can eat on the deck."

A sandwich in front of the television suddenly held little appeal. "It'll take me a few minutes to get there."

"I don't mind waiting."

After they said good-bye and the line disconnected, Claire remained seated on the edge of the mattress and scanned the bedroom, which she'd been meaning to redecorate ever since Ron had moved out.

It was definitely time for fresh paint on the walls. Something bright and colorful would be nice, as well as new bedding to match. She might go so far as to replace the furniture, too.

Maybe, in the morning she would call Vickie and ask if they could add a shopping trip to their spa-day agenda, something they'd always enjoyed in the past.

Actually, the idea intrigued her. So did the thought of returning to Sam's house and joining him on the deck, even if they would have to tiptoe around their feelings.

In spite of an almost overwhelming urge not to

dawdle, she did run a brush through her hair and applied a dab of lipstick and mascara. Then she slipped on a pair of tennis shoes and headed downstairs.

She stopped in the kitchen, where her cell phone lay on the counter, and shoved it in her pants pocket more out of habit than need. Then she snatched her purse and keys from the table and headed for the laundry room.

The hint of a breeze whispered through her hair—or so it seemed—and she paused in the doorway that led out of the house and into the garage. Her senses went on alert, and for a moment, she felt uneasy. Unbalanced.

Don't wait, something inside of her urged. *Go now.*

She shook off the compulsion to obey, as well as any questions regarding her sanity, locked up the house, and climbed into the car instead.

As she slid behind the wheel, she couldn't help muttering, "That was weird."

She backed out of her driveway and, after closing the automatic garage door, headed down the street. When she reached the stop sign, she made a left instead of a right, just as if she'd been instructed to do so by someone in the passenger seat.

But there was no one there; she knew because she'd looked.

She turned onto Peachtree Circle, then Chinaberry Lane—another alteration from her usual route. Yet the closer she got to Mulberry Park, the more convinced she became that this was exactly where she needed to be.

Up ahead, the headlights illuminated something that lay in the gutter where the sidewalk met the blacktop road. A bag of . . . laundry?

No. *Not* laundry. A small crumpled body.

Oh, dear God.

Erik.

No. *Not* Erik.

She hit the brakes, then shifted the transmission into park, leaving the car in the street, the headlamps on, the engine running. In what felt like one fluid movement, she threw open the door and rushed to the injured child's side.

A bloody face from a nasty head wound would have made it difficult to recognize the boy, but the red T-shirt that was a size too small, the jeans with the gaping hole in the knee, and the dark hair in need of a trim told her who it was.

Trevor.

His skateboard lay off to the side—in the street.

Oh, God. *No.* She checked for a pulse while she pulled her cell phone out of her pocket, then dialed 9-1-1 and reported the accident. "Hurry. Please. He's unconscious and bleeding."

When assured that paramedics were on the way, she took Trevor's hand, her mind slipping into an instant replay of the day Erik was struck by a full-size SUV and thrown into the bushes at the side of the road.

She'd jumped off her bike and run to her injured son, clawing her way into the brush until she found him lying bent and battered, his blood seeping into the ground, his essence gone.

Trevor's hand, as Erik's had been, felt cool and lifeless in hers.

A strange sense of déjà vu settled over her this evening, and she tried to ignore it, focusing instead on the differences: Erik had been on a Sunday afternoon bike ride with his parents and had been dressed in full safety gear, while Trevor had been outdoors at night on his skateboard, alone and without any protection at all.

Still the similarities plagued her, as did an onslaught of questions.

What had happened? Why was he out so late? And where were the helmet and pads Claire had given him?

She directed her questions at God, yet they seemed to dissipate in the air, just as they had three years ago when she'd begged and pleaded with Him to no avail.

Even the unexplained compulsion that had seemed to lead her here like a whisper on the wind had grown still. And just as she'd had no idea where it had come from, neither did she know where it had gone.

"Hang on," she told Trevor. "Help is coming."

As a siren sounded and red lights flashed, she struggled to claim a sense of relief.

Near Trevor's body, on the sidewalk, she spotted a sheet of paper folded several times over. It was crumpled a bit. On the outside, light from her headlamps enabled her to read: *To God From Trevor.*

Had he been on his way to the park so that he could place it in the mulberry tree?

Aw, Trevor. I never should have answered that very first letter.

What had she been thinking? She'd never expected it to come to this.

Two paramedics—one a blond woman—jumped out of the ambulance, rushed to the stricken boy and began working on him.

"Rico," the female said, "Get his vitals. Then let's strip and flip."

Then the thirty-something blonde, who appeared to be calling the shots asked Claire, "Did a car hit him?"

"I don't know," Claire answered. "I have no idea what happened. I was just driving and spotted him lying here."

The blonde, who'd lifted Trevor's eyelids to look at his pupils with a light, glanced up long enough to ask, "Is he your son?"

"No."

Trevor *could* be her son, though. If she volunteered to take him as a foster child. To be the mother he deserved.

"He was riding a skateboard," Claire added, as if that could somehow explain all of this.

"BP is one-ninety-two over one-thirty-six," Rico said. "Pulse forty-eight."

"Do you know who he is?" the woman asked.

"His first name is Trevor. He lives in an apartment complex off First Street with a guardian. Her name is Katie. That's about all I know."

"Get the C-spine on and get his head in line on the backboard." The woman who appeared to be in charge glanced at her watch. "Four minutes and counting. Let's get oxygen started, then we're out of here."

As the duo worked together, they carefully placed a still unconscious Trevor on the backboard and then onto a gurney.

"Can I ride with him?" Claire asked.

"Sure. Get in."

A bearded, long-haired man who'd been standing to the side—Claire had no idea who he was or what he'd been driving—volunteered to move her car and leave it at the curb.

"The keys are in it," she told him.

After the paramedics loaded Trevor into the ambulance, the man handed her both the keys and her purse, leaving her vehicle now parked safely on the side of the road.

She thanked him.

The stranger, his blue eyes bright and compelling, nodded toward the ambulance. "Now go."

Claire nodded, shrugging off the thought that his breezy, whisper-soft voice sounded familiar, and focused on the injured child.

Just as she had the day Erik had been struck by Russell Meredith's SUV, she moved as though she was on autopilot, climbing into the ambulance and buckling up for the race to Pacifica General.

As the sirens roared and the red lights flashed, she watched the paramedics work on the boy. Rico began an IV in each of Trevor's arms.

Where was Katie? *She* was the one who should be here with him, the one worried about his well-being.

Claire reached into her purse with stiff and trembling fingers and withdrew the telephone number Trevor had given her. Then she opened her cell and dialed.

One ring. Two. Three . . .

A click sounded, followed by the canned voice of an answering machine. "Hello, you've reached Katie and Trevor. We're not able to get to the phone right now, but please leave your number."

Claire responded to the prompt. "Katie, you don't know me. My name is Claire and I have some very bad news. Trevor had an accident and is being transported to the hospital by ambulance."

With the siren blaring in the background, that last piece of information probably wasn't necessary.

"I'm not sure when you'll get this message," Claire added, "but you can reach me on my cell." She recited the number. "I'll be waiting with Trevor until you arrive at the ER."

"No answer?" the blond paramedic asked.

Claire shook her head. And there was no telling when Katie would get the message—especially if she was out partying with her friends again.

The blonde radioed the base hospital and recited Trevor's vitals. Claire wasn't an expert, but his condition hadn't seemed to change since they were taken at the scene. "The patient is unconscious and appears to have a skull fracture. We'd like permission to take him to Pacifica General. Our ETA is six minutes."

In the meantime, now desperate enough for a miracle, Claire began to pray silently.

"*Please* let him live," she pleaded. "Don't you have enough kids in Heaven?"

As Walter drew near Pacifica General, he heard an approaching siren and let up on the accelerator. As the ominous sound grew louder, he glanced in the rearview mirror, spotting the flashing red lights of an ambulance racing to the ER. He pulled to the right and allowed the emergency vehicle to pass.

Poor soul, he thought, as the ambulance turned into the hospital entrance.

Walter eased his pickup back into the street and followed the same path until he reached the Y in the driveway, where he veered to the right toward visitors' parking.

There was a time when coming to the hospital had unnerved him, but not so much anymore. Besides, he was eager to check on Maria and the baby.

That same crooked grin, the one that had begun the moment he'd laid eyes on the four-pound, two-ounce newborn, was tweaking his lips again, and another surge of pride washed over him.

Imagine that. There was a new kid in the world, a boy who would soon be walking and talking and throwing a ball.

Earlier today, he'd stood at the window and watched Walter Carl snoozing in his little bed in the NICU nursery. The precious sight had been awe-inspiring—and a little scary, too. But he and Maria had been assured the little guy was doing as well as could be expected.

It had been after two o'clock this afternoon when he'd finally left the maternity ward. He must have been a sight, too, with his feet dancing on clouds and his tail dragging the ground. In his daze and his obsession with the miracle he'd just witnessed, he'd forgotten to stop by and see Hilda on his way out, so he would visit her first tonight.

She probably wondered what had happened to him, and he couldn't wait to share the news with her. If she was up for a wheelchair ride, he'd take her to the fourth floor to see the new baby.

As he neared the lighted entry, he glanced at his wristwatch. Whoops. Nearly nine. He hoped no one threw him out before he got a chance to at least talk to Hilda.

He entered the lobby, tipping his head at the lady wearing a pink smock, then made his way to Hilda's room, only to find her alone and crying.

"Hey, there." He slowly eased toward her bed. "What's the matter?"

She swiped at her tears with the back of her hands. "Nothing."

Walter wasn't what you'd call an expert on women, but when one was crying and said it was for "no reason," he knew better than to believe her. "Is there something I can do to help?"

She shook her head, then reached for a tissue from the small box near her bed. "No. I'm afraid nothing can be done."

"Suppose you tell me about it anyway."

She dabbed at her eyes and sniffled. "The doctor said I can't go back to work for a couple of weeks."

"And you're crying because you'll miss Analisa?"

"Yes, but it's more than that. I'll get some disability payments, but they'll take a while to kick in and . . ." The flow of tears began anew, and when she'd gotten control, she dropped her hands into her lap and tore at the damp and wadded tissue.

Walter took a seat next to her bed. He lifted his hand to place it on hers, then drew it back, afraid she'd think he was too forward. "Why don't you try me, Hilda? Sharing the load is what friends are for."

She sniffled again. "It's just that I . . ." She turned to him, her red-rimmed eyes searching his. "I've lost so much already, and while I'm not thrilled with the apartment in which I live, it's the only home I have. I just hate the thought of moving again."

He wasn't sure what to say, what to offer. "I have a pickup, so I can help with that."

"Thanks, but it's not just moving boxes and furniture." She took a deep but wobbly breath, then let it out slowly. "I used to have a house, the single side of a duplex my late husband and I bought back in the sixties. It's where we lived when we were first married. And then about ten years later, when the other side became available, Frank insisted we buy it, even though it was a financial stretch for us. 'It'll be a good investment,' he'd said. 'Something to provide extra income in our old age.'"

It seemed like a fine plan to Walter, and he wondered what had happened, how she'd lost it.

Always one to clam up about his own problems, he hated to push for more information. So he figured he'd just keep quiet, much the same way Carl used to do when Walter had rambled on about Margie's death and the grief that had led a brokenhearted widower to drink himself into a stupor more nights than not.

Hilda cleared her throat. "Last year I lost the duplex plus the bulk of my savings, so I had to move into an apartment. I also had to come out of retirement. Thank goodness Mr. Dawson didn't hold my age against me and hired me to care for Analisa."

In spite of his intent to keep still and let her share as much or as little as she felt comfortable with, Walter asked, "How'd you lose the house and your savings?"

The floodgates opened again, and she bit down on her bottom lip before meeting his gaze. "I feel so foolish. I swore I'd never tell *anyone* about it. But keeping it in is eating me something fierce. And . . ." She sniffled.

Walter reached for another tissue and handed it to her, wishing there was more he could do. "I'm not one to repeat tales or sit in judgment when a good friend makes a mistake."

"A *good* friend?" she asked, a hint of a smile stealing her frown.

"Well, *I* thought we were."

She reached over and stroked his arm, letting her hand linger. "I suppose there isn't anyone else in this world who's been a better friend to me in the past few days."

Another sense of pride spread through him, the fourth or fifth such rush in the past twenty-four hours.

"But Walter, I swear, you can't tell anyone."

Rather than move his right arm, which bore the warmth and comfort of her touch, Walter used his left index finger to trace a cross over his chest. "I give you my word, which is about all I have left these days."

Hilda looked toward the door, saw that they were alone. "After Frank died, my friend, Barbara Mason, and I made a pact to look out for each other as we grew older. I'd spent most of my life taking care of other people's children and had never remarried or created any kind of family of my own. Barbara was estranged from her relatives . . ." Hilda glanced at Walter and slowly removed her hand. "And for good reason, too."

He arched a brow, but she didn't continue about her friend's problems.

"Anyway, since we were both alone, we thought we could face anything together. But three years ago last spring, Barbara passed away unexpectedly."

"I'm sorry to hear that." Walter, missing the warmth of Hilda's touch, rested a hand on his own forearm.

"It's been tough."

"I know. I lost my best friend, too, and I'm still struggling with it."

"Grief is a terrible thing." Hilda fiddled with the tissue she held in her right fist. "I probably don't have to tell you how lonely I was. Nor that I was feeling sorry for myself. Maybe that's why I lost my senses when I met Melvin Burrows and allowed greed to lead me astray."

"Who's he?"

"Melvin was a handsome and charming man I met one day while playing cards at the senior center. He was younger than me by about ten years, which bothered me at first, but . . . well, like I said, I was so lonely. And he was so nice. He would take me out to dinner wherever they had those crazy karaoke machines. Then, after ordering a bottle of expensive wine for us to share, he'd get up and sing some of the old hits, dazzling me with his Barry Manilow impressions. I'd never been courted like that."

"You were lonely. And I can see why you'd like to be wined and dined and sung to." Walter figured Melvin had a real gift of gab, and while he wanted to dislike the man intensely, he felt a stab of jealousy, too. There was no way he'd ever sing to a woman, even in private, let alone with a microphone in front of a crowd of strangers.

So he'd never be able to compete with a charmer. He

hoped that's not what it took to turn Hilda's head.

"Before long, Melvin came to me and told me about an opportunity he had to invest in a real estate project that was sure to quadruple in less than six months, but he was a little short of cash and offered me a chance to buy in as his partner."

Aw, man. Walter had an idea what was coming . . . And if he was right, he'd like to get a hold of that dad-burn cheat and let him have it.

"It was supposed to be a sure thing, so I took a mortgage out on the duplex."

"And Burrows never came through," Walter muttered.

"I should have been happy with what I had, not trying to make more. And now look at me. What'll I do if I lose my job, Walter?" Her tears began all over again. "I won't be able to pay my rent, and then where will I go? To a state-funded nursing home?"

"Not so fast. Whatever happened to Burrows?"

"Melvin felt so bad about things going to pot that he quit calling me. And then he moved away."

"A real man wouldn't have left you in a lurch like that, Hilda."

"What do you mean?"

"If I had been responsible for a woman losing her home and her savings, even if I weren't sweet on her, I would have felt obligated to do something about it."

"But Melvin lost his money, too."

"Are you sure about that?"

"He told me he did . . ." She furrowed her brow. "I

suppose, deep inside, I suspected that might not be the case."

"You very well may have been the victim of a scam, honey." The endearment had slipped out, although she didn't seem to notice, and he was glad she hadn't. "You need to talk to the police, Hilda. There's a possibility you could get your money back. Or at least be entitled to some sort of restitution from that swindler."

"You think that's possible?"

"Sure." Walter reached out and took her hand in his, giving it a little squeeze. "And if you'd like, I'll help you file the complaint."

"Aw, Walter." She blessed him with a smile. "You're a good man."

The way her eyes lit up made him almost believe her. But he shrugged off the compliment, afraid to put too much stock in it until he saw that glimmer of admiration a few more times.

"Hey," he said, changing the subject. "Maria from the park had her baby this morning."

"She did? It came a little early, didn't it?"

"Five-and-a-half weeks. What do you think about me getting a wheelchair and taking you for a little spin?"

"Where to?"

"First to say hello to Maria, then to see the most beautiful little boy in the whole world."

"You've seen him?"

Walter grinned. "Actually? I watched him come into the world."

Hilda arched a skeptical brow, and Walter beamed as he got to his feet. "I'll tell you all about it on the way to the maternity floor."

She glanced at the clock on the wall. "As much as I'd like that, it's almost nine o'clock. Visiting hours are nearly over, and they'll be shooing you out soon."

"All right. I'll come back early in the morning and take you to see them."

She laughed, and his chest filled with a warmth he hadn't felt in years. Life seemed to be falling nicely into place, which could almost restore a man's faith and make him believe that all was right in the world.

A siren sounded in the distance, and Walter glanced out Hilda's window, only to see the flashing lights of another ambulance bringing someone else to the hospital.

Well, maybe life wasn't going so well for *everyone*.

Chapter 17

Trevor had suffered a seizure while inside the ambulance, and Claire had known without being told that his injury was life-threatening.

When they'd arrived at Pacifica General, she followed the paramedics as they pushed the gurney though the ER and handed Trevor over to the doctors and nurses who quickly took charge.

"Are you his mother?" a red-haired ER nurse asked.

Claire didn't respond right away. She was too caught up watching a doctor intubate Trevor to secure his airway. They'd done that to Erik, too, and it was an instant replay she'd never wanted to see repeated.

"Excuse me," the nurse said. "Are *you* the boy's mother?"

Claire shook off the staggering memories and turned her attention to the woman speaking. "No, I'm not his mother. He has a guardian, but I haven't been able to reach her. What'll happen if she doesn't show up?"

"The trauma team will do everything necessary to save his life."

"Even surgery?" Erik, who'd also suffered a head injury, had been handed over to a neurosurgeon almost immediately upon his arrival at this same hospital. And Claire and Sam had been asked to sign consent forms.

"Yes." The nurse had placed a hand on Claire's shoulder. "Are you all right? You look a little pale. Would you like to wait somewhere else? Or perhaps go home?"

"I can't leave him. But maybe I should sit in the waiting room." Claire snagged the woman's gaze, hoping to pin down a promise. "Will you let me know as soon as he regains consciousness?"

"Yes, we will." The nurse showed her to the door that led back to where a hodgepodge of people seeking emergency treatment waited.

Claire then took a seat next to a young man with his hand wrapped in a bloody towel. To her left, a woman held a lethargic toddler.

It seemed like just moments ago when she'd been on

her way to Sam's house for . . . Oh, no. *Sam*. She reached for her cell and dialed his number, letting him know where she was and what had happened. "I'm sorry. Trevor doesn't have anyone else, so I need to stay."

"I understand. Is there something I can do?"

"Just keep a close eye on Analisa and don't ever let her have a skateboard. And if you do decide to buy her one anyway, make sure she always wears a helmet. But other than that? No, there's nothing you can do."

They agreed to talk again in the morning, and Claire said good-bye. Next she tried to call Katie again, only to hear the same we-can't-come-to-the-phone recording. It seemed useless to do so, but she left a second message.

A matronly woman wearing pale blue hospital scrubs and an ID badge approached. "Mrs. Harper?"

Claire stood, hoping for news that Trevor had made a turn for the better, that he was conscious and needing someone at his bedside.

"Since we've been unable to contact Trevor's guardian, we've notified the police. They're sending an officer to the apartment building. Sometimes neighbors can provide more information."

Claire nodded, wishing she herself could do more. "How's he doing?"

"They've taken him to surgery. I'm afraid that's all I can tell you."

Claire's stomach clenched and twisted into a fist-size knot. For a moment, she feared she would be sick and thought about making a mad dash to the restroom.

As the woman in scrubs—a nurse?—walked away, Claire sat back down, helpless to do anything but wait.

On a whim, she unsnapped her purse and pulled out her cell to make sure it was still working. Sure enough, the phone was on, the battery charged, the ringer on high. She went so far as to check whether she'd missed a call, but she hadn't.

From across the room, a cough sounded. She turned to see an old man hacking away until he turned red in the face. He'd covered his mouth with his hand, but she wondered how many people in the ER would end up with the same ailment.

As she put away her cell, she spotted the folded paper Trevor had been carrying.

To God, it said.

A growing rumble of guilt roared through her mind, rocking her to the core. If she hadn't given the boy reason to expect a divine answer to his letter in the first place, he wouldn't have been heading to the park tonight.

And he might have been home right now—safe in bed.

She wanted to shove the evidence of her wrong-doing back into her purse, as though she could avoid culpability. But because Trevor's plea might provide a clue of Katie's whereabouts or reveal what had provoked him to write a message that couldn't wait until daylight, she slowly unfolded the paper.

As she did so, she realized he'd written on two

sheets, both lined, with the left edges hastily ripped from a spiral notebook.

Dear God,

Analisa said you can make miracles happen. At first I didn't believe her. But then you gave me the skateboard and I knew she was right.

Me and my dad need you to help us really bad. He's in jail, but he isn't a bad guy. Not like robbers and killers. He's just my dad. And he's really sorry about the accident.

The people who work there can let him go, but they won't do that unless they believe he's sorry. And he really is. You've got to believe me. He didn't even see the kid or know that his car hit him until the next day. Katie said that's what got him in the most trouble. Because he didn't stop.

I'm sorry too. Analisa said the kid who died is happy now. Is that true? I hope so. Being dead doesn't seem like it would be much fun. I don't know all that much about heaven though. Just that my mom is there.

Her name is Susan. So if you see her will you tell her that I love her and miss her? I have a picture of her. It's in my room, but it isn't the same as having her.

My dad said that it is good that she died because she was so sick before. And Analisa said heaven is a cool place. Sometimes I wish

I could go live there with my mom. But I don't want to leave Katie all by herself. Can you help Katie too? Her boss doesn't pay her much money even though she works super hard and is tired all the time.

Analisa said that you will fix things for us. All I have to do is believe that you can do it. So that is what I am doing. I won't even tell you how to fix things. I'll just let you do it your way.

Thank you very very much.

Your friend, Trevor Meredith

Reality slammed into Claire with such force, it took her breath away.

Trevor was Russell's son.

She had no idea how long she'd sat like that, her stomach trying to right itself, her mind grappling to get a handle on the news. It seemed like forever that she clutched the pages of the note. Yet before she could actually come to grips with any of it or wrap her heart around the pain Russell and his family had suffered, the automatic ER doors swung open again, and a young woman rushed inside.

Her dark hair, most of which was contained by a ponytail, looked as though it hadn't been combed in a while, and her expression suggested she'd been in a frantic rush to get to the hospital and hadn't given her appearance any thought. She wore faded black jeans, a white T-shirt, and a brown vest with a name tag attached to the chest. Claire couldn't read it from where she sat, but she didn't need an introduction; she knew who'd just arrived.

As the woman scanned the waiting room, her eyes wide with fright, Claire noted only the slightest resemblance to the well-dressed, attractive young brunette who'd testified for Russell three years ago.

Still, without a doubt, Claire knew they were one and the same. So she stood and made her way toward Trevor's guardian. "Katie?"

"Yes?" A wounded gaze latched onto Claire like an exhausted swimmer reaching for the only lifeboat in a stormy sea. "Where's Trevor? What happened? A police officer told me he was badly hurt and then brought me here. He didn't know very much."

"Trevor suffered a serious head injury. He's in surgery now."

"But I don't understand. He was in his room . . ." Katie took a step back, then swayed, reaching for a chair to steady herself. "Oh, God, I've been so sick . . ." She shook her head, as though trying to clear her scattered thoughts. "This can't be happening. He was in bed for the night. We both were . . ."

A part of Claire wanted to comfort Katie, while another warned her to keep her distance.

"After dinner, I was dizzy and lay down for a minute to rest my eyes. The next thing I knew, the police officer was banging on my door." Katie looked at Claire—*really looked*—and recognition dawned. Still, confusion played across her face. "What are *you* doing here? What do you have to do with any of this?"

"Actually, I met Trevor at the park a while back, but I had no idea who he really was until a few minutes ago." Claire pointed to a chair in an empty corner of the waiting room. "Come over here and I'll see if I can fill you in on what happened."

When they'd each taken seats, Claire explained how she'd befriended Trevor, leaving out the part about the letters to God, of course.

"So you're the 'nice lady' he met. Analisa's babysitter."

Claire nodded. "He's a good kid. And I was drawn to him. He's one of the park regulars."

"I told Trevor he could go to the park for a little while each day, but I had no idea he was hanging out for hours at a time. In fact, I'd gone to look for him this afternoon to let him know I'd decided to go into work after all, but I couldn't find him anywhere. After I got home tonight, I scolded him for disobeying, then sent him to his room as a punishment. That's where he was *supposed* to be." Katie's brow furrowed, then tears welled in her eyes. "Oh, no. He must have run away . . . Did he call you? Is that why you're here?"

"No, that's not what happened." Claire couldn't even begin to explain how she ended up on Applewood, how an indefinable feeling sent her on an unplanned route. Nor did she feel comfortable telling Katie what Trevor had been planning to do. "I was driving to a friend's house when I saw him lying at the side of the road. So I called an ambulance, came to the hospital, and waited until you could get here."

"What happened? Was he hit by a car?"

"He was riding his skateboard and must have fallen and hit his head. I think he was on his way to the park."

"In the dark?" Katie grimaced. "And what do you mean his *skateboard?* He doesn't have one."

"Yes, he does. I assumed you knew about it."

"No. I didn't. In fact, about a year ago, Trevor asked his father if he could have a bike and was told, 'Absolutely not.' Russ said that . . ." Katie paused, as though seeing the need to choose her words carefully. "Russ adores Trevor and is a real worrywart. Even more so after the accident. So he wouldn't have approved of a skateboard, either."

Claire hadn't liked thinking of Russell as a father, as a man who'd been taken from his child and had to parent from a distance. She hadn't wanted to identify with him at all. Yet now she was being forced to consider a lot of things she hadn't been able to think about in the past.

"This is *my* fault," Katie said.

"No, it's not." *Accidents happen*, Claire wanted to add, but she didn't. She couldn't.

"Russell asked me to look after Trevor, but I haven't been able to supervise him as much as I should. I trusted him to follow my rules, but I guess that was too much to expect from a nine-year-old. I don't want to sound like I'm making excuses, but it's tough enough to pay the rent and the utility bills without adding the cost of summer day camp to the budget."

It was a Catch-22 in which too many single parents found themselves, Claire realized.

"At one time, I'd hoped I could stay home with him, that there'd be enough money so that I wouldn't have to work, but . . ." Again, Katie paused. This time her words hung out like dirty laundry on the line.

Claire hadn't needed to hear the rest, hadn't wanted to. The civil suit must have broken Russell financially, although she wasn't going to beat herself up about that now. And apparently Katie, who could have blamed Claire for at least some of her problems, wasn't going to throw rocks about that at this point, either. Not when Trevor was fighting for his life.

As it was, grief and guilt had wormed their way into the stilted conversation, which she could understand. Yet a few false assumptions were coming to light, making things even more awkward.

The assistant district attorney had painted Katie, a onetime foster child with no family of her own, as a greedy young woman who'd roped herself a wealthy executive and who would lie to keep him out of jail. But Katie had taken on the job of raising Russell's son, and even though whatever money and property he'd accrued over the years appeared to be gone, she'd stuck it out.

As if there weren't enough ugly and discomfiting thoughts to deal with, regret reared its head and pointed a gnarly finger at Claire, who'd thought the worst of Trevor's guardian and made assumptions she'd had no business making. She'd even gone so far as to report her suspicions to child protective services.

How did one go about backpedaling on a claim like that? She didn't know, but she would make some calls first thing in the morning.

"Did they say how long the surgery would take?" Katie asked, drawing Claire from her self-incriminating thoughts.

"No. They didn't."

Katie's shoulders slumped, and she exhaled the breath she'd been holding. "What am I going to tell Russell? He'll be devastated if . . ." Again she glanced at Claire and clamped her lips, cutting off any further explanation.

"Come on." Claire stood. "Let's tell someone at the front desk that you're here. Maybe there's some news they can share with us."

Claire led Katie to the ER receptionist. Moments later, a nurse's aide escorted them both back to a special room where the family and friends of surgery patients waited.

They didn't talk much; they were probably both caught up in their own thoughts and fears. Yet as grueling as it was to stay, Claire couldn't bring herself to leave Katie alone. Nor could she deny her own sense of helplessness. Her own instinct to reach out to a God who'd seemed distant, uncaring, and silent for the past three years.

Once upon a time, Claire had believed in miracles.

Maybe she still did. Especially when God appeared to be the only one who could help.

She closed her eyes, bowed her head, and silently cried out for a miracle. But as she began to open herself up to spiritual discourse, she couldn't help laying her own pain upon the Throne, her own failures. Her guilt.

Confession, they said, was good for the soul. And maybe they were right.

She'd been so caught up in her own pain, her own loss, that she'd failed to see that tragedy had struck two families that fateful day.

Who knew why some children were spared and others taken? It was beyond her understanding. But it wasn't beyond God's.

As her prayer deepened, as she opened her heart and mind, the first sense of peace she'd felt in years began to fill her battered soul. Before she could get anywhere near enough of it, the neurosurgeon came into the room looking for Katie.

"We managed to do some repair work," the doctor said, "but it will be a long time before Trevor is out of danger. We lost him twice on the table, and we're not sure whether that caused any permanent brain damage."

Katie's tears gave way to heart-wrenching sobs, and Claire fought against an onslaught of her own. Surely there was something she could do.

You know *what needs to be done.* The voice, the barest of whispers, had returned.

And it was right. Claire *did* know what to do.

She reached for her cell and dialed Sam's number. Then she stepped into the hall to speak to him in private. As she apologized for the late night call, the emotion she'd been struggling with all evening bobbed in her throat.

"Don't worry about the time," Sam said. "What's up?"

"You know the boy I told you about? He's Russell Meredith's son. He's just had surgery, and they don't know if he'll survive."

Sam didn't respond immediately, and she suspected it was because he was sorting through the news just as she'd had to.

He finally asked, "Are you okay, Claire?"

She pressed her lips together, then cleared her throat. "So far so good. But you have to do me a favor."

"Anything."

"Pull strings, make calls. Do whatever it takes. I want Russell released from prison."

"The parole board hearing isn't until Thursday."

"That could be too late. Surely there's something else you can do. Trevor is in a coma and on life support. He might not make it through the night."

And if that were the case, Russell ought to at least have a chance to say good-bye.

Sam stood barefoot in the kitchen and watched the morning coffee dribble into the carafe, waiting to hear from Jake.

After Claire had called last night, Sam hadn't given the time any thought at all. He'd quickly contacted his friend and colleague. Jake had been too concerned about his client to care about being awakened from a sound sleep.

When Sam had shared the tragic news and Claire's request, he and Jake had put their heads together, agreeing to do whatever they could to facilitate Russell's release, even if it was just a temporary furlough that would allow the father to visit his comatose son.

Sam had just begun to pour himself a cup of coffee when the phone rang, and he snagged it immediately. "What'd you find out?"

Instead of Jake's voice, it was Claire's. "Trevor's still alive. That's about all I can tell you."

"I'm sorry. I thought you were Jake Goldstein."

"Russell's attorney?"

"Yes. He and I talked last night, and he's doing what he can. He plays golf with a retired prison warden who has connections. And a family that attends his temple has a relative who's on the state parole board. So that's another route we can go. I also have a call in to a friend of mine who works at the governor's office. We're trying everything we can."

"Thanks. I appreciate that."

Sam, more than anyone, knew just how difficult this situation had to be on Claire. "How'd you sleep last night?"

"I didn't. I'm still at the hospital. I couldn't leave Katie alone. She's falling apart, and I can understand why. She's young and feels as though she's let Russell down by not watching Trevor closely enough. I was wrong about her, Sam. She's been pedaling as fast as she can to stay on top of the rent and the day-to-day living expenses. Neither she nor Russell wanted to apply for state aid, even though that stupid civil suit nearly bankrupted them."

It had been Ron's decision to sue Russell for wrongful death, and Sam had merely done his job. The jury had been sympathetic and awarded the Harpers over four million dollars. Now, Sam suspected, Claire was also struggling with the result of that ruling, as well as everything else.

"You know," Claire said, "for the first time in ages, I prayed last night. And it felt good. Right."

"I'm glad."

"I just wish I had Analisa's faith," she added.

"Speaking of Analisa, don't worry about her today. I'll take her to the office with me."

Claire caught her breath. "Oh, no. I completely forgot . . ."

"Hey, it's not a problem. I'll just pack her coloring books and crayons. She can pretend she's the assistant receptionist. And if I can get away for a while, I'll come by the hospital a little later. This has got to be tough on you, Claire."

"It is, but I can't seem to imagine myself being anywhere else right now."

"Trevor is lucky you came by and found him."

She paused. "Maybe. But on the other hand, if he

didn't think God answered letters that were placed in trees, he wouldn't have been out at night."

"Trevor's accident wasn't your fault, Claire."

"Intellectually, I know that."

"I guess that's the first step." Sam glanced up and saw Analisa standing in the doorway, Lucita in her arms. He offered her a smile, then returned to his conversation with Claire.

"Keep me posted about Russell," she said. "All right?"

"Absolutely."

When the line disconnected, Sam felt a tug on his bathrobe and glanced down to see Analisa looking up at him, her eyes glistening with apprehension. "What happened to Trevor? Is he okay?"

That wasn't something Sam wanted to discuss with her. What had she overheard? Claire had done most of the talking, but he must have said something.

While Sam tried to choose an appropriate response, his niece pressed him for an honest answer. "I heard you say Trevor had an accident."

"Yes, he did."

"Is he hurt bad?"

Sam's old man hadn't always been truthful, and both Sam and Greg had sworn they'd never lie to their kids when they became parents. But what about in a case like this? Under the circumstances, would Greg still feel the need to be honest with her?

And if not, what if the boy died? Analisa would not only lose a friend, but she might think Sam had betrayed her by keeping the seriousness of the injury a secret.

"Trevor fell off his skateboard," Sam admitted. "And yes, he was hurt badly."

Analisa drew Lucita close, like a mother cradling her child. "Is he going to die?"

"I hope not. The doctors are doing everything they can."

"But sometimes doctors *can't* fix people. You and me better pray right *now*."

"I'll listen while you do it. God doesn't know me very well."

"He knows *everyone,* Uncle Sam. Even *you.* But I'll pray and show you how. It's really easy." Analisa slipped her hand into his.

Sam had never understood his brother's faith, so it was a bit staggering to see his niece take the lead. It was a bit surprising, too, especially when God had failed to heal her mother or to spare her father.

Analisa led him to the kitchen table, where she took a seat and waited for him to join her. "Let's hold hands."

Surely hand-holding wasn't a prerequisite, although what did Sam know? Either way, he complied.

Analisa bowed her head and closed her eyes. "Dear God, please make Trevor get better right away, just like Mrs. Richards did. But if you want him to go to Heaven instead, will you show him my mommy and daddy? They'll be nice to him."

Sheesh. Sam didn't know what to say.

When she said, "Amen," Sam opened his eyes, thinking it was all over.

Instead, Analisa tugged on his hand. "You have to say 'Amen,' too, Uncle Sam. It lets God know you were praying, even though I said the words. And it lets Him know we're all done."

"Sorry. *Amen.*"

"Can we call Mrs. Richards at the hospital and tell her about Trevor? That way, she might want to go see him. And she can pray, too."

Sam doubted the child would be able to have visitors, but Hilda ought to be told. He glanced at the clock on the microwave. "It's too early now. I'll call her around eight."

"All right." Analisa slid off her chair. "Me and Lucita are going to go back to my room and color a picture for Trevor."

As she padded out the door, Sam poured himself a cup of coffee, grabbed the portable phone, and took them both out on the deck. The sun had only been up an hour or so, but the birds, a couple of red-breasted robins, were awake, chattering in the branches of the fruit trees that lined the rear of the yard. The neighbor's cat, an orange tabby, slunk along the top of the wall that separated the properties, its ears alert to the sound of breakfast.

Sam sat there for a while, one with nature. Or so it seemed.

Out here, it appeared as though a new day had dawned and life was going along just as it should. But in Sam's corner of the world, that wasn't the case. Russell was still behind bars, his son was lying in the intensive care unit, and Analisa just might be facing another loss that would break her heart.

While she believed that everything would work out, whether on earth or in Heaven, Sam feared her faith—as innocent and pure as it was—would crumble if Trevor didn't pull through.

How would her father have handled this situation?

Sam owed it to Greg to do right by Analisa, but how did a guy go about getting advice from someone who was dead?

Yet even if Greg were still alive, the brothers had grown so far apart that it would have been tough to talk about a subject like this anyway.

Sam had blamed their differences on opposing world views, but it had been more than that. They'd each blamed the other for their mother's death.

In the end, Greg had found peace through God and prayer, but Sam hadn't wanted him to.

As much as he hated to admit it, there were times when he vaguely remembered Greg telling him about a church event going on that night, but as long as Sam could blame his brother for not being home, it had eased his own sense of responsibility.

"It doesn't matter anymore," Greg had told him about a year ago in an e-mail Sam hadn't thought to save. "Mom's at peace. You've got to believe that."

Sam had chuffed when he'd read that part, disregarding his brother's faith, just as he'd always done.

"Talk to God," Greg had gone on to say. "He'll reveal that to you, just as he has to me."

Yeah, right.

Go peddle that spiritual mumbo jumbo elsewhere, Sam had wanted to tell him. And he might have, if he'd actually responded to Greg's e-mail.

Yet, deep inside, Sam had wanted to believe he could find inner solace and comfort. Maybe that's why he'd been drawn to the beauty of the outdoors, to the calming breeze. He'd found only a hint of what he'd been seeking, though.

Maybe Greg had been right. Maybe the only way Sam could find lasting peace was through the Creator Himself. But Sam hadn't been kidding Analisa when he'd said he didn't know how to pray.

Should he bow his head and fold his hands? Should he kneel?

Instead, maybe he ought to find the nearest church or confessional with a minister or a priest ready to listen to the burdens on his heart—burdens that now included Claire, Russell, and Trevor in addition to the other worries and guilt that had plagued him.

As it was, Sam placed both hands on his coffee mug and peered beyond the steam that snaked into the morning air, hoping to find some common ground on which he could communicate with his Maker.

Once, when Greg and Sam had been teenagers, Greg had talked to Sam about prayer. "Sometimes," Greg had said, "when I'm out fishing by myself, I use the quiet time to lay my heart before God. Then I listen. It's hard to explain just how it happens, but we share a conversation like two good friends."

Sam had scoffed at his brother's words back then, but maybe it was time to seek that personal relationship Greg had often talked about.

"Okay," Sam said out loud. "I believe you're up there. *Somewhere.* And I've got a lot of things to talk to you about."

A stillness fell over the yard.

Using his foot, Sam pulled out the empty chair and nodded toward it. "This could take awhile, God. So maybe you ought to have a seat."

Chapter 18

Everything seemed to be falling nicely into place. Last night, after Walter had visited Hilda, he'd gone upstairs to see Maria and the baby. A nurse had shooed him out of the hospital around nine-thirty, but not before he learned that Maria was being discharged the next morning. He volunteered to provide her a ride, and she seemed very appreciative when she accepted his offer.

On the way back to his place, he stopped by Hilda's apartment to check on her cat and birds. Then, feeling more useful than he had in ages, he'd gone home and fallen into a deep and restful sleep, which was a nice change of pace.

He woke well after dawn, showered and fixed himself his usual breakfast fare, a cup of coffee and a bowl of oatmeal—both instant.

Now, after parking his truck in the visitors' lot at Pacifica General, he strode through the lobby, whistling a carefree tune. It was just after eight, which was earlier than the nine o'clock time he and Maria had agreed upon, so he stopped to see Hilda first.

He was becoming an old hand at hospital visitation, and as he passed the third-floor nurses' desk, he nodded at a blond LVN before making his way to room 311, where Hilda sat in bed drinking a glass of juice with a straw.

"Good morning," he said from the doorway. "Is this a bad time?"

"No. Not at all."

He eased into the room. "How are you feeling?"

"I can't complain. I'm just eager to go home, and the nurse said it would be another couple of days yet." She pointed to the chair that sat adjacent to the foot of the bed. "Have a seat."

"Okay, but just for a little while. I really can't stay long."

"I don't blame you for wanting to get out of here. I sure wish I could, but since I don't have anyone at home to watch over me, they're insisting I stay longer."

"I can do that. Take care of you, I mean." The offer had slipped out before Walter could give it any thought.

"You're a good man, Walter."

No, not really. But he was trying. "Next time you see the doctor, tell her you've got someone who'll look out for you. I can sleep on the couch at your place or just come by in the morning and stay until dark."

"Thank you. I'd appreciate that."

With his courage bolstered, he decided to get a little bolder. "You know, I was thinking. Maybe, after you recover, we can go out to dinner and see a movie some night."

One of her eyebrows arched at the datelike suggestion, and he got the sudden urge to reel the words back in.

"We can go as friends," he added. "Or whatever."

Hilda tossed him a pretty smile. "*Whatever* sounds interesting."

His heart took a spin around his chest, and he couldn't help feeling like a teenager again. Well, at least an elderly widower who had a lot more life left in him.

"How are Maria and the baby doing?" Hilda asked.

"They're fine. Maria's being discharged this morning, but little Walter Carl has to stay for a while longer."

"Why is that? Is everything okay?"

"Since he was born too early, he's not sucking as well as they'd like him to. So they've been feeding him through a little tube that runs from his nose to his stomach. Once he's able to eat better on his own, they'll take it out. And when he gains some weight, they'll let him go home."

"Good. I'm glad to hear it."

"Me, too. Maria wasn't happy about having to leave him behind, but she knows he's in good hands. Besides, it'll give her time to get her strength back, to check on the other kids, and to get the nursery ready for him."

"Looks like everything is working out for her."

"Well . . ." Walter didn't want to go into details, even if both women had become his friends. If there was one thing he had going for him, it was the fact that he was trustworthy and knew how to keep his mouth shut, but something told him to share a bit of Maria's dilemma. "She needs to go back to work, but can't leave those kids with just anyone. I'm not sure where she's going to find a decent sitter. She can't afford to pay much."

"With two youngsters and a newborn, she almost needs live-in help."

Walter agreed.

"Too bad I can't do it."

Yep. It was. If Hilda didn't have to worry about paying rent and utilities, it would take some pressure off her. But before Walter could give the possibility any kind of what-if thought, Hilda's phone rang, and she answered.

"Hello?" A smile stretched across her face. "I'm feeling better every day, Mr. Dawson. Thanks for asking. And while you're on the phone, I wanted to tell you that I'm sorry for the inconvenience my illness has caused you. Hopefully, I can go back to work for you soon."

Walter watched as Hilda's smile dimmed and the creases on her forehead deepened.

"Oh, *no*. When?" She listened intently, then thanked Mr. Dawson for the call. "Of course. Tell her I will."

She pulled the receiver away from her ear. Instead of putting it where it belonged, she held it in her lap.

Walter got to his feet. "What's wrong?"

"Trevor, the little boy from the park, is downstairs in the intensive care unit."

Walter's gut cramped, putting a squeeze on the breakfast he'd eaten earlier. "How bad is it?"

"He's in a coma, and the doctors aren't sure if he's going to live."

All the fear and discomfort Walter had once felt in a hospital setting came rushing back full throttle, and he feared that his legs would give out on him.

"That poor child." Hilda slowly shook her head.

She was right. It didn't seem fair that the little boy was facing death before he even got a chance to live. Walter had half a notion to raise his fist and shake it at whoever was responsible for deciding when someone's number was up. But he wouldn't. With his luck, he'd step outside and be zapped by a thunderbolt.

"According to Mr. Dawson, Analisa wants me to pray for the child," Hilda said, "but I'm afraid I'm not very religious. It's been a long time since I've turned to God."

It couldn't be any longer for her than it had been for

Walter. God didn't listen to men like him. Never had. Not even when he'd been a boy like Trevor and was virtually a ward of the streets and raising himself. Nor when he'd hunkered down in a frozen trench at the Chosin Reservoir and held Lonnigan while he died. And certainly not when he'd waited day and night at a hospital just like this one, begging for Margie to be spared.

"Do you go to church?" Hilda asked.

"Huh?" Walter actually glanced over his shoulder to see if she was talking to someone else. "Who? Me?"

She nodded.

"One of my foster mothers used to send me to Sunday school when I was a kid."

Irene McAllister had been confined to a wheelchair and hadn't been able to attend too often, but she'd made Walter go and had given him pennies to put in the offering plate. Instead, he'd hung on to them so he could stop by the Kesslers' store on the way home to buy himself a bag of lemon drops.

"I'm not much of a churchgoer, either," Hilda said, "although I've gotta tell you, Walter. You've been such a blessing to me that I may have to start making more of an effort."

He supposed she deserved a thank-you for her comment whether it was true or not, but the walls of the hospital room were closing in on him, and he feared he wouldn't be able to catch his breath if he stayed much longer.

"You know," he said, backing toward the door. "I'd

better head to Maternity and make sure Maria isn't waiting for me."

"All right. I understand. Will you be coming back to visit me tonight?"

No. Yes.

He didn't know. "I'll have to give you a call later."

She nodded, as he continued to back out of her room and took off down the hall. He didn't even acknowledge the LVN who looked up from her work and smiled.

The few people he passed on the way to the elevator blurred together with the corridor walls.

It just wasn't right. And it wasn't fair.

When Walter arrived at Maria's room, she was dressed in street clothes and appeared ready to go home. "They're sending up a wheelchair and someone to take me to the curb out in front. It's hospital regulations."

Walter nodded. "I'll go get my truck and wait for you there."

"Are you okay?" She reached for his arm, clutching a bit of his sleeve. "You look a little pale."

He almost told her what had him twisted in a knot, but figured it was best to wait. What if she insisted upon staying and visiting the boy? Walter couldn't handle that. He needed to get out in the open where he could breathe, where he could look up to the heavens and beg God to take him instead of Trevor.

So he forced a smile and patted the top of her hand, which still rested on his forearm. "I'm fine. But I could use a little fresh air. That's all. We'll talk more on the way home."

As he sat in his pickup, the few minutes he expected to wait for her had stretched out to a half hour, but he didn't care. He was glad to be outside. Still, he scanned the windows on the east side of the building, wondering if little Trevor was inside any of those rooms and deciding that it wasn't likely.

About the time he thought it would be a good idea to head back inside and see what was keeping Maria, an orderly brought her to the curb where a sign indicated it was for loading and unloading patients. Walter pulled up and waited for her to get in. Then he began the drive to her house.

"I've got some bad news," he began.

"What's that?"

Walter stared out the windshield, afraid to catch her eye as he told her what had happened to the lonely little boy who'd reminded him so much of himself.

"Oh, no!" She made the sign of the cross over her chest. "I'll ask my cousin Rita to take me and the kids to St. Peter's after I get home. We'll pray for him and light a candle."

Walter hoped it would help.

"Would you like to come with us, too?" she asked.

"No, I'd rather not." Walter suspected he'd be even more uneasy inside of a church than he was in hospitals.

A few minutes later, he dropped Maria off at her

house, where Rita, a stocky young woman, met them at the door with a smile and a hug.

It was about all Walter could do to carry Maria's bag inside and stick around long enough for an introduction. As soon as he could politely tear himself away, he went back to his pickup. But instead of heading home, he drove to Mulberry Park, pulled into one of the empty stalls and shut off the ignition.

He'd been in a daze ever since hearing word of Trevor's accident and sat behind the wheel for a while, waiting for his thoughts to clear.

But they didn't.

Finally, he climbed from the truck and headed toward the mulberry in the center of the park, where Carl's bench sat empty.

Other than a woman and boy walking a collie mix and a perspiring male jogger stretching after his run, the park was practically deserted.

The midday sun burned summertime bright, but there was a light wind today, one that rustled the leaves in the trees and mussed Walter's hair.

He took a seat on Carl's bench, draped an arm over the backrest and stretched out his feet. He wasn't sure how one was supposed to approach God. Respectfully, he supposed, although he didn't know the rules or what to say. "Now I lay me down to sleep" came to mind. And "Bless this food which we are about to receive." Still, he'd never been any good at this sort of thing, even as a kid in Sunday school.

One day, seventy-some years ago, the pinch-nosed

lady who led music and played the piano asked if any children had a particular song they wanted to sing. Walter had quickly raised his hand and, when called upon, suggested "Show Me the Way to Go Home."

The pianist had harrumphed then, ignoring his request, and had chosen a little red-haired girl who'd wanted to sing "Amazing Grace."

Walter hadn't meant to be a wise guy suggesting a barroom ditty. He'd just liked the tune.

Still did, actually.

He supposed he'd always been out of step and, to be honest, he wasn't sure why he'd ever been born.

"Even my own mother didn't want me," he muttered out loud. "She just put me in a wicker laundry basket and left me behind the Lone Oak Motor Lodge."

If ol' Charlie Klinefelter hadn't gone looking for his dog before the snow started falling that night, Walter would have frozen to death as a newborn.

"And no one else wanted me, either," he said, his voice lowering to a drawn-out whisper.

He'd stayed with the Klinefelters for a few years and had taken their name, but by the time he was eight, he'd lived in five or six different homes. He never had understood why no one had stuck him in an orphanage. Instead, for some reason, the folks in the community had just passed him from one family to another.

One home in particular had always stuck out, but Irene McAllister, who'd been crippled when her Ford sedan had stalled on the train tracks, eventually died from complications of the accident.

From the age of thirteen on, Walter had more or less raised himself, and as soon as he was old enough, he'd joined the army. He'd found a family of sorts there, too, but seen some of them killed and others wounded. Eventually, they'd all gone their separate ways.

Walter blew out a bone-weary sigh and glared up at the sky. "What were you thinking when you let me come home from Korea instead of guys like Lonnigan and Schwartz?"

There were others who hadn't survived either, soldiers who'd been just as brave as Walter—even more so when you considered they'd had more to lose. More reason to come home in one piece—like families who'd loved them.

Nope. It hadn't been fair.

Then there was Margie, who'd had two boys who weren't quite raised when she'd died. Boys who needed her even more than Walter had.

"Margie was called home," the preacher had said.

Home.

She'd *had* a home—on earth. And it had been the only real home and family Walter had ever felt remotely a part of.

"What's the deal?" he asked, his voice ringing out louder than before. "Do you have some big set of dice that you shake up and toss?"

The breeze blew a strand of hair onto his forehead, and he raked it away with his fingers. "Sorry. I don't mean to be disrespectful. But I just don't get it. You can understand that, can't you?"

The thumb of his outstretched arm brushed across the brass plate that proclaimed Carl Witherspoon a loving husband and father, which was merely another reminder of how unfair things had been.

The Fairbrook Community Church had been packed the day of Carl's funeral. If Walter had been the one to drop dead of a heart attack, instead of Carl, they could have just done away with the whole memorial. In fact, they could have just lowered the box into the ground and been done with it. No fuss or flowers would have been necessary, not when there wouldn't have been anyone to cry or mourn.

"So why spare me, God, and not the others?"

Walter hadn't really expected an answer. Nor had he expected a memory to surface that triggered the feelings he'd had for the only real mother he'd known.

He'd thought about Irene a lot over the years and realized that she'd probably loved him more than anyone else had. And that she'd been the only one who'd believed he would amount to something.

"Maybe you'll grow up to be the president of the United States," she'd told him once.

But when Walter had been about Trevor's age, Irene's health, which had never been good after her accident, began to fail.

She'd called him to her bedside and admitted she was dying. Then she'd taken his face in her hands. "But don't you worry. You'll be just fine. And you won't be alone. God will always be with you. And He's going to use you in a powerful way someday."

Good thing Irene wasn't here to see that Walter hadn't amounted to much. Not that he'd done any serious jail time or been a complete loser.

"God has plans for you," she'd insisted. "Plans to prosper you and not harm you. Plans to give you hope and a future. All you have to do is believe in Him and trust Him. And He'll see you through."

She'd said it like she'd had some kind of word from God Himself. Walter had kind of put it all out of his mind back then. But now, thinking back on it, he wondered if she'd known something he hadn't.

Was that why Walter had been spared? First from the winter cold? Then from enemy fire? Because God had a plan for him?

If so, it was certainly difficult to see why. Or to understand what that plan was.

Had Walter somehow dropped the ball? Forgotten to do his part?

"You'll hear God's voice if you seek Him with all of your heart," Irene had told him time and again.

Was *that* what had gone wrong? Had Walter merely asked for things and not stuck around long enough to listen for a response?

At a loss and unsure of what else to do, Walter bowed his head and removed his arm from the backrest so that he could clasp his hands together in his lap. "Here I am, Lord. What you see is what you get. I've made a lot of mistakes in the past, and I have no business coming to you at all. But I'm tired of the pain, the sorrow, the loneliness. And I don't want to go it alone. I'll give you my heart and my life, what's left of it anyway."

The breeze swirled around him, and for the first time in what seemed like forever, Walter sensed a spiritual presence, a connection, and he just sat there, taking it all in.

"Irene said you had plans for me, Lord. So if you'll just show me what they are, I'll try to keep my eyes and ears peeled so that I can get the job done."

Walter wasn't so bold as to press God into action, especially when he figured the Almighty was smart enough to know He'd better hurry since time was running out—for Walter *and* for Trevor.

"By the way," Walter said, his head still bowed, his eyes still closed. "If you can spare a miracle, I'd be eternally grateful if you would heal that little boy."

Claire didn't know how Sam or Jake had managed it, but before the end of the day, Russell Meredith arrived at the hospital, accompanied by a prison escort.

In court, he'd worn expensive suits and ties like those of any sharp young executive. But now, dressed in a pair of worn jeans and a white T-shirt, his dark hair long and in need of a trim, he resembled an ordinary blue-collar worker, a man who did his own yard-work and took out the trash.

He stood in the doorway of the ICU waiting room, pain and worry etched across his face with sharp, bold strokes. His eyes bore evidence of a long, hard cry.

As he carefully scanned each occupied chair, Claire suspected he was looking for Katie.

When his gaze locked onto Claire instead, her heart ached for another grieving parent. Unable to do anything else, she stood and made her way to him. "Katie just took a short break. She'd been here since last night and went home for a quick shower. She'll be back soon."

"My attorney said that you stayed the night here, too."

Claire glanced down at the clothes she'd been wearing for nearly twenty-four hours. A quick trip home and a shower would do her good, too. "Katie is pretty torn up. I didn't think she should be here by herself."

Of course, now that Russell was here, Claire had an excuse to leave—if she wanted one.

"Have you been able to see Trevor yet?" she asked.

"I just left him." Russell's eyes filled with tears. "Seeing him like that, hooked to a ventilator, his head bandaged, his blood pressure and oxygen levels being monitored . . ."

"It's tough." Claire hadn't meant to remind him that she knew just how he felt—the helplessness, the worry, the fear . . .

"Do you mind if I talk to you?" he asked. "Just for a few minutes?"

Her heart skidded to a halt, then started back up again. Part of her wanted to say no, to find an excuse to leave. But she supposed it was time they faced each other. "Sure."

"Not a day goes by that I don't think about that accident and wish there was something that I could do to make everything all right. I wanted to contact you a hundred different times, but my first attorney adamantly advised me not to."

She doubted she could have handled talking to him before. Could she now?

"You have no idea how sorry I am."

Claire was sorry, too. Yet where there'd once been anger, there was merely shared pain.

"This may not be the best place or time, but if you wouldn't mind, I'd like to explain my side of the story. All of it. Not just the responses my attorney coached me to make."

Somehow, she had a feeling this might be the perfect place to talk, so she pointed to a couple of seats against the far wall where they could have some privacy. Russell glanced at the escort, who nodded an okay.

As they sat side-by-side, one parent to another, Russell began his story. "A little more than four years ago, when my wife was diagnosed with an aggressive form of pancreatic cancer, I was the rising star at a new software company. I'd been working day and night to provide for my family, and her death just about killed me. I tried to gain control of my life and my grief by pouring myself into my work, and before long, I was offered a partnership. I knew Trevor was hurting, too,

337

but since he never really cried, I assumed he was doing okay. But I was wrong."

"The lack of tears isn't always a sign that someone is grieving well." Claire ought to know. She'd had enough counseling sessions in the past.

"I know that now. I picked up on Trevor's depression during his visits to me at prison, so I read everything I could get my hands on about the subject, especially when it came to kids. Anyway, about a year after my wife died, I met Katie, who was a waitress at a diner down the street from my office. When I was with her, I didn't hurt anymore, so I began to spend more and more time with her. I thought having a new lady in my life would be good for Trevor, too."

Claire could understand why. In the time the women had spent together at the hospital, she'd come to realize how devoted Katie was to Russell and his son. "Katie loves you both very much. And she's tried to take good care of Trevor while you've been gone."

"I know. And I've grown to love her, too, but at first . . . well, it took awhile to get over my wife, to let myself love again."

Again, Claire knew what he meant. Some people found it difficult if not impossible to rebound after tragedy like that. And she was one of them.

Russell cleared his throat, then leaned forward in his seat, placing his elbows on the armrest of his chair. "Three years ago, on a Sunday afternoon, I was driving home from the office. It had been two weeks since I'd allowed myself some time off, and I was mentally exhausted and growing increasingly frustrated by a problem we were having with a new software program the company was developing."

Claire recalled one of Russell's coworkers had testified that he'd been working that day.

"My cell phone rang while I was on my way home, and it was Katie, complaining—*again*—about how often she watched Trevor for me and how little time we spent as a couple. I'd been under more pressure than she could have possibly understood, and something inside me snapped. I blew up, telling her I was tired of her crap.

"Up ahead, I spotted a man and woman—you and your husband—riding bikes and passed them, just as the road made a turn. I swear I didn't see a child with you."

Erik had been riding in front of Claire and Ron. As the road curved, they'd momentarily lost sight of him, but she let Russell tell his side of the story.

"The glare from the setting sun had grown worse, and so had Katie's complaints and the tone of her voice. I felt a bump, as though my car struck something, and I took a quick glance in the rearview mirror. All I saw was the movement of some shrubbery along the side of the road."

Claire and Ron had just come around the bend in time to see Russell's SUV strike Erik, throwing the child and his bicycle into the bushes. At that moment, their lives had slammed into a wall.

As if in slow motion, they'd quickly thrown down

their own bicycles and climbed through the brush to find their son.

"When I got home, Katie was waiting on the front porch in tears. She apologized for not being more understanding. I was sorry, too, and we made up. I'd meant to check the side of my vehicle for any damage caused by the shrub, but it slipped my mind once we went inside."

"Had you been drinking?" Claire asked.

"Not a drop." Russell took a deep breath, then slowly let it go. "The next day, the newspapers and television stations ran a story about a hit-and-run accident that had caused critical injuries to a boy riding a blue bike. But it wasn't until later that evening that I even heard about it. When I did, an uneasiness settled over me, and my stomach churned. Knowing that I'd traveled along that road about the same time the accident occurred, I went outside to check the passenger side of my SUV. That's when I spotted the dent and the streak of blue paint."

He hadn't turned himself in until late that second night, about the time Claire and Ron had agreed to remove Erik's life support.

"As soon as I realized what had happened, I called a criminal defense attorney, and he came over to my house. After we talked, he accompanied me to the police station, and I turned myself in."

Erik had died the next morning, before Claire and Ron had learned the driver had finally come forward.

"You may not believe me," Russell said, his eyes red

from tears he'd shed before and filling with new ones now, "but I'm truly sorry for causing your son's death. In my heart, I know that accident could have happened to anyone, but I'll carry the guilt to my grave."

Claire would be hurting until the day she died, too. But seeing Russell suffer, watching as his own child battled death, did nothing to ease her pain. And in fact, it seemed to make it worse.

"It's taken me a long time to get to this point, Russell, but I forgive you. I'm also sorry that you're in the same situation that I was once in. No parent should have to go through something like this."

Russell nodded, then dropped his head and studied his hands. Claire wondered if he would be able to forgive himself. She tried to put herself in his shoes. What if she'd struck Trevor with her car last night? How would she feel if she were responsible for all of this?

She couldn't even imagine coping with the guilt.

Something shifted deep inside, something that had kept the pain and grief lodged permanently in her chest, and a balm of peace washed over her.

Before she could fully acknowledge the freedom she'd been granted to live and love again, a nurse came to the doorway of the waiting room.

"Mr. Meredith?"

Russell stood, his eyes announcing his fear. "Yes?"

"Your son is awake and asking for you."

Chapter 19

Claire checked the blue and yellow streamers that swooped across the patio, as well as the table decorations, one last time before her guests arrived.

In the past, she'd loved throwing parties, but there hadn't been much to celebrate lately. However, a lot of things had changed in the three weeks since Trevor had awakened from his coma without any sign of brain damage—a miracle that had touched everyone who knew him.

As Claire straightened the vase of flowers that adorned the buffet she'd set up on the countertop of the built-in barbecue on the patio, she glanced at the chocolate birthday cake that rested in the shade. The bakery had done a nice job decorating it with buttercream frosting and piped roses.

Everything was ready for Walter and Hilda, the guests of honor, and the others Claire had invited. She'd even sent an invitation to Trevor and his family. With Russell out of prison, she hadn't hesitated including them, but wasn't sure if they would come.

Sam had promised to arrive early and help with any last minute details, and although Claire had it all covered, she was looking forward to seeing him. They'd had several dates already, each one nicer than the last.

Expecting him any moment, she glanced at the face of her bangle wristwatch to check the time just as the doorbell rang.

Her heartbeat kicked up a notch as she strode through the living room, opened the door and greeted Sam and Analisa with a smile. "Come on in."

Sam brushed a kiss across her lips, and she stole a moment to savor his musky scent.

"Guess what?" Analisa tapped on Claire's hip. "I made you something. See?"

"You did?" Claire took the paper the child handed her.

"It's another picture for your fridge." Analisa grinned and crossed her arms, while Claire took note of a brown animal, with a long tail and a yellow banana in its mouth.

"How cute is this? A monkey, just like the ones we saw at the zoo last week."

"His name is Ralph. Do you want me to put him up for you?"

"Would you please? You're such a good artist. You might have to make room for him, though." Claire's refrigerator was loaded with artwork these days, especially since she was still babysitting Analisa for Sam.

"That's okay. I'll move pictures around and put the newest ones in front."

As Analisa dashed off, Sam lifted his arms, and Claire closed the gap between them, eager to share another kiss, this one deeper and more intimate than the one he'd given her when he arrived.

As the kiss ended, Sam continued to hold her close. "I've got dinner reservations for us tomorrow night at

Antoine's. And Hilda said she and Walter would babysit."

"Those two are becoming quite a team."

Walter had taken care of Hilda during her recovery, then came up with a plan that would work out well for everyone involved, especially since Sam had gone along with it.

Hilda had recently given up her apartment, moved in with Maria and would soon provide daycare for the Rodriguez children so Maria could go back to work. On the way to the office each morning, Sam would drop off Analisa at Maria's. There she would have breakfast with the other children and play until Sam picked her up. Then, when school started in September, she would catch the bus and ride with Danny to Applewood Elementary, where they would both attend second grade.

Instead of heading to the park each day, as Walter had been doing in the past, he was going to help Hilda look after the little ones.

Sam ran his knuckles along Claire's cheek. "You and I are becoming a good team, too."

Before Claire could agree, the doorbell rang again.

"I'd better get that." She slowly drew away from Sam's embrace and answered the door, seeing that most of her guests had arrived together in Maria's minivan. The kids dashed in first, followed by their mother. Hilda and Walter brought up the rear.

"It was so nice of you to throw a joint birthday party," Maria said as she entered. "Hilda and Walter have really been looking forward to it."

"I thought it would be fun to help them celebrate. Besides, we all have a lot to be thankful for."

"That we do," Hilda said, as she followed Maria inside.

Walter, who held the handle of the baby carrier and brought in the sleeping newborn, chuckled. "I just hope we don't set the house on fire with all those candles."

Claire laughed, then turned her attention to the newborn baby. "Just look at him. He's so much bigger than the last time I saw him."

"Isn't he something?" Walter beamed at the child as though he were the grandfather. "I wouldn't be surprised if he grew up to be the president of the United States someday."

As Hilda and Claire began to ooh and aah over the infant, Analisa came running back into the living room, excited to see that her friends had arrived.

"Hey, guys." Sam gathered the children together. "Let's all go out in the backyard. If you want to play tag, I'll be 'it.' "

Claire realized Erik's swing set would have come in handy today, but Ron had taken it down right after their son's death. "I couldn't stand looking at it," he'd told her.

Ron would probably be glad to know she'd finally boxed up Erik's things, most of them anyway, and placed them in the garage. She was going to have the Salvation Army pick them up one of these days. But she wasn't procrastinating for any reason other than she kept forgetting to make the call. Sam and Analisa were keeping her so busy she just hadn't found the time.

"Walter?" Hilda caressed the elderly man's arm. "If you'll carry that little guy outdoors for me, I'll keep an eye on him while the others play."

"You betcha, honey." Walter watched as Hilda made her way toward the sliding door that led to the patio, following Sam, Maria and the children, then turned to Claire. "Thanks for having the party. Hilda hasn't celebrated her birthday in years, and it's been even longer for me."

"You're welcome. It's been fun."

"I'm glad. It's about time you started enjoying life."

"Yes it is." Claire gave him a one-armed hug. "And now that you mention enjoying life, how are things going for you?"

"Great." His grin bore evidence that Claire hadn't been the only one to experience a heart-healing, faith-renewing miracle that July day. "In fact, you might not know this, but I've been stopping by to see Trevor on Sunday afternoons. And guess what? I just found out that Russell learned how to play chess while he was in prison."

"Sounds like a match made in Heaven," Claire said with a smile.

"You're right about that." Walter's grin broadened, happiness glowing in his eyes. "If my old buddy Carl could see me now, he'd sure be proud. I'm becoming the friend and mentor that he used to be to me. And that's not all. Russ has been encouraging me to call my stepsons, and last night, I finally did. Blake was a bit reluctant, but Tyler's willing to see me next week. I told him I couldn't do anything to change the past, but I was a new man these days. And that's the truth. God's hand is surely on my future."

And God's hand was on Claire's future, too. She'd already enjoyed lunch and a day at the spa with Vickie, which had been a long time coming. They'd even made plans to go shopping together next Saturday. But more than that, the wrongful death settlement from Erik's accident would have a positive purpose.

Over the last two weeks, Claire had decided to utilize a portion of it to create a charitable foundation called The Heart of an Angel. The decision alone had done wonders for her healing process, and she'd already begun to gather some enthusiastic board members, including Sam, who was handling the legal details.

A knock sounded, followed by the doorbell.

"While you get that," Walter said, "I'm going to take this little guy outside."

Claire smiled as she watched him go, then opened the door and found Trevor, Katie, and Russell on the porch. "I'm *so* glad you could make it. Come on in."

It was heartwarming to see Trevor healthy and whole again, a bright-eyed smile dimpling his cheeks.

Claire gave the boy and Katie each a hug, then

reached an arm out to Russell. As they shook hands, she noticed that he'd had his hair cut, and that his face bore a bit of color, suggesting he'd spent a lot of time outdoors lately.

"Thanks for inviting us." He released his grip, and his voice softened. "And thanks for the money you sent. You didn't have to do that."

"I know. But I wanted to." Claire had thought it was only fair to return part of the settlement money to Russell. That way it wouldn't be so hard for him and Katie to start over. "Consider it my wedding gift."

"All right, I will." Russell slipped his arm around Katie and drew her close. "When Jake dropped off your check, he told me you were creating a foundation to help disadvantaged kids."

"It seemed like the right thing to do and a good way to perpetuate Erik's memory."

"If you need a Web site designed, or if there's anything at all I can do to help, just let me know."

"Thanks. I'm sure I'll be taking you up on that." Claire offered him a genuine smile, one straight from the heart, then pointed to the sliding door. "Everyone's outside if you'd like to join them."

Trevor, who'd been standing between his father and Katie, inched toward the lamp table and picked up a silver-framed photograph of Erik standing beside his bike. "Hey! How do you know this kid, Mrs. Harper?"

Claire wondered if the boys had met, but couldn't imagine how they could have. "That's Erik, my son."

Trevor's eyes grew wide. "Are *you* his mom?"

Claire's gaze ping-ponged from Trevor, to Russell and Katie, then back again. "Yes, I am."

Trevor showed the picture to his father. "This was the kid I told you about."

Russell's brow furrowed as he studied the photo, then he looked at Claire. "After Trevor came out of his coma, he insisted he'd met God."

"You met *God?*" Analisa, who apparently had spotted Russell's car and raced in from the yard to greet Trevor, entered the living room and approached her friend. "For *real?*"

"Yeah, it was Him. He didn't have to tell me. I just knew who He was."

"How'd you know?"

"Because there was so much love in His eyes that I couldn't even see His face. And His robe was made out of weird threads of light or something. Then He showed me these green fields with tons of flowers in all kinds of colors I'd never even seen before. And there was a stream there, with water that was as clear and sparkly as blue diamonds."

Claire didn't know what to say. She'd heard stories of people having near-death experiences. And the doctor had said they'd lost Trevor on the operating table—twice. He certainly seemed sincere. Could he have really seen those things?

"There was a boy with God." Trevor pointed to Erik. "*This* one. He talked to me and said, 'Tell my mom that I'm happy here and not to worry about me. Let her know that I'm going to see her again someday.'"

Tears filled Claire's eyes, and emotion clogged her throat.

"The boy, I mean Erik, was telling the truth," Trevor added. "I could tell he was super-happy because it was so cool there. I *really* wanted to stay, but God told me I couldn't. He said I had stuff to do before I could come back."

While Claire was at a complete loss for a logical explanation, in her heart she knew Trevor had seen Erik. She bent down and gave him a hug, holding him close, just as she'd once held her son. "Thank you for sharing that with me."

In the past few weeks, Claire had come to believe that Erik was in Heaven. But now she'd been blessed with confirmation.

"Do you want to go outside and play?" Analisa asked Trevor.

"Okay."

As the kids headed toward the sliding door, Analisa asked, "Do you know what I'm going to do?"

"What?"

"I'm going to write another letter to God and thank Him for letting you see Heaven and a real live angel."

"You don't have to write letters. All you have to do is talk to Him. When I was in Heaven, it was like His heart already knew exactly what mine was feeling, and I think it's the same way when we're here."

Claire stood in awe at what she'd just heard. Trevor had been in the presence of God and seen a glimpse of

Heaven, something most people would never witness and live to tell about.

Yet in her own way, Claire had experienced God, too.

She'd learned that His voice was a whisper in the breeze and a sense of peace within a storm. And that His biggest miracles occurred when a heart listened and obeyed.

For those who believed, Claire realized, death wasn't the end.

It was merely . . .

The beginning.

Center Point Publishing
600 Brooks Road ● PO Box 1
Thorndike ME 04986-0001 USA

(207) 568-3717

US & Canada:
1 800 929-9108
www.centerpointlargeprint.com

DATE DUE

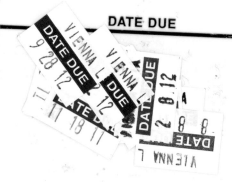